C000171248

THE
THIRD
BLACK BOOK
OF
HORROR

Selected by Charles Black

Mortbury Press

Published by Mortbury Press

First Edition

2008

This anthology copyright © Mortbury Press

All stories copyright © of their respective authors

Cover art copyright © Paul Mudie

ISBN 978-0-9556061-2-0

This book is a work of fiction. Names, characters, businesses, organisations, places and events are either the product of the author's imagination or are used fictitiously. Any resemblance to actual persons, living or dead, events or locales is entirely coincidental.

All rights reserved. No part of this publication may be reproduced, stored in a retrieval system, or transmitted, in any form, or by any means (electronic, mechanical, photocopying, recording or otherwise) without the prior permission of the author and publisher.

This book is sold subject to the condition that it shall not, by way of trade or otherwise, be lent, re-sold, hired out, or otherwise circulated without the publisher's prior consent in any form of binding or cover other than that in which it is published and without a similar condition including this condition being imposed on the subsequent purchaser.

Mortbury Press
Shiloh
Nantglas
Llandrindod Wells
Powys
LD1 6PD

mortburypress@yahoo.com
http://www.freewebs.com/mortburypress/

Contents

Dedicated to Hugh Lamb

*****

Acknowledgements

The Scavenger © by Rog Pile 2008
Takashi's Last Symphony © by Gary McMahon 2008
A Sense of Movement © by David A. Riley 2008
Last Night © by Joel Lane 2008
Widow's Weeds © by Paul Newman 2008
Out of Her Head © by Christine Mortimer 2008
Family Ties © by Steve Lockley & Paul Lewis 2008
Death-Con 1 © by Sean Parker 2008
Like A Bird © by Mike Chinn 2008
The Spoon © by John Mains 2008
The Lake © by Franklin Marsh 2008
Synchronicity © by Craig Herbertson 2008
In the Thicket © by Paul Finch 2008
John & Jenny and the Lump © by John Llewellyn Probert
2008
In an Old Overcoat © by Frank Nicholas 2008
The Looker © by Julia Lufford 2008
What We Cannot Recall © by Gary Fry 2008

Cover artwork © by Paul Mudie 2008

*****

Also in this series:
The Black Book of Horror
The Second Black Book of Horror

THE SCAVENGER

Rog Pile

"Chambers? Mr Austin Chambers?"

"Speaking."

"My name is Ventham. That is, Reverend William Ventham. I understand that you perform consultations?"

"I do tarot readings, if that's what you mean."

It was early in the morning, too early for a telephone call, and already I was forming a picture of some frustrated country clergyman who, for reasons of his own, had decided to embark on a one-man Crusade of Light. That kind of thing happened.

As more and more churches closed their doors, and people came groping through the fog of their own confusion to the mystics and fortune-tellers – to people like myself – what more natural reaction than to be resentful of those whom, it must seem, were stealing their flocks away. At least, so ran my train of thought while I wondered whether the best thing to do would be simply to hang up. Then he said something that stopped me.

"I need your help. I would like to make an appointment. Today, if possible, at my house."

I don't get men of the cloth ringing up for appointments every day, but the weather looked bleak and I didn't want to set a precedent. I said, "I'm afraid that I don't make house calls. If you'd like to come here, though—"

"I'm afraid, that's impossible. I can't get out. I believe that you usually charge fifteen pounds for a consultation. I am not a rich man, but I'll double that sum; I will also pay you for any time and travelling expenses you incur."

It was tempting. I'd just got my car back from the garage after an expensive overhaul, so needed the cash; but something about it didn't seem right, and I smelled a hoax. "Suppose that I turn up at your address, and someone answers the door and tells me there's been a mistake?"

"I believe I can persuade you that I am genuine; as a matter of fact I anticipated just such a reaction. I admit that this is an unlikely request. Have you opened your post yet?" he asked, apparently irrelevantly.

I hadn't; I'd been woken by the telephone.

"Among your letters there should be a white envelope with a type-written address, postmarked Edgecombe. Please open it."

I put down the receiver, got out of bed shivering, and found the envelope, just as he said. I tore it open, picked up the receiver again, and tipped out the envelope's contents. Five ten-pound notes spilled onto the desk-top.

"It's all I can afford at the moment," he said. "Now will you come?"

"You're going to a great deal of expense, reverend. Surely there must be another card-reader you can consult, closer to home?"

"I read a book of yours once, some years ago, Mr Chambers. My memory of it convinces me that you are the only man who can advise me."

"Reverend, what is this all about?"

"I believe someone wants me dead. I believe that I am the object of a malevolent and vicious form of psychic attack," he said. Then the telephone went dead. I got up and made a cup of coffee, and fetched down the AA atlas to look for Edgecombe. I switched on the radio for the weather forecast. It was cold enough for snow, and they said it would.

I didn't get lost too many times looking for Edgecombe. Once I had to reverse up a lane when a lorry met me half-way down it. The driver was a burly fellow, what I could see of him, with a pipe clamped in his jaws, and clearly believed that he had the right of way. He barely slowed the lorry, and I had to reverse my Wolseley promptly before its radiator was stove in by the advancing lorry. Later, I was brought to a halt by a herd of cattle which moved past on either side, their flanks slowly steaming. The cowherd bringing up the rear switched at them with a stick and gave me no more than a glance. By the time that I pulled into the narrow streets of Edgecombe I'd already decided that the simple pleasures of country living were possibly overrated. I pulled the car into the square with its small white granite War Memorial. It wasn't difficult locating the Vicarage. The church spire was the tallest building thereabouts and poked over the cobwebby trees that rose above the nearer rooftops. I would have liked to have stopped in a pub for a quick one, but the dark, grimy windows, closed doors and deserted streets of the village didn't suggest hospitality, so I drove up the street in the direction of the church.

Surrounded by high laurel bushes beside it, I found The Vicarage.

It was one of those little cottages which might have modelled for the cover of a chocolate box; until one looked closer and noticed that the half-open gate was actually off its hinges, some of the windows were cracked, the holes stuffed with rags, and the paintwork was peeling. If God wasn't actually dead he was definitely undernourished in Edgecombe. I didn't find this reassuring. Ventham believed that someone wanted him dead. It was always possible. But it struck me that a man living alone in this neglected and isolated place might ultimately need to fill his existence with some form of fantasy. The whole place was like a signpost to despair. I walked up the overgrown path and noticed the hulking broken-backed silhouette of the church through the screen of hedge and bare trees. Before I had time to knock, the door opened, and the Reverend William Ventham said: "Come in, Mr Chambers. I can't tell you how pleased I am that you were able to accept my invitation."

*

"They say that not a sparrow falls without God seeing," Ventham said. "But I have yet to hear anyone suggest that He might reach down and catch it. You could hardly have failed to notice that the parish of Edgecombe is not what it was."

He spoke apologetically, as if he was seeking to make amends for the short-comings of the Almighty.

"The place was failing even before I came here – years ago. Once, would you believe, this place was famous for its public houses? Did you drive through the village on your way?"

I nodded. The tiny hamlet might have been deserted if I hadn't noticed some of the drab curtains twitching. Broken windows and twitching curtains formed the core of my impressions.

"There is still one pub open, I believe, but running at a loss. Most of the cottages are owned by weekenders, out of the city; and a good many of those are up for sale. The youngsters have moved away. Who can blame them? There are just a few doddery old people, myself – " he grinned " – among them. I still open the doors of the church on Sunday mornings, but no-one attends; they even go away to be buried."

He stood with his back to the window; through it, I saw the still-impressive silhouette of the church spire. A little man, he must once have been plump, but now his clothes hung loosely on him. When he took off his glasses there were white strain marks around his eyes. I noticed that he was slightly hunch-backed.

"Now you're going to ask me why I don't apply for a posting to some other parish, some place where life would be more fulfilling. I've tried that." He grinned again, this time with a trace of bitterness. "There's a new breed of clergyman today. They wear duffle coats and run discothèques in the crypt on Saturday nights. I'm too old to adapt to that. I'm afraid I've become... an embarrassment. I think I must face the truth, that it suits them to have me tucked away here; somewhere where I can be forgotten, where I won't get in the way. When I die, I've no doubt they'll close the church. That's if it doesn't fall down before then. The roof and spire are already in a dangerous condition."

He was rambling, and I shrugged, a little impatient. "So how is it that you expect me to help? You must know that although a tarot-reading might provide a clue to a problem, the answer to it still remains with you. And you are already clearly aware what that problem is."

Ventham turned away and faced the distant spire, then, his head lowered in thought; he turned back to face me. "I must admit to a small deception," he said. "Frankly it was a pretext to get you here." Something in the way that he said this made me uneasy, and he must have sensed it. He continued: "I was afraid that you would dismiss me as a crank. You published a book some years ago, *Earthly Powers; Malignant Beings.* I've read it. I found it interesting."

My curiosity must have shown then, because he quickly went on, "I read a lot. There's nothing much else to do here. And I see no reason to limit myself to exclusively Christian literature. I believe that unexplained phenomena should be the concern of all thinking people. I was particularly intrigued by your argument that elemental forces, spiritual forces, are always present to be harnessed to the will of the determined individual; harnessed and directed for good or evil purposes. And lately I've become convinced that those very forces are being directed specifically against me – or what I represent."

"The Church?"

"This is a pagan place, cut off from the world, lost in time. And the old ways survive. I know they do. They must feel that the Church has let them down. Or perhaps they never wanted it in the first place; see it as some kind of presumption on their lifestyle."

"Yet on your own admission, the church here hardly presents a threat to their way of life."

"Again," he said, "perhaps it's not so much the church, or even me; but what the Church stands for. I think I need hardly remind you that, not so long ago, a combination of ignorance and religious fervour led to the deaths of thousands of innocent human beings. 'Witch-hunts.'" He made a disgusted sound.

"They wouldn't have known a real witch if..." He broke off and seemed to make a determined effort to compose himself. "Memories are long in a place like this. Families go back a long way. At first there were the accidents. Oh, yes, I really believed they were accidents to begin with. They were nothing dramatic, not at first anyway. Just small things going wrong with the car. Electric power-points malfunctioning. Then I began getting telephone calls. They were disgusting. They threatened me, told me that I had to leave. They would kill me if I didn't.

"But the noises are worst. They come at night. It's very quiet here. You can hear the slightest sound. At first I thought it was foxes. But it kept coming back. There is nothing here to attract a fox. Lately it's begun coming closer. And it *scratches*, as if it wants to get in."

"Couldn't it just be a dog?"

"Of course, I thought of that, too. But one night I watched from upstairs. I could not see it very clearly, I admit; but what I saw was not a fox. I sensed that it knew I was there. I am sure that it knew I was watching it, and *it wanted to be seen*. It was mocking me. Then when it moved closer I saw that it was walking upright, on its hind legs, like a man."

Ventham shivered.

But all the same, he had so far told me nothing that could not be explained by accident, stress, or, at worst, the work of a vindictive hoaxer. I knew I could not tell him that. It must have seemed to him that fate had played him a cruel trick when it had deposited him in this lonely, miserable spot; and now he was looking for a pattern, some clue to show him that he still had a purpose here. He could hardly fight the passing days themselves which alone, in the end, would deliver him; he had to find some more palpable object to fight and vent his frustration on.

"Have you considered an exorcism?" I said. "If so, you must know that you are better qualified than I am to perform one." It was a valid suggestion. If nothing else it would be a positive

10

means to channel out some of the frustrated energy which was the real monster here. He seemed to consider the idea for a moment. Then: "Do you know," he said thoughtfully, "I think that I would like that card-reading now."

*

I think that no card-reading I have ever conducted ranks in my mind as so dreary as the one that took place that afternoon, in that gradually darkening house. Ventham had lit no fire, and the chairs we sat in, facing one another across a small table, were palpably damp. Before we began he got up to close the curtains and switch on the light, a yellowish sixty-watt bulb. Then I sorted the pack and gave it to him to shuffle, and I spread the cards. Five of them. None of them held hope for much optimism; and I knew that no careful euphemisms or light philosophising would disguise their real nature from him. The first was the Five of Cups.

It showed a black cloaked figure, standing alone, in a desolate landscape underneath a grey sky. A storm threatened in the distance. It was only too clear how well the card related to Ventham's own situation. I began to interpret it. "The man is looking down, intent on the three cups which have spilled at his feet; he only sees what he has lost, and does not notice that behind him two more cups still remain upright. Perhaps not so much has been lost as he thinks; or perhaps it is that, made bitter by what has been wasted, he refuses to turn and carry on with what is left."

"Is that a church in the background?" Ventham pointed.

"Strictly speaking it's a keep or stronghold; but in your case that is analogous to a church, yes. You see here a river comes between the man and the church. But in the distance there is a bridge. So he can still enter it if he wishes." I wondered why I had almost said 're-enter.'

The Nine of Swords came next, hovering over the sleepless figure in its narrow bed, hands clasped to its face as if just awoken from some awful nightmare. I always remembered Aleister Crowley's version of this card. Nine poisonous, chipped, and dripping swords. They showed old memories which lingered and festered in the mind, to be projected against others and perpetuated in their turn. Ventham did not comment while I interpreted this card, and I quickly moved on to the next.

Before I could speak he said, very quietly, "What is the significance of the dogs?"

I was puzzled. It was the Four of Swords. It showed the effigy of a knight at repose on his tomb, beneath the window of a chapel. And then I saw it, too; There *was* a dog – crouched at the knight's feet. I had turned up that card hundreds, perhaps thousands of times. It meant seclusion from the world, exile; some said that the picture illustrated the practise of a knight spending one night alone in prayer and meditation before setting out to battle the next day. The tomb-effigy raised this idea to another level; this was the final rest before the greatest adventure.

The light falling through the window was the dawn of a new day after the sleep of death.

But I had not noticed the dog before. And there was something inexplicably baleful about the creature. "Effigies of knights were often shown with dogs at their feet," I said. "Generally, this is believed to show the knight's affection for an animal that had followed him through life, and his hope that it would accompany him into the next world. Of course, there is a correlation to the Egyptian practise of burying a noble with his possessions, and indeed his animals and slaves." I was talking smoothly enough, but inwardly I was shaken. Up until that moment I would have been prepared to stand up and swear in court that no dog appeared on that card. The dog's yellow eyes seemed to burn from the image as if there were pin-pricks in the cardboard, shining light from behind. I wondered if I had covered my confusion successfully; but when I risked a glance at Ventham he seemed oblivious to me, transfixed by the image.

The fourth was a major card, The Moon. "It seems to glow, but its light is not truly its own, only reflected. So it shows illusion, or self-delusion. Often it appears in connection with stress or even mental illness." I wondered how much of this Ventham was taking in, but I did not dare risk another glance. "Under the Moon is a path leading between two towers. The road of life. The space between the towers resembles a womb, where a man may be reborn. In some ways it can be likened to the experiences of psychiatry or spiritual enlightenment, which are often accompanied by frightening traumatic disturbances."

I was afraid that I was being about as subtle as a sledgehammer, but I could hardly stop now. "To reach this place of rebirth the traveller on the path has first to pass the keepers of the towers, who are a dog and a wolf."

I heard Ventham say, almost inaudibly, "More dogs."

"The dog shows the docile, domesticated side of man's nature, the wolf, the wild and unrestrained. To give way completely to either force can have disastrous consequences Dogs obviously provided the key to Ventham's particular trauma, so I decided to enlarge on the theme a little. "In some tarots the card shows the towers guarded by Anubis, the jackal-headed god of Egyptian lore. He is the keeper of doors and gateways, Lord of the Threshold. Also he is the god presiding over cemeteries, which are gateways to the next life. It's a fairly widespread tradition. In Haiti, the voodoo Baron Samedi holds nearly identical status, as god of crossroads and graveyards. Apart from being the guide of the dead, conducting souls to their place of rebirth, Anubis also has connections with the Greek Hermes and Roman Mercury – messengers of the gods."

Ventham repeated the last part of this sentence carefully, as if it meant something very important to him. I was relieved. I had not been at all sure that any of this made sense to him at all; frankly I suspected that he was only trying to prolong my stay – and I could hardly blame him for that. This was a desolate place, and any visitor must have been welcome company. The last card, though, offered little chance for optimism, no matter how careful my interpretation. It was the thirteenth-trump. It showed the land on the other side of the towers, a war-torn valley presided over by a grim skeletal rider.

"Death," Ventham said; "but for whom?"

"It need not imply physical death," I pointed out.

"Sometimes I wonder if that might not be infinitely preferable."

Before I had a chance to think of a suitable rejoinder (which I am not sure I could have done) he abruptly stood and moved away from the table. "I really must thank you. It's been fascinating, most enlightening. If you're not in too much of a hurry, now, there is something I would like to show you." So I was right; he didn't want to be left alone. But my heart sank when he said: "The church is very old. Beginning to show it, too, I'm afraid. But there is something in it which I think you may find interesting."

*

I have never really felt comfortable in churches. Following a rigorous 'religious' upbringing which had forbidden me the delights of fairgrounds, cinemas and other worldly pleasures that most children took for granted, I had spent years overcoming an almost crippling introversion. Until finally I had passed between the 'towers' of my own life to enter a more fully rounded existence, when Christianity became just one more religion to be studied as my interest in alternative beliefs grew. We walked through a chilly, untended graveyard to the massive doors of the church, and passed into a gloomy interior which seemed, if that were possible, even colder and less inviting. I looked around, wondering how many years it had been since a child had been baptised at the now-tilting font; how long since the pews, designed more for boxes than human beings, it seemed, had seated an uncomfortable and dwindling congregation. I found that I was quite unable to imagine the sound of human voices raised in song. What on earth could have inspired singing of any kind in this dismal tomb, unless it was defiance of their hostile surroundings? I thought I could understand why people would turn to the older religions, the worship of moon and trees and the turn of the seasons. What else could be so natural here where civilisation seemed completely to have foundered?

"This is what I wanted you to see."

He was standing over to one side, beneath a stained glass window, close to the door. There was not much light from outside; the sun was masked by the surrounding trees. I could just make out something in the shadow near the wall. I walked closer, peering through the darkness. Then I started back with an acute feeling of shock. The effigy of a knight cast in age-blackened metal lay atop a tomb. Its hands were clasped on its chest in prayer. And crouched at its feet was the shape of a huge, unbelievably malevolent dog.

*

I don't know when I have had a less agreeable experience. The old man kept his eyes fixed on the figure the whole time, with an expression which seemed to mingle repugnance and unhealthy fascination. He urged me to touch it, to more closely examine the craftsman's work; and I felt a strong sense of distaste when suddenly remarking; "Here. Touch it here," he grasped my arm by the coat sleeve and guided my hand to the dog's cold grimacing muzzle. The memory left a lingering impression long after I had left that desolate church and its keeper and was at last back behind the wheel of my car and headed for home.

All the time that we were in the place, Ventham had talked, an incessant whining tinged at times with the smugness of the scholar who knows his subject too well – has become obsessed, taken over by it, until there is nothing else. "They say that a dog at a knight's feet is the mark of the Knight Templar," he had said. "Of course one doesn't place too much stock in such ideas. But there does seem reason to believe that the Order survived in one form or another long after its supposed suppression in the thirteenth century. And if, as you suggested earlier, the animal was only a semblance of a favourite pet, then what of those knights shown with lions? How many knights, one wonders, had lions as household pets? Myself, I am inclined to believe that these were the symbol of some other, perhaps affiliated, cult."

It was part educated conjecture and part nonsense. The man had been alone too long; and with no-one to challenge and refine his arguments he had become obviously unstable. "Some say their cult was evil," he said; "and of course there *were* unsavoury incidents. The selling of Sultan Abbass's son into the hands of the enemy, to be carried across the desert in a cage to Egypt, where he suffered protracted torture and finally death; that was – regrettable. And yet when they were at their greatest strength and could have ground any country in Europe beneath them, they did not. They had power, but they used it wisely, to combat the enemies of Almighty God."

At this point I had begun to make my excuses to leave. I had heard enough. I had my own views on the Knights Templar, but I saw little point in discussing them here. Ventham seemed past the point of reasonable argument.

Before I left I had given him what advice I could – which frankly didn't amount to much. Past experience had taught me that 'psychic attacks' fell generally into two very basic areas. One involved the malicious direction of another person's will to destroy or enslave the victim – which covered anything from bone-pointing to modern brain-washing techniques. The other was the more subtle, self-induced kind, which occurred when the subject placed himself – willingly or not – in a situation or environment likely to arouse paranoid reaction. Anything, in other words, from a séance to a lonely country vicarage. The resulting effects could be anything from hallucinations to production of the stigmata.

But the greatest danger arose when the fears which lay unsuspected in a man's subconscious began to take on shape and invade his everyday, waking life. From what Ventham had told me, I knew that in his case that stage had already been reached. The cause of his fear hardly mattered; he might even genuinely be the victim of some malign external influence. The important point was that he believed the thing he was afraid of could kill him. So it could.

Once again, without any real hope that he would follow my advice, I suggested exorcism; but still it remained with Ventham to carry it out. It seemed clear that only by drawing on the strength of his own beliefs would he be able to restore his confidence, both in his church and himself. I couldn't help him there; our faiths lay worlds apart.

The motorway stretched away and then blurred into a frayed string of ring-roads. The lights of town appeared ahead. I had been glad to enter the motorway; the winding country lanes surrounding Edgecombe had had me seeing monster shapes in every fallen tree and bush. I suspected that the long afternoon I had spent in the cold, damp house listening to Ventham had affected me more than I realised. I sneezed and guessed that I'd caught cold into the bargain. I remembered the damp chairs in the vicarage. The ring-roads dissolved into genteel suburbs and before much longer I was turning the car into the drive of my own house. I stopped the car to get out, walking into the light of the headlamps to open the garage door. As I grasped the handle a shadow flickered across the metal door; something loping quickly in front of the headlights. I turned just in time to see the dog vanishing into the darkness. I felt an odd crawling feeling up my spine; then I shrugged it off and opened the door and drove the car inside. Ventham and his damned dogs.

All the same, I was shaking slightly when I entered the house, and poured myself a stiff drink. After another one I began to feel better; but still I was disturbed. If I could be so easily rattled after one afternoon in the place, what of Ventham, cooped up there years on end? Was he only a little unstable, as I'd thought? The telephone rang. I tried to ignore it, hoping whoever it was would hang up; but in the end I got up and answered it.

Ventham's voice crackled over the line.

"I thought you would be home by now," he said. "I wondered if you'd had a pleasant journey."

"As a matter of fact, I'm rather tired. I was about—"

"You know what country roads are like. Sometimes... animals... run into the road. People have terrible accidents."

"No. As you can hear, I've arrived safely. Now if you don't mind, reverend, I feel I need some sleep."

But the voice on the telephone was oddly persistent. "Dogs are the worst, of course. I think dogs must be the cause of many accidents, don't you agree? Did you see any dogs on your journey?"

"As a matter of fact..." I stopped. I had a sudden intuition that something was terribly wrong. "What exactly are you driving at? What's this all about?"

"Ah, I thought so. So you *did* see it. They were treated with contempt by the Jews, you know. Dogs, I mean. And yet they filled an important role in that society, clearing the streets of rotten garbage on which they fed. Scavengers. You could almost say that in a sense they were purifying agents, clearing away the corruption which might otherwise have spread disease. It is said that even the body of the witch-queen Jezebel was left as food for them. I think that is a fitting end for one who challenged the authority of God."

I listened while the mad old voice droned on and on, "'Thou shall not suffer a witch to live.' You must be familiar with this quotation, I think? After all, isn't that what you are? You try to conceal your true nature behind a facade of modern psychiatric mumbo-jumbo; and you fool a great many people. But in the end you are still a witch, one of those false prophets warned against in the Bible. You divert and distract people from what is true. God's holy word. Because of you many lost souls have been led onto a false path and will suffer damnation. For that, Mr Chambers, you must pay." He paused briefly, as if considering. Then he said: "I am a merciful man, Chambers. I give you the space of one hour in which to prepare to meet your God. For I have summoned an avenging angel, and at the end of that time he shall come and smite thee. Beware dogs, Mr Chambers." Then the line went dead.

Beware dogs.

I had never encountered a totally insane mind before. I wondered if it was possible that the crazy old man had really succeeded in bringing some ghastly elemental force into the solid, everyday world of trees and stone. In theory it was possible; the only question remaining was whether Ventham was capable of doing it. I remembered the malevolent creature sculpted out of bronze in the church; the loping shape silhouetted against the car headlamps. And suddenly I knew that it was true. Ventham had raised a demon, and unless I did something to prevent it, it was coming to kill me. I got up and went to the door and made sure that the lock and bolts were secure. Then I began a methodical tour of the house, checking each of the doors and windows in turn. All the time I knew that it would take more than wood and glass to keep the damned thing out. My only chance lay upstairs. There, in a room facing east, I had built a simple place of retirement; my 'temple', I called it. But even there I knew I could not be sure of safety. And I couldn't remain there forever. I needed some means of fighting back; I needed to find some way to reverse the evil that Ventham had directed against me. I found myself wondering why he had invited me to his home in the first place; surely not just to see what I looked like.

A dog. How would he send a dog to find me?

And then I remembered, the image shining with a hideous clarity in my mind, and again I saw that hand gripping my coat-sleeve, thrusting my hand against the cold muzzle.

The maniac had given it my scent.

I hardly remembered anything of the next hour. I know that I prepared myself in my upstairs room, while sometimes, from downstairs, I heard sounds – sounds of something moving around the house. I tried to concentrate on my preparations and to shut out the noises of it pushing at doors, windows. And scratching, always scratching. I stood in the east-facing room, slowly moving from quarter to quarter of a thin chalk circle drawn on the bare boards. At each of the four quarters stood respectively a lighted candle, a wine-glass full of water, a small dish of earth, and another dish in which lay a feather: symbols of the four elements. The room was devoid of curtains or furniture of any kind. A little way beyond the circle, near the door, was a smaller circle with a triangle drawn inside it. I began to visualise a wall rising up from the floor around me. I concentrated on it, watching it build brick by brick. At first it seemed misty, translucent; but as it rose higher than my head, it grew in solidity. I could even see the imprints of fingers in the hard mortar holding the bricks in place. When I judged that it was strong enough I began to work on the smaller circle. This was a circle of pure energy which I visualised as blue-white light. I had barely completed my preparations when I heard it. The thump of a heavy weight against the outside door. Then, almost innocuous in itself, the doorknob rattled as hands which were never intended for that purpose tried to turn it. The door creaked.

There was brief silence.

Then a rending of wood rang through the house, followed by the crash of some enormously heavy body against the floorboards, and I knew Ventham's demon was in the hall.

Down in the hall I heard it moving about, making hard scraping sounds against the hall floor; but worst of all was its *snuffling*, quick and hard like a dog on the scent as it cast about to find me. No more room for doubt then; Ventham had raised a hound of hell, and it was sniffing me out like a rabbit.

The sound came nearer, until it was on the stairs. As it

climbed. I could hear each successive stair creaking under its weight. I didn't know exactly what form Ventham's avenging angel had taken, but it was something heavy. Finally it was on the landing outside. I had deliberately left the door ajar, knowing that wouldn't stop it anyway. Something moved in the darkness of the landing and padded stealthily into the room. It was on the other side of the wall.

I could hear its breathing and the scratch of claws against the floor, then the rasp of rough fur as it brushed against it. Then it began to scratch the heavy bricks and it began to growl. I couldn't see it but as it followed the wall around, I sensed its growing frustration as it found no means of entry. For perhaps a minute it stayed in one place, puzzling over this impenetrable circular barrier. Then the wall shook as it launched a furious attack on it, pounding repeatedly with hammer-blows that shook the structure to a foundation that existed only in my mind.

Mortar crumbled and fell.

I visualised reinforcing rods of steel inside the bricks; but it was a mistake because the visualisation was too complicated, I couldn't hold it in my mind. Now the bricks themselves began to crack and large pieces became dislodged and fell. A large part of the wall fell away, and the creature redoubled its efforts. And now I could see it as well as hear it.

In dreams, some say, a being half-man, half-animal can show the nature of the true inner self. After the successive masks of character and personality and the objective and subjective views of the individual have been stripped away – beneath all the fantasies and illusions concerning that person – finally there is only the true self that is revealed. The thing which stood before me now seemed deliberately to parody that idea. It stood a little over five feet tall – about Ventham's height. It stood awkwardly upright, as if its limbs had never been intended to hold it erect. It wore a sort of surplice made of rough sackcloth, which was darkly stained and in rags. Its head and limbs were covered in tufts of uneven wiry reddish hair. It resembled images I had seen of the Egyptian Anubis; except that its head was the snarling blunt-muzzled mongrel head of the creature in the church. The huge muzzled head turned about as if sniffing out a trap; and as it turned briefly in profile I saw that, like Ventham, it was hunch-backed. It moved towards me through the ruined wall and stepped straight into the smaller circle.

It stopped.

It tried to move forward, to reach me, but to its bewilderment could only beat up against an imprisoning wall of light. Entering the circle it had passed through a one-way gate. It began to snarl, foam dripping from its gaping mouth, all the time hammering against the light-wall with huge stubby appendages which were neither hands nor claws. I knew I could only hold it for a short time. On the floor at my feet was a pair of fire-tongs I had earlier liberated from the grate; beside them lay five ten-pound notes.

I have always been careless with money. Now that carelessness might save my life. I remembered the telephone call that morning, the envelope on the doormat; I remembered tearing the envelope and spilling its contents onto the desk-top. I prayed silently that my memory had not failed me and I had not in some way handled the notes. The notes with Ventham's scent on them.

In one swift movement I gripped the bundle of notes in the tongs and thrust them out at the creature in the smaller circle. Some of them just fluttered feebly and fell to the floor; one landed inside the circle at the demon's feet.

For an instant it ceased its snarling. Its snout tipped back, sniffing; it seemed confused, questing for the source of the new odour. Then it saw the notes lying on the boards, and smelled Ventham's scent on them. Recognition showed in its yellow eyes. And something else. Ventham's scent on witches' money! The sound it made was beyond all description; throwing back its head it howled, a dismal noise which seemed to encompass brute fury and betrayal. The next moment its pounding fists cracked through the light-wall: I saw a spider-web tracing running all around its surface, jagged pieces falling and dissolving as they touched the floor. And as the wall frosted over completely with cracks and dissolved, I saw that the circle was empty. Somewhere far away I heard the ghastly cry of a hound.

I remained in the circle the rest of that night; at some point I fell asleep. When I woke, grey daylight filled the room. Automatically I made myself go through the banishing ritual, dispersing the last of the protecting mental wall. Then I began to freshen myself for the journey. I knew I would have to go back to Edgecombe before I could be sure it was over.

*

The vicarage was much as it had been when I had left it the previous afternoon, except that the front door was open; without stepping inside I knew that the house was empty. The broken-backed church loomed through the trees and I turned towards it, along the footpath I had followed with Ventham the day before.

I found him lying in the mud below the steps leading into the church. I thought I could imagine how it must have happened. When the demon had smelled his scent on the money, Ventham would have been aware of it; after all, it was his will that had animated the creature. From the card-reading I knew that he had suffered a death wish, clearly expressed in his reaction to the Death card. I had counted on that as the final trigger to reverse the dog-thing's attack. When he realised that it was coming for him, he must have turned to the one place that he felt would offer him sanctuary – the church, which in his own perverted fashion he had genuinely believed he was trying to save. It had caught him on the path, just in front of the doors, and after rending him with its claws, had crushed him against the granite door-post like an egg.

I ascended the steps into the church. It was not long before I found what I was looking for. In the vestry, something that stank like rotting meat hung from a pole set into cracks in the floor; it was covered with a cloth. Flies crept and buzzed lazily around it.

I found an old curtain to wrap it in and somehow managed to get it down from the pole without touching it. I did not have to uncover it to know what it was. Ventham's ramblings had given me the clue. There was a legend that the Knights Templar had worshipped the head of an ass. I dumped the stinking thing in a stream at the back of the church.

I only stopped once on my way out of the village, to telephone the police from a kiosk. I gave a false name and the address of a derelict cottage standing opposite. As I stepped from the kiosk it was beginning to rain, a heavy persistent drizzle. That was my last impression of Edgecombe. I drove away, leaving it with its broken windows and drab closed curtains, in the rain, leaving Ventham under the solid doorposts, like the towers in the tarot card, where he had finally met the Keeper of the Gate.

TAKASHI'S LAST SYMPHONY

Gary McMahon

"...sometimes I become very anxious because I can't find the energy or strength inside myself. It's not something we can get on demand. Sometimes it comes when I hear a favourite song..."

Takashi Miike

Later that night I went upstairs to my friend Takashi's place.

It was the beginning of spring and the rains had come, slashing the streets with broad cleansing percussive strokes, clearing away the litter and the stains of another dreary day in the city. I was feeling low, run down – possibly developing some sort of flu virus – so had stayed home from work for a few days. I surfed the Internet all day, scouring swingers' sites and message forums dedicated to low budget horror films. My mood was bleak, so the entertainment I sought reflected this vacant inner landscape.

Which was why I decided to visit Takashi.

The last time I was up there, we'd had some sort of drunken argument. I recalled a sweet *saké* high followed by a crushing combative low.

Takashi was fiery by nature, a westernised Japanese artist with severe emotional problems; he hated himself for turning his back on what he perceived as his cultural heritage, but loved the convenience of our way of life and embraced it fully, like an addict with his drug of choice. He was a soul in torment: a man on the edge – and that was even before you even considered his less than harmonious past.

I turned off my computer and leaned back in the chair, listening to the slow whirring sound of the hard drive shutting down. Rain pelted the windows like snatched notes from a piece of unknown music, forming smeary abstract pictures on the glass; the night world beyond was grey and formless, and did nothing to lift my sombre spirits.

I drank cold coffee from a chipped Star Wars mug, took a bite from a sandwich I'd prepared hours ago. The coffee was bitter; the bread stale. My reflection stared back at me from the blackened screen of my computer terminal, eyes nothing more than holes carved into a jaded, sickened skull. I pulled faces at myself, but the reflection didn't seem to want to obey; I got up from the chair, feeling afraid of my own disobedient image.

I could hear my neighbours fucking through the thin apartment walls. Nora and Teddy were a couple of sexual adventurers, always picking up some young stud in a club and bringing him home for the night. I tried to decipher the theatrical moans and groans and grunts, with the intention of counting how many people were present.

It was impossible: there could have been anywhere between one and five bodies in the room, rocking the bed and making small impacts against the paper-thin wall.

Noticing the blinking red light, I walked over to my answerphone machine and pressed the button to hear a message left the night before, when I'd been sleeping off another thick, pounding headache.

"Hi Jake. It's me. Just calling to say that I'm sorry I walked out the way I did. It was messy, lacking any closure.

"We need to talk, but we can't stay together. I'll come over later tonight, after the gig, and we can go out for a late drink, preferably somewhere neutral that stays open all night."

The message ended in static.

Sandra: my ex. She had left me for a photographer she met at the wedding of a friend I'd never even heard of. Some girl called Kiri. What a fucking stupid name.

Sandra had been performing at the ceremony, singing a couple of numbers before the main event and then the song that would form the basis of the first dance. She was a great singer, my Sandra, and had always loved her music. She played keyboards and provided backing vocals for an up-and-coming local band, a bunch of studied slackers who called themselves The Auditioners.

But if Sandra had planned to see me last night, why didn't I hear her arrive? Was I so soundly asleep that I'd missed her knocking on my door? I felt like kicking myself. Even if, as Sandra had said in her message, that was the end for our brief duet, I'd missed an opportunity to make myself feel better about things by telling her a few home truths. Or at least making some up.

The sounds of fucking from next door increased in volume. I covered my ears with my hands and tried to recite Beatles lyrics to keep out the clamour. When I got to the chorus of 'Penny Lane' I gave up, feeling even more depressed. I hate The Beatles.

My headache intensified; the pain was like a muffled backbeat inside my head, distant foreign music that I could not recognise.

Closing the curtains and checking that I hadn't left the oven on, I left the apartment and made my way across the landing, heading up to Takashi's place. I knew he'd be in; he never went out. Just stayed at home working on his 'installations' – ridiculous works of art created from what he called 'found objects'. Last time I was up there, he'd been putting the finishing touches to a piece called *Havoc*: the figure of a child made from empty baked bean cans and broken beer bottles.

The man wasn't right in the head, but I liked him all the same. He made me seem normal.

The stairwell was tight and dark, like a birth canal – I'm still not sure where that image came from, but it disturbed me all the same.

My footsteps echoed in a way that made them seem to originate below and behind me, making me feel pursued. Stalked. The ceiling light wasn't working, so I climbed in darkness, expecting someone to jump out at me at any minute. Paranoia nibbled at the back of my neck, giving me uncomfortable little love bites.

I jogged up the final flight, turned the corner and stood

before Takashi's door.

Something inside me – some crazy intuition – almost convinced me to turn back, retrace my steps down the shadowed stair core, and resume my nocturnal surfing. I wish now that I'd listened to whatever voice was trying to sing or speak.

I knocked on the door, expecting a long wait: Takashi was half-deaf and rarely heard visitors announce themselves outside his apartment. When he was a child, possibly about seven years old, his mother had inserted a piano wire into each ear, pushing them in far enough to burst the eardrums and retard the boy's hearing for the rest of his life.

My strange friend had escaped an even stranger family.

The door opened instantly and Takashi's small face peered out into the gloom.

"Lights still busted?" he asked, smiling.

"Yeah. That landlord needs a fucking good talking to."

He opened the door and beckoned me inside, turning his back on me to pad along the hallway on his little bare feet. Not only had he removed his shoes, but he was also stripped to the waist. His wiry torso was coated in a layer of sweat, and glistened like snakeskin in the oily darkness.

"I have something to show you," he said, his quick, brittle voice snatching at the air like strumming fingers. "My new project."

I watched his lean back disappear into shadow, and followed him into the depths of his apartment. There was a funny smell, but that was nothing new: there was always a funny smell in Takashi's place, a different one every time. This one held the dull tang of hot metal.

"Another sculpture?"

He didn't answer, which I took as an ominous sign. One time when I popped up to see him, he was working on a huge collage. A six-foot by four-foot canvas decorated with his own blood, semen and faeces. He'd called it *Infidelity*, and said it was about sexual indiscretion. Apparently someone had bought it, but I was never brave enough to ask whom. Just the fact that it had sold was unnerving enough. I mean, who would want to own *that*?

I thought about Sandra, and her unfaithful ways. The bitch had screwed me over, but really I couldn't blame her. I'm not the easiest man in the world to be with – I have issues. In the old days, I would have been called complex. These days, I'm just fucked up.

I walked into Takashi's spartan living room, squinting against the dark. What little furniture he possessed – TV, stereo, low occasional table and a single tatty armchair – had been pushed back against the walls to create a big open space at the centre of the room. Something hovered in that space, something I didn't really want to look at.

It must be a piece of installation art, I thought, perhaps meant for the lobby of one of the large law firms or advertising companies in the city. I knew that Takashi made a lot of money out of ignorant businessmen looking to acquire some easily purchased culture.

Takashi was up against the far wall, his back pressed to the smooth plaster. I could just about make out his stunted shape in the darkness, his tiny head with that shock of tousled black hair, his skinny little arms held tightly at his sides. With his cowed demeanour and upright posture, he resembled a naughty schoolboy sent to stand in a corner to atone for a silly prank.

I glanced around the room, looking for a light source. The windows had been boarded over with timber ripped from packing crates and when I glanced upwards I saw that the light fitting had been torn out of the ceiling. Strands of wire poked through a black hole like spiders' legs. As I watched, I half expected them to twitch in anticipation.

"Behold," said Takashi, his tongue twisting the words into a kind of clipped, singsong version of English. "My new piece. I call this one *Begotten*."

I stepped closer, trying to make out something familiar in the confusing pattern before me. Long hair? A bent arm? A

29

pale, slender leg?

What was this?

"Takashi... what have you been up to?"

"Working. I dedicated this one to my mother."

I knew that Takashi's mother had disowned him when he'd left Japan to pursue a career in the arts. Then, after sending him a series of terrible, abusive letters, she'd hanged herself from the branches of a tree outside the family home in Osaka. According to Takashi, the woman had suffered a mental breakdown shortly after her husband's death, and her mind had been warped ever since.

Takashi's mother was the widow of a renowned pianist – a classically trained musician who died in a freak accident when a stage on which he was performing collapsed, killing the entire orchestra and several members of the audience. For several weeks before she killed herself, all she could hear was the music ringing in her ears like her late husband's screams. Suicide was the only way to shut it off.

I wondered, not for the first time, what kind of horrors Takashi had run away from in coming here to the UK. I knew about the abuse, both mental and physical, but I could only imagine the actual tortures carried out in their family home.

"Are you okay, man? I mean, have you been getting those headaches again?"

He giggled in the darkness, and that was when I began to feel afraid. Takashi had been on the verge of a breakdown himself ever since I'd first met him when I moved into the building three years ago. I found his near-madness appealing in a twisted kind of way, but if he finally snapped I didn't want to be around to wallow in the aftermath.

Then I heard another sound. The dreaded sound of Takashi snapping – a soft moan, the slapping together of dry lips. The clicking of fingers.

I backed up a step, but then realised that Takashi had moved behind me, leaning up against the closed door.

"Listen, mate, I think we'd better call a doctor. You seem

ill."

He giggled again. "No, no, my friend. I've never felt better."

I took a step forward, regaining the ground I'd given up. Takashi began to drum his fingers against the hollow door, his long nails providing a sharp percussion. It was the soundtrack to a nightmare.

Drumming. Like mercilessly trained fingers on piano keys.

Drumming.

As I took yet another step forward, moving closer to his latest creation.

"What do you think? Be honest – I want to hear a genuine *emotional* response."

Drumming.

I waited for my eyes to grow accustomed to the darkness, watching in latent terror as the artwork began to take shape. Yes, I *had* seen human hair, an arm, a leg. But that was where the humanity ended.

She was young, perhaps in her mid twenties, and had been rather beautiful before Takashi had got his hands on her. Piano wires hung around her head in a skinny Medusa hairnet, passing through the flesh of her cheeks, lips and throat. What blood had spilled, Takashi had painstakingly washed away, leaving her taut white flesh unmarked by impure liquors. The puncture wounds had puckered around the wires, gripping them, trying to heal and absorb the invasive material.

The wires also supported the body, looping silver knots that attached her to the ceiling joists like a languid angel caught in mid flight.

Her hands had been cut off and the wounds cauterised; piano keys dangled from the stumps, pushed into the truncated wrists like long cartoonish fingers.

Drumming.

Bile rose in my throat, but I had no choice now. I had to look at the scene that Takashi had orchestrated: his symphony to a painful, unbearable childhood.

"She made me practice on toy pianos when I was a baby.

Every day. Every night. Hours spent battering my fingers against hard plastic keys just so I could be like my daddy." His voice was like a torch song, low and mournful.

And his fingers drummed against invisible keys.

The girl's mouth had been smashed in, but with a slow, careful violence. Her lips were gone, sliced off with a surgeon's precision, and yet more piano keys had been forced into the cavity, musical teeth for a mouth that would never sing again.

"I hated those fucking pianos."

The final touch was the feet. Of course, they'd been sawn off, and what took their place was nothing less than inspired. Two tiny plastic toys, children's pianos. Somehow he'd managed to attach the absurd novelty items to the nubs of her ankles. Judging by the five or six empty tubes of Superglue scattered on the floor nearby, it had been a tricky and time-consuming procedure.

The drumming stopped.

"Your comments, please?"

I swallowed bitter vomit, bowed my head before such an amazing sight.

"It's beautiful," I whispered. And it was. It really was.

Then, locking the door and moving slowly away, Takashi approached his work of art. He sat on the floor beneath her, cracked his knuckles, and began to play a tune on those ridiculous toy pianos; a lilting melody for his mother as the girl's limp legs swayed above his nodding head.

"Her favourite," he said, smiling. I didn't know if he meant his mother or the poor, mutilated substitute that hung limply before me.

Then, to my eternal horror, she moved. Piano-key fingers flexing, misty eyes opening in a narcotic awakening, overstuffed mouth twisting into something approaching a chemically blissed-out smile.

It was only then that I noticed something my mind had blocked out, something I should have anticipated. It was

32

obvious really, a rather predictable encore to please the crowd in the cheap seats, but for some reason I'd failed to read the right notes, or even to follow the correct song sheet. I blame the jet-black wig he'd used to cover her dyed blonde hair, and of course the distraction caused by her multiple musical disfigurements.

The girl was Sandra.

She had always loved her music.

For John Llewellyn Probert

A SENSE OF MOVEMENT

David A. Riley

His mottled face set in a look of anger, Malcolm trudged along Anvil Avenue, wilfully ignoring the cold on his back, where the wind cut through the holes in his sweatshirt. Damn her, damn her, fuckin' well damn her, the ungrateful bitch! He stared at the houses across the road, their red brick walls almost dazzlingly bright as the sun sank towards the high-rise flats behind him. A short distance further on, the road was blocked by a haphazard jumble of bulldozers, cranes and JCBs, left for the weekend like abandoned toys where some of the houses had already been demolished to make way for a town centre by-pass. Dust from shattered bricks and pulverised plaster slowly drifted across the road towards him, blown by the cool September wind.

Pausing for a moment, Malcolm rumbled a belch of stale beer from his lunch in the Grapes as he gazed morosely at the tall Victorian terraced houses, his large, heavily veined drinker's nose sniffing at the smell wafting from them. Somehow their look of woeful dilapidation so closely matched the flood of self-pity that had risen inside him that he suddenly, fervently wished he hadn't drunk as much beer as he had last night. If he hadn't he might have held his temper. But, with three weeks holiday pay burning a fist-sized hole in the pocket of his jeans, he'd felt entitled to a bit of a binge, and the night had started well enough, with him and Linda making the rounds of the local pubs.

Angrily, he rubbed his knuckles. Blood slowly seeped through the makeshift bandage he'd wrapped around them. It still looked wet, and he knew he should have gone to the Infirmary to have them stitched. He'd probably be left with a row of scars when they finally healed. Though Bill Sutcliffe, the cheap, conniving, sleazy bastard, was fuckin' well worse off than him. For all he might have temporarily lost a few lumps of skin, Bill would be short two of his teeth for the rest of his life, left on the floor of the Swan. That should cramp the bastard's style, Malcolm commiserated with himself, feeling a vague semblance of satisfaction – marred only by the fact that Linda went off with Bill afterwards, and was probably looking after him right now.

Irritably, Malcolm kicked out at a stone on the kerb. It arced across the road and bounced off the door of one of the derelict houses opposite. As he followed its flight, a flash of sunlight from the attic window of the house dazzled him. Instinctively he jerked his head from the glare. When he looked back again a frown slowly formed in his eyes. For an instant he thought he saw something move behind the window and look down at him. Although there were no curtains, the strong sunlight across the glass was far too bright to see anything inside the room. Only a vague, almost illusory sense of movement, an impression of something nearing the window, could be seen from where he stood. Distracted from his rancour, Malcolm wondered if kids had broken into the house. Despite the throbbing ache in his head and the odd spell of queasiness, that still persisted from time to time in disturbing his stomach, it was a pleasant evening and he was in no hurry to go home. When he thought about it, in fact, he was in no kind of hurry at all, not without Linda, who'd lived with him for over six months.

Again he glanced up at the attic window. As the sun dipped beyond the flats, it seemed as if the movement he sensed inside the house became increasingly distinct.

Slowly, he strolled across the road. In a strange way the house seemed to draw him to it as flies buzzed through the fading sunlight around him. They buzzed unheard, as Malcolm stared up at the window, fascinated by whatever was moving behind it. It may have been a face, drawing nearer the glass, but it was still too vague for him to be sure.

In a half-hearted attempt to restore some sense of normality, Malcolm told himself there was nothing there, but he knew that

35

there was. Something that looked down at his face as he looked up at it.

What happened next took Malcolm by surprise, leaving him gasping for breath and halfway certain he was cracking up.

Like a film in which a reel had been accidentally missed by the projectionist, with no image of whatever happened in between, he found himself suddenly walking downhill more than five blocks away into town. Anvil Avenue and its condemned rows of empty houses lay far behind him. Sweat covered his face and his side was sore from a violent stitch, as if he'd been running. A cold flush added to his feelings of alarm as he stopped in his tracks and stared about himself. Confused, Malcolm tried to think back over what had happened, but no matter how hard he tried to remember he could not recall leaving the front of the house he'd been staring at. In fact, Malcolm thought, with a dim awareness of unease, the last thing he could remember was an impulse to go into the house.

A young couple passed him on their way into town. Their amused curiosity, as they glanced at his face, made Malcolm attempt to pull himself together. He was feeling light-headed, and as he hurried on home he told himself that he must have been out walking too long.

Perhaps it was his need for a reassuring reason to explain what happened that made him realise deep down that something dreadful must have occurred. That night, despite being so overwhelmingly tired that he turned the television off long before ten, he barely slept. Whenever he somehow managed to escape the turbulence of his racing thoughts, nightmares sent him crying into wakefulness again. There were voices in his dreams that no lips had ever formed, that no lips *could* ever form, voices that called in distant chants. There was a figure there, too. Hooded like a monk, it reached out for him from clouds of mist, calling, beseeching, irritably ordering him to obey. And there was an awareness, too, of terrible deeds carried out beyond men's sight, of deaths and mutilations and of sacrifices to dark and evil forms. He seemed to hear his name called out, but it was an echo of an echo that was swept deliriously into oblivion when he awoke.

Next day he felt too ill to go out. His temperature was over a hundred and he felt incessantly sick. Viewing his face in the bathroom mirror, as he forced himself to shave, it seemed as if all the life had been drained out of him.

But he could not rest.

Not properly.

The house seemed stuffy and hot, and it wasn't long before he dressed himself in an old sweatshirt and a pair of slacks, then sat in the sun at the front of his two up, two down terraced house, watching the weeds as they swayed back and forth in the narrow strip of garden.

It was late afternoon before he felt well enough to go for a walk. For no particular reason, except perhaps for a feeling of curiosity about what happened when he went there, he headed for the condemned streets he'd strolled along the day before. Puzzled about what happened when he was here last time, he looked up at the attic window as sunlight blazed across its small, square panes.

A cloud shadow swept across it, and this time there was no mistaking it. Nearer, nearer, black within the shadows, *something* moved. He felt drawn to it. Dizzy and sick, his mind suddenly seemed to slip into a daze, a sensationless daze in which memories and even thoughts themselves were dissolved into oblivion.

With a cry he broke free. Fear pounded the blood through his aching head as he turned and ran down the hillside street as dusk overran it with shadows.

Not daring to stop till he was safe within a crowd, his chest was heaving when he finally slowed to an unsteady walk. Nearby, people were queuing up outside the Apollo Cinema on King William Street. More were waiting by the edge of the pavement for a bus, mopping their faces in the cloying heat of an Indian Summer. There was the sound of cars and the reassuring normality of the smell of hot burgers and chips as he passed McDonald's, its gaudy lights glowing bright against the spreading darkness of the sky.

A few minutes later Malcolm pushed his way through a small crowd of drinkers outside the Castle; he hurried on into the pub. Standing behind the bar he saw Jenny Finch, her plump face shining with perspiration as she flicked a few strands of dark red hair from her brows.

"Hi Malc," she called as he leaned against the bar in front of her, still gasping for breath. "Lager, is it?" Thin strands of dyed hair clung to her forehead like streaks of paint. She'd been married twice, and was battered by her last husband for more than three years till she got a divorce.

"And something for yourself, sweetheart," Malcolm said, looking up and sensing that his own smile probably looked as false as hers. He handed her a crumpled ten pound note. Perhaps a few drinks would help to settle the ache that ground inside his head. He felt better already, drawing a sense of well-being from the familiar smells of beer and leather and old upholstery in the pub.

"I'll have a half of lager with you, if that's all right," Jenny said, placing his pint in front of him. She turned to the till and got him his change.

There were only a handful of drinkers in the pub, and Jenny, seeing that none of them needed a refill yet, poured herself a glass of lager, before returning to Malcolm.

"Cheers," she said as she sipped her drink.

"Cheers." Malcolm smiled. It came easier now, less restrained – less tense.

"What are you up to tonight?" Jenny asked. She held her drink in both hands. "Meeting someone?"

He shook his head. "The night's my own. No ties."

"No ties?" She cocked her head to one side. "Last I heard you were living with Linda Barton."

"Was."

Jenny smiled, her small teeth showing. "Nothing lasts, does

38

it?"

"Not often," he said, smiling back.

Later that night, with seven more pints inside him, Malcolm felt better than he had for days, especially when Jenny came from behind the bar as Harry, the landlord, sorted her pay for the night.

"A taxi's going to pick me up in a few minutes," Jenny said. "Perhaps we could share it."

Malcolm shrugged. "Why not?" He watched Harry saunter towards them; the landlord's broad red face was creased into a knowing wink as he gazed at Malcolm from behind Jenny's head. "I've some booze back at the house. We could always get a takeaway from the Chinese on the way and let the night last a few hours more," Malcolm said.

"Oh, yes?" Jenny turned round, took her money from Harry, who went off with a chuckle. "And just how many hours were you thinking of?" she asked.

*

His bedroom felt hot and tense in the darkness, like a prison cell deep beneath ground. Struggling from his sleep, Malcolm grabbed for the edge of the hole he dreamt he'd been thrown or stumbled in, he did not know which.

"Hey! Watch out! You're hurting me"

There was a click as the bedside light came on. Jenny sat up. Blankets tumbled about her lap as she held the side of her face with one hand.

"You hit me," she said.

Still entangled in his strange, dark dreams, Malcolm blinked his eyes at the light.

"I'm sorry," he mumbled, unsure what he'd done. His throat felt drained of moisture.

"I should think so too." Jenny leaned out of bed for her handbag, took out a mirror and inspected her face. "If I have a bruise, you're for it."

Malcolm examined her face for himself. "You'll be all right," he told her.

"I'd damn well better be." Irritably she shrugged his arm off her shoulders as he tried to give her a reassuring hug. "You didn't used to be like this, writhing and muttering in your sleep all night. God knows how many times you woke me up with your kicking. I've hardly had a half hour's sleep all night."

"It was just a nightmare, that's all," he muttered.

"That's all? If I had nightmares as bad as yours I'd be worried. I've never heard anything like it. If I didn't know better I'd think you were on drugs or something." She picked up a packet of Berkleys and lit one, puffing it hard to control her nerves. "Half the time you seemed to be jabbering away in a foreign language."

"A foreign language?" Uncertain, he tried to pick through the jumbled scraps of what he could still remember from his dreams. "Like chants, d'you mean? Something like that?"

Jenny shrugged. "Could've been. You went on enough. Jabber, jabber, jabber! Like a drunken priest rushing through Mass. You know what I mean?"

*

When Jenny grumblingly left after breakfast, Malcolm decided to have another look along Anvil Avenue. He'd seen the house again in his dreams. That much he could remember, though the rest was so weird – so disjointedly weird – that he felt confused. The only thing that didn't was the feeling of menace the half seen figure in his dreams had filled him with.

Demolition men were hard at work when he finally reached the condemned street. Thick clouds of dust filled the air as the walls of a house shuddered, then ponderously crashed to the ground with a sullen groan, though it would be a while yet before they finally reached the one he was interested in. Its front garden choked with thigh high nettles, there was little more than a narrow gap along the path from the rusted wrought iron gate. A notice pasted to the sun-bleached door announced its impending demolition in thick, block letters and row after row of finer print.

Malcolm glanced at the attic window, but the reflection of the sky in its empty panes was too bright for anything to be seen inside.

"Evil place, ain't it?" One of the demolition men strolled over, a mug of hot tea in one hand and an inch-thick sandwich in the other.

"What d'you mean?" Malcolm asked.

"Never heard tell of it?" The man grinned through a mouthful of corned beef, onions and bread.

Malcolm frowned. "Should I have?" He wondered if he was being set up.

"Osbert Cunningham. Surely you've heard tell of him? It were in all the papers a couple of years back. Black magic. Got taken away to the loonybin. Certified. And about time too from what I heard. A real nutter, he was. His place has been empty ever since. Well, you can tell that, can't you, just lookin' at it? If we weren't gonna knock it down in another few days I reckon as how it'd fall down itself. Look at it!" The small man strolled down the path, his thick work trousers impervious to the nettles. He kicked the door with his heavy boot. Springing open, it jammed on the floorboards inside with a high-pitched squeal, and a strong, stagnant smell of decay swept out. The man pulled his face as he returned to the road, grinning. "Almost bad enough to put me off me grub," he said, before munching another mouthful of sandwich.

"Osbert Cunningham?" Malcolm frowned. Never a close follower of the news, apart from the sports pages of the *Sun*, he had only the vaguest recollection of the name.

"Don't tell us you've never heard tell of him. Damn near got himself jailed a few times o'er the years for what he got up to. Evil owd bastard, he was. Dead now, I should think. Must've been damn near eighty when they put him away. My cousin, Jimmy, he was here at the time. He'd been sent by the Council

to help clear it out. Unsanitary, they said. Health risk, like.
There was that much horrible crap in here they had to wear
face masks. Owd Osbert had to be dragged out. A couple of
coppers broke in first with a warrant. Bust in the door with a
hammer. Then the blokes from the nuthouse went in for him.
They had to use a straight jacket on him to get him out.
Laughin' and shriekin' and callin' out names. Jim said as how
it sounded as if the silly owd bastard were tryin' to call
somethin' up. But they soon put stop to that, I can tell you.
One of the doctors pushed a bloody great needle in his arm to
calm him down. Or knock him out. I don't know which.
Anyway, they got him out of there at last, though by then a
crowd had gathered on the street, shoutin' and jeerin' and
damn near ready to lynch the owd bastard, they hated him that
much. Or feared him. I'm not sure which. Least ways, they
used to fear him. Perhaps now he'd been trussed up like a
Christmas turkey, ready for the oven, they'd forgotten just how
much they feared him before, though they hated him still. That
hadn't changed. It was as much as the coppers could do to
clear a path to the ambulance so they could get him away in
one piece."

"And no one moved into the house after him?" Malcolm
asked, viewing it nervously.

"Don't look like it, does it? Leastways, if they did I don't
reckon as how they stayed here long. Do you?"

Malcolm shuddered, unnerved by the workman's words
more than he cared to let on.

"I'll tell you somethin', though," the man continued, clearly
intent on telling him the rest of his tale. "Jim and the others
workin' with him were far from keen to clean the place out."

"It smelt that bad?"

The man laughed, spitting bread. "Naw, it wasn't the smell.
They're used to that where Jim works. They've had to clean
out worse smellin' places than this. Take my word. Naw, it
wasn't the smell. It were some of the things they found inside.
Or some of the things they *thought* they found inside. The way

A Sense of Movement

Jim talks when the mood takes him – that or the booze, if you know what I mean – it were like some'at out of one of them there Hammer Horrors, you know. Said as how some of them thought they saw some'at in the dust, starin' at them. Anyhow, they cleared out the ground floor and most of the bedrooms, but then, when they got to the attic bedroom, well, that's when they said as how they'd had enough. Jim said there were some'at about this place that was too much for what they were bein' paid to bother with. 'They can do it themselves if they want it clearin' out,' he says. 'Too fuckin' horrible for me.' Personally, I think he lays it on a bit thick. Though I know one thing. However bad it is it won't stop *us* from knockin' it down when we come to it, things starin' at us from the dust or not!" He guffawed loudly. "Have you ever heard owt like it, eh?" He looked at the house, at the half open door. "When we've done with it, it'll be nowt but a pile of flattened bricks, that's all. Just like the rest of them. You can take my word for that."

Malcolm wiped his face. Sweat covered it, cold against his skin. He grunted something, unable to stand it here anymore. He waved goodbye, then hurried as quickly as he could down the road into town, stumbling his way across the ruptured tarmac where tufts of grass had sprouted through.

*

Too confused and unsettled to stay in that night, Malcolm went to the pubs instead, intent on getting as drunk as he could. He bought himself a bag of fish and chips on the way, then went from one pub to another till he lost track of time and had to be helped back home by a couple of friends. Despite his drunkenness, though, the nightmares returned. The robed figure was clearer now as it beckoned to him, its emaciated arms covered in sores, though he could not see its features completely. Parts were missing, or had been dissolved. Terrified by the sense of malignancy that radiated from it, Malcolm tried to flee, but clouds of corruption barred his way.

Like waves upon waves of vile-smelling fog, they forced him towards the creature's arms. He turned away from it as he fought the miasma, but his lungs were clogged with the evil stench. He could barely breathe. "Help me, God help me!" he cried, filling his mouth with the doughy vapours.

The black arms reached towards his face till their brittle fingernails touched his cheeks.

His body drenched with perspiration, he woke up tangled amongst the blankets on his bed, staring at the darkness. Even though he knew it was only a dream, even though he knew that none of it – none of it at all – had really happened, that it was his own mind playing stupid, idiotic tricks on him, none of this could do anything to lessen the effects of the nightmare on him. What was wrong with him, Malcolm did not know. Too much booze? Too many pints over too many years? Was that it? Had it weakened his brain so much that he was hallucinating now like a drunken old wino?

When morning eventually came, he made himself something to eat, then washed and shaved before forcing himself to go out, even though the day was overcast, with the threat of rain not far away amongst the swollen, angry banks of clouds that hung above the town.

Bored, he wandered through the shopping centre, gazing without interest at shop windows. By eleven, when the pubs had begun to open, he was ready for a drink. On an impulse he headed for the Castle with the hope of seeing Jenny Finch. Perhaps he could patch things up. God knows, but he needed someone for company.

The pub was quiet when he entered. Over the bar a portable TV was showing a chat show. Later it would be tuned in to whatever races were being televised today for the regulars who flitted between here and the nearest bookies down the road. In the meantime, Harry lounged behind the bar, smoking a cigarette as he gazed through a copy of the *Mirror*.

"Will Jenny be in this afternoon?" Malcolm asked when he'd ordered a pint.

Harry shrugged. "She sometimes pops in for a half if she's been in town shopping. Otherwise she'll not be in till eight to work behind the bar." Harry handed him his beer. "If you ask me you'd be better off getting yourself some sleep than messing about with her. You look shagged out already." Harry grinned knowingly.

Malcolm tried to match his leer. "She's worth it, Harry. Take my word."

"I don't doubt it, old son. I don't doubt it one bit. Not when I look at the rings under your eyes," he laughed.

Malcolm wished that what Harry evidently thought was the reason for whatever ravages had been inflicted on him were true. But even sex with Jenny Finch seemed beyond him now. He'd never felt so tired. Or so worried... as if part of him really did believe that what he'd been dreaming about was real. Or partially real in an uncanny way. Malcolm gulped at his beer, knowing that he would have to down a few more before he would begin to feel like his normal self.

By half past three he was almost drunk. Seven pints of lager, two pork pies and a bag of cheese and onion flavoured crisps, and he felt fit for anything. Jenny Finch hadn't turned up, but that didn't matter anymore as he leaned against the bar, half listening to the racing commentary on TV. He drained his last pint, then looked at the clock. For an instant, as he gazed up at it, he saw the shadowed face of the thing from his dreams staring at him. The horrifying shadow beneath its moth-eaten cowl seemed to shift, and its features became nauseatingly clear, leprous and evil like a mask shaped from a pile of old fungus. The beer he'd drunk seemed to turn in his stomach, and he had to force back the vomit that rose in his throat.

"Anything wrong?" Harry asked.

Malcolm felt his face pale as blood drained from it.

"Your fuckin' beer, that's what," he grunted against the nausea that gripped him.

Harry laughed. "There can't be that much wrong with it from the amount you've drunk this afternoon."

45

In a daze Malcolm headed for the gents. What the hell was wrong with him? He splashed cold water in his face from the sink, then soaked a paper towel and wiped himself with it. Malcolm pressed the wet towel to his eyes. Never, he thought, *never*! The fuckin' thing could never have been there. He knew it. Whatever he thought he saw above the bar must have been his own imagination. Like all the rest.

Breathing deeply, he stared at his face in the fly-spotted mirror above the sink, then returned to the bar, where Harry cast him a look of concern.

"Feeling better now?" Harry asked.

Malcolm made an effort to grin back at him. And failed. "I will when I've had a whisky to settle my stomach."

"You sure?"

"Why not? It can't be worse than your fuckin' beer, you old sod." A nagging ache pulsed behind his eyes, and he knew that he wasn't well. But some whisky would soon sort that out, he was sure.

When he'd downed the first, he ordered another, then tried to sort out what had happened. As the whiskies spread their reassuring heat through his stomach, easing the tension in his abdominal muscles, it seemed to become easier to think. Much easier, in fact. And he soon realised that he had allowed himself to become obsessed by the house on Anvil Avenue. A half seen shape had been enough to persuade him that something sinister lay inside the house, when all it probably was, in fact, was a tattered length of torn curtain that had been left hanging behind the window. You're a fool, a stupid, impressionable fool, he told himself as he finished off another whisky.

Abruptly, he stood up, swayed for a moment, then took a deceptively strong grip on himself. "I'll be back in a while," he told Harry. "I'm just goin' to sort somethin' out. Somethin' I should've sorted out before."

"Take care," Harry called as he left.

Cold gusts of wind blew into him as he hurried down the

street, trying to clear his brain. At the bus station in the Boulevard he bought a large mug of coffee in a snack bar, drinking it while he waited for the next bus to arrive that would take him to Anvil Avenue. Already car headlights were coming on as the sky darkened. Shop windows glowed through the rain-swept gloom.

Twenty minutes later Malcolm stumbled from the bus. Although the avenue was still a couple of streets away, some of the effects of the demolition work could already be seen. White dust, darkened by drops of rain, lay across the tarmac road. Odd pieces of shattered masonry were strewn here and there, dropped by some of the trucks that ferried the rubble away. Through a gap between the terraced houses he glimpsed vehicles parked along the avenue: JCBs, bulldozers, cranes and trucks, stilled for the night. Malcolm glanced at his watch, and decided that the demolition men must have knocked off early because of the weather.

As he walked towards the house – old Osbert's house – he became aware of a feeling of unease, small to begin with, but increasing as he drew nearer. The front door still stood partially open. Heavy drops of rain dripped from its ornate lintel. More, swept into its gloomy hallway by the blustering wind, staining the walls inside.

Grunting to himself, Malcolm clenched his fists in a futile gesture of determination as he strode across the last few yards towards it. Before he was even fully aware of what he was doing, he'd marched down the path through the nettles and was inside the house. For a moment he gazed up the intimidatingly bare staircase to the landing above – and felt an almost overwhelming impulse to turn round and run. But from what? What on earth could there be in an old house like this for a grown man to run away from? It was ridiculous. He knew it. Clenching his fists yet again – his fighter's fists – Malcolm was determined he wasn't going to be obsessed by a drink sodden nightmare. He'd show himself now, once and for all, there was nothing here.

Nothing at all.

For a moment, as his hand rested on the banister rail at the foot of the stairs, he hesitated again. He grunted deep inside his throat, then pushed himself forwards and mounted the stairs so fast that the blood was pounding through his head as he looked along the short, filth-strewn landing towards the next flight of stairs that led to the attic. Dust and debris lay everywhere. Over everything there hung an oppressive smell of damp and neglect. He strode towards the final set of stairs. Forbiddingly narrow, with strips of paper hanging from the walls on either side, the banister rail at the foot of the stairs felt cold in his hand as he reached out for it. He tightened his grip, ignoring his qualms, ignoring the voice that shrilled out at him from somewhere deep inside his head to turn round and run. The door at the head of the stairs was shut. A thin beam of light glanced dismally across it from a dirty skylight, a dusty square of glass in the ceiling. One minute more, he told himself. That was all it would take. One minute more and he would see for himself there was nothing here.

Malcolm clung to the banister rail as he climbed the steps, his stomach tensed. On the short, uncarpeted landing at the top he reached for the door handle and pressed down on it. For an instant he closed his eyes, then pushed.

The door swung open. A cold draft wafted his face as he opened his eyes. Watery sunlight shone in cold grey beams across an empty room. Only heaps of dust lay scattered across the bare floorboards in front of him.

With a sigh of relief Malcolm stepped into it and crossed towards the window. He gazed at the avenue far below as cloud shadows raced along its rubble-strewn surface, one after another. As he stood watching them, something stirred a memory at the back of his mind – something he had all but forgotten.

He turned.

Inexplicably, he felt his beer-filled stomach tighten with apprehension as the room was plunged into darkness by a passing cloud. For the first time Malcolm remembered when he came here before. He remembered pushing the door open and peering in, uncertain if the floorboards would take his weight. He remembered it so clearly he could not understand how he could have possibly forgotten it till now. Could his own mind have made him forget? But why? Why should it?

As the memories became clearer, he heard something move. There was a strong smell of dust and damp clothes.

Malcolm tensed, feeling aware of being watched. Someone was standing in the shadows behind the door, he was sure, even though he could not make anything out in the growing darkness.

Beads of sweat dripped from his chin as he wondered if someone had followed him into the house.

Panic struck him as his memories warned him that, unlike before, he had gone much further into the room this time. He tried to speak to whoever was stood behind the door, but his tongue wouldn't move.

In the gloom he saw the dim impression of a lip. The lip began to move on the unseen face.

Malcolm tried to scream. Old Cunningham, he remembered (though he could not understand why this thought should strike him now) had been stopped before finishing whatever it was he was calling up. Had it been too late to stop something from answering, though? Something part-formed?

The dark, twisted scab of a lip began to smile.

He could see that now.

As a black hand, which looked to Malcolm like a burned leather glove, moved towards him…

*

The old man, lying in a drug-induced sleep, smiled to himself on the hospital bed, his face outlined by a distant light.

A nurse, passing by on her tour of the ward, caught sight of the movement of his lips. Poor old thing, she thought as she glanced across his wasted, geriatric features, though she knew well enough who he was. Dreaming again, she supposed, though what kind of dreams a man like Osbert Cunningham could be having she preferred not to think. Let the doctors who examined him waste their time with things like that, she thought. The evil smirk on the old man's lips was bad enough. What went on in the murkier depths of his mind was almost certainly many times worse.

"*His soul!*" the man whispered, viciously. "*Now grasp his soul!*"

Hurrying towards the lighter part of the ward, the nurse felt a shudder of revulsion as the old man chuckled in the gloom behind her, a sound of satisfaction in his crackling voice.

"*NOW GRASP HIS SOUL!*"

Alarmed at the gloating in his high-pitched voice the nurse looked back and saw old Osbert's long, thin, almost fleshless hands rise from beneath his blankets.

Plucking... and plucking... at the empty air.

Like claws.

LAST NIGHT

Joel Lane

"Let's not talk about last night." That's what you said when you finally stumbled out of the bedroom this morning to sit in the armchair the way a tramp sits in a bus shelter: breathing into your cupped hands, staring hard at nothing. Well I'm sorry, Conor, but I want to talk about last night. Because last night was typical. It was just like every other night, to quote your favourite singer.

You hiding in a corner at the Meercat, drinking yourself slowly but surely into a blind alley of rage. Then falling to your knees outside the pub, drooling and weeping, fighting with yourself. Telling me I don't understand. If you have to get like that to understand, thanks, I'll stay ignorant. I'm the one who has to talk you up off the pavement, half-carry you step by tense step to my house. Not that you're heavy, I admit. You're as skinny as one of your own roll-ups, and you have the same smell. The smell of despair.

When we get indoors you're barely conscious, fading in and out like a phone in a train tunnel. I pull you through the door and guide you to the bathroom, where you vomit so hard I can hear you cry out with pain. I would hold you, I swear it, but the smell makes me too sick. When you come back I hug your bony form, pour you a glass of water and sit you down somewhere not too close to my books and records. You start to revive and jab at your mobile, texting fuck knows who with your profound insights. Finally I get you to bed and you're twisted across the mattress, still half-dressed, almost choking. I slept on the couch again last night.

It would be worse for you if you were alone, I know that. So I take care of you, and in return you put up with my criticisms. That's what love is. You've told me about some of the times on your own. Getting lost in the city, then blacking out. Waking up in the park at dawn, or at the back of a bus in a

51

depot twenty miles from home. Trying to pull on your identity like torn clothes. And there was that time they found you in an alley near the cathedral where all the shops are boarded up. They must have dragged you in there before helping themselves to your wallet, wristwatch and clothes. They even tore out your nipple ring.

I didn't see you for a while after that. Thought you'd left me for good. But then you came back, knocking at my door in the middle of the night. Your face was marked with new scars. You didn't say a word, just kissed me. Your mouth tasted of Jack Daniels and blood. We made love so intensely I could feel the bruises weeks later. You were the wounded soldier of my childhood dreams, the gypsy who pressed me to him in the shadow of the city wall. And I worked all night long to make you come. You didn't have to try so hard with me. I was always helpless when you stroked me, held me in your tobacco-stained mouth.

It's different now. You only seem to want sex when you're too wasted to do anything about it. Sometimes I wish you'd hurt me, twist my arms, give me something to feel besides a dry compassion that feels like numbness. Not that I fancy you much when you're trapped in the pit of self-disgust. At those times you're barely aware of me, your mind spinning with the memory of the people who've sneered at you and the reasons why. Your face a thin mask, hard like *papier mâché*. Your mouth smeared with foam, as if you'd just brushed your teeth. I'd rather try and curl up on the sofa, lie there alone smelling the damp in the skirting-board, hearing the traffic go past on the main road.

There was one time I saw just a little of what you were going through. I usually drink while you're drinking, just to stay in touch, but this time I was really trying to keep pace with you. Near closing time I needed the toilet urgently. I went through and stood at the urinal, nearly choking from the smell of bleach they used to cut the other smells, when I saw you stagger towards a cubicle. Two men came after you. They pulled you back from the door, and I saw their flaky hands tugging at your sleeves. Their vacant grey faces. I even heard some of what they were saying, but that was just the drink talking.

I remember how it was when we started. When the only shadows in your world were home-grown. You'd meet me after work, first slipping into the pub for a quick pint or two. Then you'd turn up at my house or wherever else we were meeting, alert and vivacious, a Celtic dreamer, primed with those little sardonic quips that made me want to kiss you. We'd drink and talk and cuddle, and slowly you'd work yourself up into a vortex of staring madness. Lately I've become afraid of walking home alone, in case I meet someone like you.

So let's talk about last night. Last night was your life. And it's easier than talking about this evening. I was just getting ready to go out when there was a knock on the door. Two policemen were going from house to house, asking about a missing cat. They say they've found some bones in the park. Other cats have disappeared, they said, even dogs. They showed me photographs. If people looked after their pets properly, it wouldn't happen. Just taking a photo isn't enough. Caring is a serious business. Everyone needs to belong, but there's only so much belonging to go round. I'm not giving you enough for the way you are. You need more.

From tonight onwards, I'm leaving the back door unlocked. How Freudian is that? To keep you, Conor. There's a claw-hammer under the bed. It's all for your sake. I know how far you came to be with me again. How what you've left behind is pulling at you, dragging you back. I'm doing my best for you. Before it ends, maybe there'll be one night we both want to remember.

WIDOW'S WEEDS

Paul Newman

Crystal chimes of young laughter and a muffled stampede beyond the closed study door snatched Daniel Tarling from contemplation of the dust motes riding the late September afternoon sunbeams like infinitesimal planets wheeling gracefully through an amber cosmos.

He caught a glimpse of jostling shadows cast under the door onto the dark sheen of lacquered floorboards and then the clatter and merriment dwindled into a pell-mell ascent to the next storey. The wild glee of the unseen playmates and his languid reverie collided in his breast to gift a wistful, indulgent smile to his lips as he turned to his host with the half-formed intention of enquiring after the girls' health and, perhaps, of making some tolerably witty observation concerning his yearning for all the careless joys of youth, although he himself was little more than a decade from college.

But the expression, mood and notion all faltered as his gaze fell upon Nicholas de Vries. Tarling's oldest friend stood to one side of the door with his back to the room, the diffuse sunlight lapping at his knees, his upper body and features obscured in the scholarly gloom wreathing the book-lined walls. He held himself rigid, right hand frozen with a cut-glass decanter tilted to within a degree of pouring, the left cradling an evidently forgotten snifter. His whole attitude, the angle at which he cocked his head, implied he was listening acutely for some specific thing. The tension across his shoulders and the muscles corded at the base of his neck strongly suggested it was not something he wished to hear.

The only sound now was the rhythmic, glottal warbling of woodpigeons in the dense coppice of elm and hawthorn which crowded close to the rear and sides of the modest country house. This, and the steady bass tocking of the large grandfather clock.

54

Tarling, perplexed and concerned, attempted to break de Vries' spell as gently as he was able. "Nicholas?"

The utterance of his name caused de Vries to start slightly and splash cognac into the glass. He steadied himself with an almost imperceptible quiver, finished pouring and carefully replaced the decanter. Cradling a snifter in each hand, he returned to the worn leather armchair opposite that occupied by Tarling and set the drinks down next to a small parcel of loosely folded oilskin on a low table of exquisitely carved teak.

"I'm sorry, Dan, it's just th…" He broke off as suddenly as he'd begun and again Tarling observed that curious attitude of pensive vigilance. Then de Vries did something even more extraordinary. He slipped out of his shoes and on stockinged feet crossed the room swiftly to snatch open the door. The passage beyond yawned vacant. Softly closing it, he took a handkerchief from his trouser pocket and, pinching it in the centre, wound it into a loose spiral and fed the point into the keyhole until it was sufficiently impacted to remain there. He glanced around at Tarling and attempted a pantomimed jocularity when he saw his guest's incomprehension, but it was a poor effort and combined with the trepidation in his eyes to quite grotesque effect. He clapped a hand across his lower face and dragged it away as if smoothing wet clay, eyes flitting around the room. Then he was moving again, crossing to the tall window with the exaggerated caution of a cat stalking a sparrow in a garden frequented by crafty dogs and pressing his forehead against the glass to peer into the flower borders directly below. Evidently finding nothing, he withdrew wearily into the room, all the while scrutinising the leathery, dark green tangle of rhododendrons bordering the tree line. His calves encountered the chair and he groped back to support his weight before gingerly easing himself down.

When he finally dragged his gaze back to Tarling's there was no sense he was in any way abashed at his behaviour nor in the slightest aware of the hectic intensity in his eyes.

"Nicholas, I—"

"Forgive me, Dan. I'm sure I can imagine how this must look but I promise you I can explain. Just not... not right at this moment."

De Vries reached for his glass and drained it without pleasure.

"Not at all, no, I..." Tarling began and, realising he had no idea what he intended to say, fell silent. De Vries' focus drifted towards the door. For the first time since the starched, unsmiling housekeeper had ushered him into the study not ten minutes earlier, Tarling had an opportunity to properly scrutinise his friend. He had lost weight, but not to an alarming degree, and his skin still bore the last fading vestiges of the deeper colouring imparted by months under the Asian sun. The flesh under his eyes appeared swollen and smudged by fatigue and his hands trembled ever so slightly when they were not gripping the studded arms of his chair. For all that, his sharp grey eyes, sharper cheek bones and unruly dark hair still conspired with a slight weakness around the mouth to give him the air of a buccaneer who has awakened to find himself an office clerk after all, his days of plunder just a salt-rimed dream of liberty.

Inspiration and social grace returned to Tarling in the same instant. "Helen. I'm so sorry. You must think me a dreadful boor. How is she? It can't be long until she reaches term."

De Vries pulled his attention back with difficulty. "Helen is well. According to the good Doctor Crane, she is very well indeed and can expect to deliver at any time. There is also a midwife of advancing years from Beauchamp Roding who attends her and assures her she can expect..." he corrected himself, "...*we* can expect a boy. A son." The muscles in his jaw relaxed a little.

"Oh, wonderful! That's wonderful news, Nicholas! And the three girls? They fare well? Little 'Ginny must be almost four by now and—"

Unable to contain himself any longer, De Vries cut across

him to blurt: "Dan, I must ask. Did you discover anything, anything at all about…" he shot a glance at the door, "…about the matter I mentioned?"

"Well, yes, somewhat. There are several accounts, but I fail to see why a mess of native superstition and legend should be of such pressing importance that you—"

"Please, Dan, I have reason. Good reason."

"—that you wire me out of the blue for the first time in – what? – more than two years with some cryptic hints about a matter of the utmost urgency that sends me rushing to the British Library on a moment's notice and then drags me out of town and up into the wilds of Essex only to find you acting like, like, well, like *this*…" he gestured with both hands at de Vries in annoyance.

De Vries slumped back, pinching at his eyes and the bridge of his nose. "Forgive me. You're right. I'm behaving like a perfect ass. An explanation is the least you deserve, my dearest friend. It would appear my manners are just another casualty…"

He trailed off and momentarily rose to retrieve the decanter. Tarling's glass was untouched yet nevertheless received another half-inch of cognac before de Vries poured for himself. He carefully lowered the vessel to the table but, straightening, paused once more as his eyes moved to the window and gazed intently into the receding obscurity of the trees as the sun slipped fractured behind their topmost branches. After maintaining this posture beyond the point of conversational awkwardness, he sat abruptly and began to speak, his attention roving around Tarling's face without once encountering his eyes.

"It occurs to me, more than ever, that one should be careful for what one wishes. And it occurs to me, also, that there are things in this life to which one should never have to bear witness, things far more terrible than one's own end."

He gnawed delicately at the inside of his lips, the act drawing them into a tight trembling line as if he were fighting for self-control and determined to prevail.

"Dan, I have been a party to... *questionable* things. Would that I had not and they might be undone. But they cannot and I fear their course is not yet run. That, or I am driving myself to distraction with the culpability, the horror of it all."

He leaned forward and emptied his glass, slurping clumsily. Tarling, noting a clammy flush about his cheeks even in the dwindling light spilling into the room, was grateful to see he did not reach for more. The drink, however, seemed to steady him and his voice was stronger, calmer when he continued.

"You will remember my frustration at my interminable days and slower progress in the offices of Maxwell, Cooper and Creatorex. You may also recall my forefathers' long association with the Verenigde Oost-Indiche Compagnie, long a source of much pride and some vanity in the family. My forebears were with one of the original ten companies van Oldebarnevelt merged to create the VOC more than three centuries ago, his instincts birthing a model for all significant commerce to come. Just think of the man's indefatigable ambition and vision, to create a single company capable of running entire countries and marshalling armies to police them, establishing an empire of commerce for the benefit of those whose investment had made its existence possible and not just to be leeched away by a hierarchy of nobles and monarchs! Even after it was nationalised shortly before the beginning of the last century, the structures and principles on which it was founded ensured its ongoing success, an international economic entity dominating and serving a multitude of nations. The Dutch East Indies is *still* a wealth beyond calculation, *still* a place where men of intelligence, diligence and loyalty can nurture a modest fortune for themselves and their descendants..."

At this he halted and the momentary enthusiasm inflecting his speech was gone when he repeated: "...and their descendants."

De Vries reached for his glass and checked himself. He

waved away the impulse with a distracted air and continued.

"Well, that was how it seemed from the dusty, stale confines of Maxwell, Cooper and Creatorex, and it took little persuasion for my father to petition Great Uncle Maarten in the old country to employ his connections in the relevant departments and obtain for me an opening as a junior administrator in the Residency of Bali and Lombok.

"I don't need to remind you how hard it was to bid farewell to Helen and the girls, and to my good friends, but it was agreed I would only leave them behind for a year, two at the most, before sending for them to join me. Long enough, I was confident, to have established myself and to have proved my worth to my new employer.

"The Christmas of '04 was supposed to have been my last here for some years but, for all that we tried to make as merry as if it were a dozen rolled into one, it was a forlorn, sad affair. The holly and pine boughs were yet fresh in the house when I took my leave, but the melancholy I carried with me was swiftly extinguished by the tedium of the voyage. There is only so much preparation that can be done and thereafter nothing for it but to chase the horizon and will it closer.

"When our vessel had been underway for several days, I conscientiously began to study all the correspondence and information sent by the staff at the Residency concerning Bali and her sister isle, but it mostly consisted of dry tables concerning the export of rice, coconut oil, cattle, pigs, dried meats, hides, tobacco and coffee, estimated populations of the various kingdoms and their shifting political allegiances – plus a few circumspect notes on the extent of the opium trade. On paper, it looked like any other minor colonial asset and would doubtless have been no more than that, but for its geographical significance regarding the far more lucrative traffic in spices from the islands to the east.

"Dried meat? Rice? Pigs? What had I let myself in for? As the banal reality of my exciting venture became apparent, my spirits sank in direct proportion to my growing boredom and I spent the remaining weeks of the journey skulking in my cramped cabin under the pretext of either diligent research or seasickness.

"Eventually, the captain had something other than distracted pleasantries and rambling anecdotes from his service to offer around yet another stiflingly humid supper table and informed the gathering we could expect landfall the following day. Surely enough, it was barely an hour past dawn on the next morning when the cry went up. I dragged myself resigned and glum from the sweat-damp sheets to dress and some part of my mind was already prying at my situation and considering ways in which I might extricate myself from it at the soonest opportunity, to move onto a more apposite appointment. In this frame of mind I emerged on deck, squinted against the glare… and fell to chuckling like the village halfwit as my worst expectations were utterly confounded.

"Although it was still early, the sun was already strong and beat the cloudless sky a shade of blanched copper. We were close in to the shoreline, scarcely more than a couple of hundred yards, and water of an impossibly luxuriant jade met fine white sands with barely a sigh. Beyond, slender palm trees fringed the beach in both directions, their frayed leaves untroubled by a breeze so gentle and warm it was a balm on the skin. Some short distance behind them began what I assumed was, from the dense confusion of foliage, the jungle proper. And strolling with graceful self-possession through this unearthly backdrop was the most entrancing vision I had ever laid my eyes on; a native girl with skin like warm clover honey, barely tapping at the door of womanhood and clad in nothing more than a boldly coloured cloth wrapped around her waist and falling to just below her knees. With one hand she steadied on her head a fully laden broad platter of woven hemp. It was clear she could not have failed to observe our ship, we heading east and she walking towards us, yet she contrived to give no indication she was even aware that we existed and, with her back straight and chin slightly tilted, our paths lightly grazed and she was gone.

"With the easy hypocrisy of the just-converted, I threw back my head and crowed into the emerald tangle in one long ululation to expel all my earlier misgivings. With no more evidence than a pretty girl on a beach about her chores, my heart was swift and decisive in reaching its verdict: I had been wrong and this was clearly a Paradise on Earth."

De Vries had become increasingly animated and sat back in a moment's reverie. He glanced up and looked Tarling steadily in the eye for the first time, a half-smile ghosting at the corners of his mouth.

"It really was, you know. Paradise. If you'd told me about it, I'd have never believed you. Certainly, I'd never before entertained the possibility that such a place could exist outside of an opium dream. For me, Paradise had always looked a little like the Crystal Palace Gardens on a public holiday, all crisp white linen and gracious diversions. Order. Safety in familiarity. But here was something I could never have imagined and I fancied the natives of this island understood something of its wonder too. There had been no trouble for more than a decade in the rival kingdoms of the south which remained unaligned with the Dutch and I found it hard to believe that such graceful, gentle and harmonious people were even capable of war and violence. Their whole lives seemed one long, complex ritual of gratitude to the unknown forces that had graced them with such an idyllic realm. In my private quarters and around the airy offices in which I passed my working days, I was forever watching my step for fear of disturbing the myriad small offerings of food or flowers set out for the teeming pantheon of their gods, given in perfect trays cunningly fashioned from large folded leaves; a sizeable portion of each meal for the esteemed household gods, smaller gifts for those lower down the pecking order and even a small handful of rice for the dire spirits who, they understood, also had their place in the scheme of things and expected at least a passing recognition of it.

"So, my first days became weeks as I passed them in a beatific haze, mostly occupied with routine administration work concerning shipments and cargoes. The Balinese speak a dialect of Malay, you know, a language so uncomplicated it took little effort to begin to pick it up with the help of one of the houseboys, and by September I had a greater facility with it than any of my colleagues, generally a good-natured sort but more concerned with cards, home and the minor intrigues of the Residency.

"I suppose I might very well have drifted along indefinitely this way and, though it shames me to say it, Helen and the girls were often ushered from my thoughts, if not my heart, by a combination of work and my growing fascination with the exotica around me. Evenings, I would often sit out on the porch in the close air and simply inhale the place. Sometimes the breeze would carry to me the subdued music of a gamelan troupe from one of the nearby villages, a haunting chain of meandering percussion accompanied by the mournful piping of a solitary flute, winding its way through the rice paddies and creepers like fat drops of rain chiming softly on copper leaves."

The ebb and flow of de Vries' telling seemed to embrace the rhythmic pulse of the music he described, lulling Tarling hypnotically so that he started when his friend suddenly sat forward, snatched up the decanter and addressed him directly as he tended both glasses. Tarling's was by now more than half-filled.

"This is the point in popular fiction where the narrator informs his readers that such a perfect state could not last – and so, of course, it could not.

"For some weeks I had been involved in correspondence concerning the wrecking of a Chinese ship, the *Sri Komala*. Sailing from Borneo, the vessel foundered on reefs off the coast of Badung, the southernmost independent kingdom of Bali, at the end of May. It was promptly stripped of its goods by the islanders in accordance with their customs. A piffling incident in the routine affairs of the region; it should have barely made it into despatches.

"Except that the *Sri Komala* flew under the Dutch flag.

"The boat's owner raised merry hell, insisting the Balinese had stolen his cargo and were therefore in violation of the treaty of 1849 expressly forbidding the plundering of wrecked ships. If we had one letter from his agents demanding compensation in full we must have had a hundred, each more exactingly formal and outraged than the last. The steady stream of complaint could not be dismissed forever and it was only a matter of time before the Governor General took a personal interest in the matter. Van Heutsz had made quite a name for himself a short time before in the victorious war in Aceh and it was supposed he sought nothing more than the quiet prestige of his new appointment to pass his remaining service. From the correspondence which crossed my desk, it was evident he had no wish to be bothered with the matter of the *Sri Komala* and so passed responsibility for making satisfactory recompense to the ruler of Badung, Gede Ngurah Denpasar. The king, perhaps predictably, repudiated such responsibility and so the matter went around and around. Eventually, van Heutsz ordered a blockade of Badung's coast but the kingdom was still able to bring in supplies from independent Tabanan a short distance to the east and it became apparent the tactic had failed.

"As the months passed and tensions grew in the Residency by the week, the dawning of 1906 was met with little enthusiasm and it seemed all other business affairs were of scant importance. Months of terse diplomacy followed, during which a significant number of new faces began to take up occupancy in our offices. As we entered September, the rainy season was still months away but the oppressive atmosphere and expectation of some kind of decisive action made it feel like a cloudburst was due any moment. Our agents had received several allegations from reliable sources that the ship's owners had beached it deliberately to make a fraudulent claim for compensation. These were remarked upon, forwarded, filed and not heard of again. The *Sri Komala* was not mentioned for almost two weeks.

"On the afternoon of the thirteenth, I wandered home contemplating how ill my bitter sense of foreboding sat with the peaceful, dusty street along which I walked and the placid domestic activity surrounding me at every hand. Upon arrival, I fought the urge for a good five minutes before I announced I would not be dining that evening and called the houseboy to prepare a pipe. The delicate, sweet resin was still on my lips and the smoke dreams unfurling in every fibre when the boy returned. I waved him away but he had not come to prepare another pipe and mutely handed over a letter bearing the Residency's seal. I remember that I stared unfocused at it for the best part of an hour before I read its contents, dressed appropriately and made my way to the beach. There I joined three others from our offices in a waiting skiff and, as the light faded to a smudged lilac, we were rowed out to a waiting vessel."

His narrative trailed off and in the silence Tarling shook himself as if to banish a creeping drowsiness. Outside, the sun had set, evening proper was drawing on and the study had become a grey mosaic of shadow. He had to blink several times to pierce the gloom with any clarity and even then de Vries remained indistinct, his words dried up and his stare once more focused on the treeline beyond the window. Tarling turned his head but could only make out the dim riot of rhododendrons and choking weeds coiling about the foot of the darker copse. While his friend sat lost in thought, Tarling rose quietly and located a lamp on the mantelpiece behind him. Cautious gropings in its vicinity secured a box of matches and he struck one. Before his eyes could adjust to its abrupt glare, de Vries bolted from his seat with a cry and was at his side in a breath to knock it from his hand.

"What the—?"

"No, no. I'm sorry, Dan, I'm so sorry. I'd just rather you

didn't. No, no."

De Vries was highly agitated, offensively so, yet Tarling could see no mitigating reason for it.

"Nicholas?"

He had received no answer as his host returned to his chair but, just as de Vries bent over the low table, something snagged his eye and pulled him to one side of the window. He peered obliquely around the heavy curtain and with a terse flapping of his arm summoned Tarling across, sharply waving him to a halt on the facing side of the frame. His voice was a low hiss.

"Look out there. Careful, slowly now. Look out there and tell me what you see."

With a show of inflated caution for the benefit of his friend, Tarling peered through the glass. The dimness of the room rendered the exterior comparatively lucent but after almost a minute of scanning the grounds immediately below the window and the thick growth beyond he was forced to admit he saw nothing.

"I swear I'm not seeing things, Dan," whispered de Vries. "Or, rather," he tittered, "I am."

His own manner momentarily startled him into silence and when he spoke again his tone was still soft but a good deal further from the hysteria which had gurgled in his throat.

"Dan, I'm really not pulling your leg nor have I taken leave of my wits. I... there! Quick, there!"

Tarling followed his gesture and caught only a shifting in the obscurity of the rhododendrons, a few agitated leaves and the nodding of a single blossom.

"Some small animal, perhaps your—"

"Shhh! Listen, Dan, listen. What d'you hear?"

He strained his hearing as if he might lift anvils with it. Nothing, but... what was that? Something so quiet, so subtle he could not even be certain it was not the blood singing in his ears. Now his voice, too, was low.

"What is that, Nicholas? It sounds like glass bottles clinking together. No, like somebody emptying out a drawer of cutlery a mile away. What is it? A chime? A distant church bell?"

De Vries stared at him with mute appeal scored in every feature and slowly shook his head.

"Then what's mak—" Somewhere within the house a door slammed. A chiding voice sounded distantly and was instantly joined by a flutter of high laughter. On impulse, Tarling raised the lower half of the sash and leaned out into the cool gloaming. The musical glee grew louder.

"Nicholas, oh Nicholas. What are you about? You'll have *me* seeing things next. Do you not know the sound of your own children's joy?"

He returned to the abandoned lamp, retrieved the matchbox and drove the darkness back beyond the window. When de Vries failed to move, he went to take him gently by the elbow but stopped when he saw the unfurled oilskin dangling limp from one hand. The other gripped a small revolver stiffly against his leg.

"Nicholas! What in God's name are you doing? What's that thing for?"

He received only a curt shake of the head in reply.

"Give it to me now. Now! I must insist."

He tugged and the weapon was surrendered without resistance. Tarling rewrapped it and went to place it on a high bookshelf.

"No, please. There…" De Vries indicated its former position and Tarling reluctantly acquiesced before taking his friend's shaking hands and steering him back to his seat. He crouched and peered earnestly into his unfocused eyes.

"What? What is it? We have known each other so long we may share anything without fear of ridicule and in complete confidence. Tell me, please, and maybe it will be that your troubles can be set at rest as easily as…" he glanced at the window, "well, easily."

De Vries stared steadily into and through Tarling's concern and when he spoke his voice was a low, monotone rasp.

"Out to meet the boats."

"What?"

"We went out to meet the boats. There were five in all. Warships. Some three thousand soldiers. Maybe more. All mustered in the utmost secrecy to forestall advance notice. We sailed slowly around to the south-east of the island and dropped anchor off Sanur early the next morning and for five days thereafter the cannons belched destruction at Badung, four miles inland. And on the twentieth, nearly the entire force put to shore and marched inland. The place was in ruins, most of it still aflame. Temples hundreds of years old lay in rubble. The dead were everywhere. The smell... oh, Dan, the smell was something that lingers still in my nostrils and I think always will. I heard later nearly four thousand were killed but it seemed like ten times that number. It was hell... but it was by no means the worst.

"The people of Bali have a custom. *Puputan.* Such a childish, happy-sounding word for so terrible a thing. You see, for these kings, surrender is a deeply dishonourable course, never to be countenanced. When confronted with inevitable defeat, all temporal power is put aside in a fight to the death, a ritual of self-sacrifice to shame the enemy. Literally translated, it means 'ending' or 'finish'. It had last occurred in 1894 in Mataram, on Lombok, and my heart tells me van Heutsz knew it could be made to happen again.

"*Puputan.*"

De Vries took a deep, ragged breath and his voice quavered as he continued.

"We were nearing the burning palaces when we saw them; the men first, with the women and children behind them and the aged following at the rear. Three hundred people, all that remained of the royal court. All wore ceremonial white dress and those who were armed carried only lances and the traditional kris, a kind of short sword with a wavy blade recalling a wriggling serpent frozen in motion. They streamed out behind their ruler, who was carried before on an ornate

67

gold palanquin flanked by his holy men. At about a hundred paces away they stopped and began pelting us with jewels. Jewels! Around me, I heard many of the soldiers laughing – a strained, unnerved sound – and some bent to collect and pocket the missiles. Ahead, the procession stopped and silence fell heavily on the ground between the two parties. All I could hear was the crackling of the many fires, a sporadic, remote screeching of monkeys and the nervous shuffling of our force.

"There must have been some sort of prearranged signal because one of the priests whirled without warning and stabbed his king through the heart. Even at a distance, the torrent of red that splashed from him was a ghastly thing to see. I felt my own heart thud dully three times and then the slaughter began. The people of Badung turned on each other in a yammering frenzy and many more rushed our lines. I screamed at them, begged them to turn back, but already our cannon and guns were firing volley after volley after volley. They fell in screaming tangles over which those behind scrambled to run on, into the next crashing hail of death. In the midst of it, I could see howling men turning their kris on themselves, on their neighbours, on the mortally wounded and on the fallen dead.

"Eventually, there was nobody left to run at us; nobody left to shoot at. A soft breeze thinned the acrid smoke and revealed the full extent of the carnage wrought. Bodies lay in bleeding heaps, some limbs still twitching, and through this hideous riot of blasted flesh the few wailing and elderly survivors picked a path towards each sign of movement and stopped it with a slash of their gore-clotted blades.

"I felt the blood running down my face and it made no sense to me when I wiped it away and saw only clear tears on my palms. Many of our soldiers were stooping to collect the gems thrown earlier but some just stared in gaping horror at the vile fruit of their labours. Later that afternoon, they would replay the scene again when they advanced on the co-ruler of that small kingdom and the survivors of the bombardment who remained with him.

"I stumbled forward and felt the sun-warmed stone underfoot become slick with so much spilled blood, pulpy with shed flesh. Memories of those moments are reduced to random images now, with no coherent whole. The face of a young man contorted in his death throes with a fierce, despairing pride. A kris writhing to the sky from the back of a girl no more than sixteen, a small patch of dusty stone hard by her mouth still dark and damp from her final breaths. The perfectly formed right foot of a child, roughly severed from just above the ankle and still snug inside a delicate sandal.

"And then I became aware of movement, followed by sound. I tottered like a drunk and forced my eyes up from the bleeding lake under my boots to find myself before an old woman. She sat cross-legged on a low step with corpses heaped behind and beside her, her knees resting against the sprawling corpse of a man a little older than she and a limp infant clutched tightly in her arms as she rocked mindlessly back and forth. A thin keening spilled from her betel-stained lips that seemed dredged from a place too deep, too primal to have originated inside something as frail as a human body. I perceived she was not mortally wounded, but a bullet or fragment of debris had left a deep gash above her left eye and blood pulsed sluggishly down her creased face and shoulder to one withered breast, to where the lifeless baby's mouth lolled against her nipple in an appalling mockery of maternity.

"I stood stupidly before them, unable to think of a single thing to say or do. I wanted to offer some shred of comfort to ease her suffering but knew nothing I could extend was worthy of her incalculable grief. I just stood there and watched her soul die, one broken moment at a time.

"By degrees, the sound of her pain subsided and I regained sufficient awareness of my senses to realise she had stopped and was staring up at me, naked hatred, fury and loss etched into every line of her features. She made no sound because she had no need to. If her thoughts were written across her forehead they could not have been clearer: 'Who are you, you in your fine, stiff suit? Who are you, with your soft pale skin and soft pale ways, that you are standing here, *here*, before me? Standing on the soil that birthed my ancestors? Standing with the life of my people staining your shoes? Staining the cuffs of your finely tailored trousers?

"'Who *are* you, standing here with nothing to say?'

"She took her right hand from where it cradled the infant's tiny head and smeared the palm across its stained lips before cupping it to her breast to catch her own blood drop by drop. I moved, I think to stop her, fearing she planned to harm herself further. But that was not her intent. With a swift flick of her wrist, she spattered her hand's contents at me, splashing a vertical line of red from my face to my groin as she spat a single unfathomable word, laden with her heart's bitter venom.

"'Rangda'.

"For an instant she showed me her stained gums in a ferocious grimace and then I was no longer there for her and she lapsed back into rocking and weeping."

Tarling's shock was plain even in the soft lamplight, but at mention of the woman's valediction his brow furrowed in recognition. De Vries did not notice. His account done, he sat in silence and stared down at the floor, his features unreadable in shadow. The air in the room was chill and the window glass now showed nothing but a dim reflection of the two men facing each other. A minute, perhaps two, passed before Tarling could bring himself to interrupt the oppressive silence. He wanted to give his friend time in which to compose himself. He wanted to offer some word of sympathetic understanding. But more than these, he wanted the terrible images the story had conjured in his mind's eye to be gone.

"Nicholas, I just don't know what to say. I can't imagine what you must have felt, must be feeling. But for whatever use it may be, I can only say to you that it must be plain you are in no way culpable."

His reply was a soft, mirthless chuckle. "Rangda."

"What? What do you mean by that?"

De Vries raised his head and his eyes burned with the reflected light. "I don't know. But I think it means that old woman knew better. Oh, certainly I can point to my insignificant place in the machine. I can insist on my ignorance of its workings. I can swear on the Good Book until my teeth fall from my mouth that I had no inkling of its course.

"But I was there. And that is enough."

Prickling at de Vries' tone of self-flagellation, Tarling considered debating the point but realised it was an argument he would not win. He fumbled for other solutions to break the spell of defeated melancholy and found none. This time it was de Vries who spoke first.

"So tell me, Dan, if you will. What did you find out on your little jaunt to the British Library?"

Tarling quailed at the prospect of feeding the other's morbidity but then considered it could probably do no more injury than was already inflicted. From an inside pocket of his jacket he took a small notepad, of the kind which can be purchased cheaply at every stationery shop and comes with a tiny pencil snug in its hollow spine, opened it and held it slightly above eye-level to catch the lamplight behind him.

"'Rangda'. Well, I suppose you may already know it translates as 'widow'?" De Vries shook his head slowly and Tarling turned to the next page. "Very well. As I said earlier, there's precious little to be found on it and what I could lay my hands on were mostly conflicting accounts by a handful of anthropologists, but where they do agree is that it's one of the island's most potent figures of myth. Or history. It's all rather confused, and from what I read I got the impression the people of that region don't draw much of a distinction between the two.

"The stories have it that in the Tenth Century, the Balinese queen was accused by her husband of practising witchcraft and banished into the forests. In a rage, she transformed herself into a..." he peered closer at his notes, "...into something

71

called a *leyal*, a demon hag. One pamphlet had an illustration taken from carvings found on temples on the island and she's certainly no beauty. All bulbous glaring eyes and tusks for teeth, with a lolling tongue and straggling hair like a nest of white snakes. Nails six inches long. Pendulous breasts perched on a belly like a medicine ball and a necklace of human entrails."

Tarling grimaced at such a repulsive notion before returning to his notes. "How long she remained in the forests is unclear but she acquired a fearsome reputation. After her husband died, the islanders simply called her Rangda. One of the accounts says her loathing of the world was compounded by the refusal of any man to consider marriage to her daughter, said to be a great beauty. In any event, the natives believe she used to creep out of the forest in the dead of night and whisper into the windows of sleeping children, teaching them the dark arts by way of revenge and instructing them in how to spread disease and to cast spells so their mothers would only deliver stillborn chil…"

He stumbled to an embarrassed halt and looked aghast at de Vries. "Oh, Nicholas, forgive me. That was utterly inconsiderate. I didn't even stop to think that Helen… that you and Helen…"

Tarling ground into silence once more as he assessed the look on de Vries' face. Not outrage, not anger nor even hurt. More a horrified understanding, a confirmation. Tarling made an intuitive leap.

"No! You can't be seriously thinking…"

De Vries straightened in his seat. "A moment, Dan. After that dreadful day, I made arrangements to leave the islands at the soonest opportunity. They were poisoned for me and I wanted no more part in their governance, but from the moment I arrived home I could not rid myself of the idea that I had brought that bloodshed back with me, like a physical thing. At every hour, in every mood, I felt it. And lying sleepless at night, I could feel a tightening constriction in my chest at the sure knowledge something was coming.

"Of course, I spoke little of the affair to Helen, always certain that the next day would be a better time to unburden myself to her. Or the next. Or the one after that. But the time never seemed right. When she told me she was with child, I felt I had no right to tarnish her happiness with so much death and so decided to keep my lips sealed on the subject.

"And then it began. Whenever I was outdoors, whenever I crossed an unshuttered window, I had the most acute sensation of being watched. As the weeks passed and the feeling grew ever stronger, I began to question my sanity, to wonder if that episode in Badung had fully unbalanced my mind. I actually became fearful of sitting near a window, always cowering in anticipation of that feeling when my flesh would begin to creep, a clammy tickle scuttling up the nape of my neck, certain the watcher lurked out there in the copse, motionless, endlessly patient. On several occasions I even fancied I caught a glimpse of something from the corner of my eye, something moving furtively in the shadows of the rhododendrons but which became still the instant I turned towards it. I would stare into those bushes for hours at a time, my mind reassembling the shadows; a monstrous face here, a foot there. Finally, I could bear it no more and resolved to see Doctor Crane at the soonest opportunity. He was understanding, very understanding and, after fifteen minutes of listening patiently, prescribed a nerve tonic and complete rest.

"I recall it was a beautiful early summer's evening on my return and, determined to make an effort to turn my mind from its insatiable gnawing, I decided to stop in at the John Barleycorn for a glass or two before taking my time about a pleasant stroll home. When I arrived back I was in a far better humour than I had been for months, was even considering the formulation of a plan to seek out new employment, this time much closer to home. Perhaps even in the locality. I was perhaps no more than twenty paces from the front door when I saw it.

"In the purple twilight, I wasn't even sure at first. It could simply have been a trick of the shadows, a slightly paler patch of whitewash in the deepening gloom of the east wall. You know how thick the ivy grows there, around the girls' window on the first floor? I wasn't alarmed, by any means, but I was curious and that led me to wander across the grass for a closer look. Even almost directly below the spot, I still could not make out what it was I regarded.

"Then it spoke. It was a frightful sound, a hoarse whisper corpulent with awful... *insinuations*. I was rooted to the spot, my gaze scrabbling at the shape to make sense of it. It clung in the fullest part of the ivy like some gigantic, obscene leech and I understood with a shiver of horror that what I had taken for a patch of exposed wall was its leprous white flesh and the shreds of dark rag it wore. A rank carrion stench drifted down in waves and I felt the gorge rising in my throat. I could not see its face, just the suggestion of a head beneath a filthy snarl of hair the colour of wet ash as it strained up towards the open window. And all the while I could hear its guttural mutterings.

"My mind was submerged in a delirium but it gradually dawned on me that this abominable thing was at the window of the very room where my children slept. Clenching every muscle in my face to prevent my teeth grinding out of fear, I silently crept around the corner of the house to the front door. Once inside, I took my gun from this study and mounted the stairs as swiftly and quietly as I was able. At the girls' door I carefully, so very carefully, pressed my ear to the panel, all the while taking tiny shallow breaths. I fancied I could hear a soft, metallic chiming coiled around a hateful sibilance and at that moment swung the door open and stepped in, levelling my pistol as I did so.

"Virginia, Clara, Eleanor, all were tucked up and evidently sleeping soundly. From the window came only a faint rustling of ivy in the breeze.

"I said nothing the next day and I've said nothing since. What could I say that would not have me committed on the spot? But it's here still. Every day, every night, I feel it out there, watching us. In the morning I sometimes find signs of a disturbance in the flower beds below the windows. Once, shortly after dawn, curious tracks in the dew that appeared to be leading away from the house, yet nothing to suggest a trail leading to it. Some nights I sit here without a light and I keep vigil, and I feel it, I feel it in here…" he rapped gently over his heart, "…motionless, invisible and as coldly patient as eternity staring back at me."

Momentarily forgetting his incredulity, Tarling blurted out: "But why is it watching? What does it want?"

De Vries cocked his head a moment, helplessly sneaking a look at the window as his did so, before answering in a tone fatigued by sorrow and apprehension. "Oh, that I think I do know. I've pondered if often these past months. On that shameful day, in that terrible place, the old woman did more than just throw blood at me. She planted something in me, deep inside, in the dark, something that's been growing ever since, nourished and thriving on my fear and guilt. And that…" he gestured vaguely at the night beyond the window, "…is the gardener." His chuckle was an unpleasant, bitter spillage, laced with irony and devoid of joviality. "Here to tend the crop."

Tarling was dismayed. "Nicholas, this is pure madness. You need care, treatment. You're driving yourself from your wits with these morbid delusions."

"Delusions? Oh, my friend, you would not think them anything so trifling as delusions had you been my ears on the long nights when I have crouched at the door of my children's room in the dead heart of the night and heard those subtle croaking whispers and the answering murmurs of my girls. As I have watched the new life grow inside Helen and thought what might really be maturing.

"This thing, this power, cares nothing for a prize as worthless as my sanity. It wishes to corrupt, to pollute those innocent streams and in so doing carry its foul poisons as far as they might flow.

"And it is my doing. All of it."

Spent, de Vries slumped low in his chair, a discarded marionette whose glassy stare took in nothing. The two sat motionless for several minutes and against the steady sound of the clock, Tarling could hear his companion's breathing lose its hectic edge, becoming deep and regular until it seemed he may be falling into sleep.

Tarling watched his friend's face intently, saw the abject exhaustion and felt impotent. His mind raced for any shred of comfort he could offer but found nothing that did not feel trite, utterly inadequate to the purpose set it.

De Vries roused himself with a sluggish tremor, glanced at the clock. "Oh, the time is getting away. Dan, you'll stay, of course? I'll have a room made ready."

"No. I can't. I really can't. I've unavoidable business in the city first thing tomorrow. My train is due in a little while and it's the best part of two miles to the station. I really should go, but I give you my word I'll return tomorrow." Involuntarily, his attention fell on the oilskin package that sat on the table between them and he was momentarily chilled. "Tomorrow. And we'll talk of this further, I promise, devise some means of putting this matter into its proper light and perhaps talk of getting you some help. I know of a good—"

De Vries cut him off: "Yes, yes, tomorrow. Tomorrow will be good."

There being nothing to forestall it, they made awkward goodbyes as Tarling's hat and coat were recovered and he left his friend with an over-firm handshake at the door.

"This will be all right, Nicholas."

De Vries grimaced. "I'm sure of it."

The door was closed quietly behind him as soon as he strode off along the thin gravel drive. The evening air was chill, sharp in his nose and throat with the promise of an early dawn frost. He was no more than thirty yards from the house when he heard a faint sound a little way behind him. He paused and half-turned but nothing broke the stillness in the smothering rhododendron border to his right, save for a rustling of leaves and the barest whisper of unseen chimes.

It was just as he made to resume his walk that he sensed more than directly saw an indistinct form cross in a swift, ungainly manner from the shrubbery to the eastern side of the house. Tarling rubbed at both eyes with the heels of his hands and peered avidly into the shadows at the foot of the ivy-choked walls. Nothing.

He was still staring when the first pistol shot cracked apart the silence, its flash illuminating a window on the first floor. Two more followed in swift succession.

"Oh, no. Nicholas, no…" Tarling was rooted with shock and then sprinting for the door. He had covered only half the ground when a woman's shriek burst from within like a crystal knife, only to be silenced abruptly by another shot. A pause, then a fifth.

He reached the door and hammered on it in a frenzy, screaming out the name of his friend, begging admission. Forehead pressed to the wood and moaning in distress, he perceived a measured step descending the staircase and crossing the lobby.

"Nicholas, Nicholas! I beg of you, open this door. Please. It's not too late, nothing's too late."

From the other side of the door he heard a low, wracked sobbing; such a sound as a soul might make as it died, one broken moment at a time.

A voice, barely recognisable as that of the man whose company he had quit barely three minutes before, uttered a single word and then punctuated it with a sixth bullet.

"*Puputan.*"

OUT OF HER HEAD

Christine Mortimer

Tracy Jordan woke with a jolt. She groaned. Her head hurt.

It was pitch-black, and she lay in the darkness trying to recall what she had been doing.

What *had* she been doing?

Drinking. She remembered drinking.

All day. Copious amounts of alcohol.

And what else? If she'd been drinking then something outrageous certainly. Her memory was hazy. She remembered she'd done something to offend Martha Briggs.

Martha Briggs, that stuck-up cow who thought she was better than anyone else who lived on the estate.

The old bitch had had the cheek to criticise her for being drunk! Why shouldn't she get drunk? What business was it of hers if she got out of her head? Old bitch... More like old witch!

No doubt she'd find out the details of what she'd done, later. They'd all be talking about it down the pub.

Sitting up, she fumbled to find the switch on the bedside lamp.

Pressed, it remained dark. The bulb must have gone. She couldn't find her cigarettes either. She must have left them in her pocket.

Tracy groaned again. She needed to pee. Needed a smoke. And to take something for her splitting headache. She'd have to get up.

Wincing, she slowly got out of bed. A tentative step, and then another, and she began to stagger across the room.

Good job she couldn't see herself in the mirror, Tracy thought. She must look terrible.

She'd barely gone a further two paces, when she stepped on something.

Something that went squish.

"Ewww!" Tracy cried in disgust, hopping around, trying to shake off whatever was stuck to the sole of her right foot.

And as she did so, she trod on her other eyeball.

FAMILY TIES

Steve Lockley & Paul Lewis

Where the hell is he? Helen rubbed one hand across her swollen belly, feeling the baby kick inside her as if it shared her anxiety. When Peter had left, his parting words were to assure her he'd be back in a day or two. But three days had passed with agonising slowness and there was no sign of him. Whenever she looked through the window, or stood on the gently sloping hill that led down to the beach, Helen was convinced she would see their small boat chugging across the sea towards her, smoke belching from the engines that Peter had repeatedly put off fixing, each time telling her he would do it on their next visit to the island. It had become a private joke. Just like the one about the pile of rubble in the garden, all that remained of a dilapidated shed Peter had demolished, that he was supposed to have cleared long ago. Christ, what she wouldn't give to be able to share one of those private jokes with him again.

He'll be all right, Helen told herself. *Peter knows what he's doing.*

And she believed that. Despite her fears and her doubts, she believed Peter was okay and that he would be home again soon. She *had* to be believe it.

The alternative was too dreadful to contemplate.

Evening was falling over Swansea Bay, casting the village of Mumbles and the hills that embraced it into shadow. No lights burned, and had not done for some time. As Helen stared at the sea the choppy water suddenly calmed, as if the weight of the encroaching darkness had smothered its energy. It was August and would remain stiflingly hot until well into the night but nevertheless she found herself shivering.

She was alone here. Utterly alone. For all she knew she could be the only living woman on earth, Eve to Peter's Adam...

"Uh-uh," Helen said aloud, shaking her head. More Biblical imagery was the last thing she needed. There was already way too much of it around. Armageddon. The dead rising from their graves. And eating the living. Funny how the good book never mentioned *that.* The stillness of the sea, the silence of the land, belied the ferocious horrors of the past few weeks. Standing there on the lonely island, with no company other than the child inside her and no one to talk to but herself, Helen still found it hard to believe this really was it. The end of everything. Of course there would be survivors other than herself – *and Peter, don't forget* – but they'd be so few and far between, so widely scattered, they could never hope to rebuild civilisation.

Helen shivered again, more violently this time, and headed back to the cottage. As much as she did not want to admit it, she knew looking for Peter would not bring him back any quicker. Shops would have been looted once the news of what was happening had spread. Medical supplies in particular would be scarce. But Peter would not give up until he had everything on their list – disinfectant, dressings, penicillin, the lot. He was like that. Single-minded almost to the point of stubbornness. Helen had never known him give up, once he had set his mind on something.

She stopped and turned to give the sea one final glance before ducking through the cottage's ludicrously undersized door. Both of them had cracked their heads more than once. Neither wanted anything done about it. The building was more than a century old and, to their eyes, just perfect. Stone walls, small windows. Snug and warm in the winter, cool at the height of summer. Their sole concession to the modern era was double glazing, but even then Peter had paid over the odds to ensure it did not spoil the look of the place. They'd bought the cottage as an investment, intending to use it maybe once or twice a year and rent it out the rest of the time. That changed after their first stay. Helen had fallen in love with the place, and even dour Peter eventually confessed he shared her enthusiasm. On the one hand the fact that it was an island made it feel isolated, yet it was only twenty minutes from the mainland in their slow-to-moderate old boat. And with only five cottages dotted around the place, it offered them all the privacy they could wish for. They had even talked about living there permanently, Peter staying in their old home in the city during the week, joining Helen and the baby at weekends and anytime else he could get away from the office. Which, considering he owned the company, was likely to be pretty often. Life, it seemed, could not get any better. Instead it got worse. Unimaginably worse.

A sudden chill wafted over her as the sun finally sunk below the Mumbles hills. Helen waddled straight over to the fireplace where she had already laid paper and sticks. On that first visit they had thought how quaint and primitive it all was; no gas and no electricity other than that provided by the generator Peter had ferried over in advance of their stay. Trouble was, the machine was so loud that Helen could not bear to have it turned on. She was also worried it might annoy the neighbours. So they lit fires to keep warm and cooked over a big old range that fed on wood and made the tiny kitchen almost unbearably hot. At first it seemed such a drastic change of lifestyle but Helen quickly got used to it and before long found herself enjoying the simplicity of it all. Putting a match to a candle and watching the flame burst into flickering life was somehow much more fun than simply turning on the light. Now, alone and more afraid than she had ever been in her life, Helen wished she could do just that. It would mean comfort in an instant.

As the fire took hold she made a mental note to check how many logs were left in the outhouse. She would also get Peter to search the other houses on the island to see if their stores were any better. None of their neighbours had made it back. Every time she thought of that, Helen had a sick feeling. It meant they were probably among the dead. Or, worse, the *living* dead. It was pure chance she and Peter had already been at the cottage when the emergency broadcasts began. Equally fortunate was the fact that they were reasonably self-sufficient. Out of habit they kept the cupboards well stocked with tinned and dried foods. Peter had turned part of the sprawling garden into a thriving vegetable patch. They would be able to manage for months before the food started to run out. Helen could not bring herself to think about what might happen after that. They'd cross that bridge when they came to it.

The logs were soon spitting and cracking. Satisfied the fire was not going to fizzle out the moment she turned her back on it, Helen made a brief tour of the cottage, closing and locking each window and door. Of course she was safe here, unless one of those creatures figured out how to swim or steer a boat. Even so, she felt better knowing her home was secure. After fastening the last of the windows she settled herself on the settee, a cushion supporting her stomach, another between her legs. It was hard enough to get comfortable in bed let alone to relax in more cramped surroundings, but she had no plans to go to bed until Peter returned. She tried the radio again but there was nothing but static and so she switched it off, anxious to conserve the batteries. From outside she heard a distant rumble, the opening salvo of an impending storm. Her mind filled with thoughts of her husband, alone in a world that had turned to hell. *Please God, keep him safe.*

Despite her unease it was not long before the heat of the fire lulled her to sleep. When she awoke the next morning, back and neck agonisingly stiff, the storm had blown itself out. At some point she dreamt Peter had returned and during the confused moments immediately following sleep she thought it was memory, not dream. The realisation that he had still not come back to her almost reduced her to tears. For the first time since she became pregnant she found she had no appetite. It was all she could do to force down a cup of coffee.

After struggling to get her Wellington boots on she ventured outside to search for damage. A branch no thicker than her wrist had been ripped from an old tree overhanging the path.

Lifting one end of it she found it was light enough for her to drag back to the log shed where it could dry, ready to be cut up and used. She knew if Peter were there he would be urging her to stop, to sit down and put her feet up. But she couldn't. There were times when she felt full of energy and had to do something with it, and others when all she wanted was to take it easy. Now was one of those times when she had to be working. Helen went to close the door before it occurred to her that the hot air would help dry the wood out faster, so she let it swing open, hinges creaking loudly. Then she started down to the beach once more.

As the path started to turn and head down towards the sea she raised the binoculars to her eyes, scanning the sea for any sign of the boat. Across the bay, the ugly steelworks of Port Talbot were obscured by billowing black smoke. Another part of the place must have gone up in the night, the resulting explosion either drowned out by, or merged into, the thunder of the storm. Turning the binoculars towards Mumbles she could see the lighthouse no longer blinked its message of warning.

What if he's gone for good? It was the first time she had allowed the thought to rise to the surface, always repressing it as something she dared not contemplate. But four days had passed and she knew she had to. If he did not come back she was stranded on the island with a baby due within weeks. It would not have been such a terrible prospect had any of the other cottage owners made it here. Then again, maybe she should be glad they hadn't. To all intents and purposes they would have brought the plague with them. Sooner or later someone was bound to die and the living would have to face the consequences. They would have to take the decision to kill someone they'd once loved. That was something she could never bring herself to do. Peter kept shotguns for rabbiting but Helen could never use one of them on him, not even if he became one of the living dead the Government broadcasts had warned about.

There was debris on the beach. Lumps of wood, bits of old fishing net and drink cans that had at some time been abandoned across the water. Pretty much anything discarded below the high water line eventually found its way to the island. Whenever they stayed at the cottage Peter loved to walk on the beach, salvaging anything that would burn to stock up the wood shed. He even seemed to gain some pleasure in bagging up the other rubbish, to keep the sands clean. That thought was still in her mind when she saw the boat, lying on its side near a cluster of rocks.

"*Peter!*"

She started to run as fast as she was able but within a few strides the baby kicked, throwing her off balance and sending her sprawling onto the sand. She called out again as she staggered to her feet, vision starting to blur.

"*Peter!*"

No reply came but she continued calling, desperately willing him to be safe. When she reached the stricken craft she saw it was empty. The medical supplies, along with tinned food and other non-perishable food, he had risked his life for, now lay scattered across the sand around the boat, almost indistinguishable from the other debris that surrounded it. But there was no sign of Peter.

Helen's first thought was that he had made his way back to the cottage by a different route. There was another path cutting up through the dunes that they rarely used because it was steep and so meandering it effectively doubled the distance. Maybe he went that way. For all she knew he could be hurt, confused. Helen grabbed some of the supplies and stuffed them hastily into a box in case the tide came in and swept the whole lot away. Then she began to walk along the beach towards the dunes.

The path seemed to defy her efforts to climb it. Sand shifted treacherously beneath her feet as she clambered upwards. Her face burnt in the strong sunlight. Another kind of heat blazed in her chest as her lungs struggled to find enough air for her and the baby. Halfway-up the path kinked to the right and Helen was forced to take a break in spite of the sense of urgency that filled her. She perched impatiently on the grass only long enough for her breathing and heartbeat to settle, then pushed herself onwards.

She found Peter a couple of yards below the crest, sprawled face down across the path, one arm out flung, like someone who'd been shot. Time solidified. The sounds of the sea, the heat of the sun, the cries of the gulls, vanished in an instant. Helen was distantly aware of the box tumbling to the ground. Then the world came rushing back at her. She cried out Peter's name and ran until she reached him. *You can't be dead! Not after coming back to me.* Helen dropped to her knees at his side and reached out for him with trembling hands, yet could not bring herself to touch him, as if she believed she could disprove the fact of his death by refusing to confirm it. Her fear of losing him had rendered her useless, paralysed.

A great spasm suddenly convulsed Peter's body. It so startled Helen that she scrambled away from him before she was aware she was moving. Her despair was replaced by a combination of shock and overwhelming relief. Peter was alive! Hurt, yes, maybe badly, but she'd take care of that. She could make him better, just as long as he was *alive*. Ashamed at her unthinking reaction, Helen moved back to his side, gripping his shoulders and helping him stand as he struggled to push himself up from the ground. "It's all right," she murmured, over and over, like a mother comforting a small child that had fallen and hurt itself. "It's all right, Peter. You're safe now, you made it back to me. Everything's all right."

Then he turned towards her, and she saw it was not all right after all.

Immediately apparent was the fact that half his face was gone. One side of it was undeniably Peter's. The other resembled something out of an anatomy textbook. Bone and muscle glistened wetly in the sun where the flesh had been ripped off in a great ragged strip. The missing skin also revealed several teeth, fixing Peter's mouth into a perpetual snarl. His eyes were like those of a fish left on a supermarket counter too long; clouded over with white. All this registered too quickly for her mind to deal with – *he's not dead, sure he's really badly injured, but at least he's alive* – leaving her bewildered enough to remain unmoving when Peter lunged forward, one blood-spattered hand reaching out and making to grab at her shoulder. It was a wild swing, poorly aimed, which was just as well otherwise she guessed it would have taken her head off. It was at that precise moment that she realised Peter was not merely stunned. He had not been driven mad by pain. Helen's brain carried on trying to conjure up a million excuses, delaying tactics to avoid facing up to the truth. Not one of them would hold any water. Peter was dead. *Fact.* And now he was trying to kill her.

Helen screamed, giving vent to her fear and grief. Momentum twisted Peter around, propelling him away from her. Helen staggered backwards. Her foot caught in something and she fell, the soft sand feeling as hard as concrete when she hit it ass-first. She bit her tongue. A sharp pain flared in her mouth, followed swiftly by the taste of blood. Helen half-rolled, half pushed herself to her feet, cradling her stomach, for one moment certain her exertions had hurt the baby. A punch-like kick inside, followed swiftly by two others, was enough to quell that particular fear.

Thudding footsteps made her spin round. Peter was staggering down the path, arms raised towards her, just a yard or two away. Helen wanted to cry. It was bad enough he was dead, but now she had to contend with *this*. The one good thing – no, the *only* good thing she could think of right then, was that she could easily outpace him. But even that belief was exposed as a cruel lie when she put her right foot down, intending to run. The ankle shrieked a siren song of agony. She must have twisted it when she fell, realisation temporarily delayed by her overriding concern for the baby's welfare. Whatever, Helen knew she did not have the time to think about it right then. The Peter-thing was almost upon her. Determination flared in her, bright enough to eclipse the hurt in her leg. *He's not going to get me. Me or the baby.*

She turned away from the creature behind her and made her way as fast as she could down the path, favouring her aching right foot as much as possible so that her movement was more skip-shuffle than walk. It was ungainly but effective. Before long, when Helen felt brave enough to risk a glance back, the gap between her and Peter had widened noticeably. By the time she reached the end of the path she had doubled the distance. There was a large stick, a piece of driftwood, on the beach close by. She grabbed it, wedging it under her arm to form a makeshift crutch. It bent alarmingly as she put her weight on it but held well enough for her to pick up her speed. By now she could no longer see where she was going. Tears had welled up in her eyes. Helen could feel them flow down her cheeks, cold against the sun-kissed skin, but she refused to wipe them away.

Even through her kaleidoscopic vision she could make out the ivy side wall of the cottage as she hobbled along the beach. Once inside she would lock the door and wait until... well, however long it took. The double glazing was tough enough to withstand any amount of bodily pressure against it. *The zombies are driven by one basic instinct – hunger.* So the Government warning had informed them. *There is no evidence to suggest they possess even the most rudimentary intelligence.* In that case the creature Peter had become would not be smart enough to use a rock to break the reinforced glass. Neither could he – *it*, she told herself – last forever. A reanimated corpse must surely need energy to keep functioning. All she had to do was remain beyond its reach for long enough and then it would cease to be a threat.

Helen left the beach. The garden's side wall beckoned. She hobbled along the dirt path leading to it. As she reached out to unlatch the back gate the improvised crutch finally snapped. The sudden shift of balance sent her face-first to the ground.

She managed to break her fall with her outstretched hands but, even so, her forehead smacked into the packed earth with sufficient force to turn the world briefly white and then momentarily black. Helen blinked, dazed, a part of her brain shouting at her to *get up and run* but the words were so distant she found it easy to ignore them. She had no idea of who or where she was. Then, in the way she would sometimes recall a vivid nightmare hours after she woke, the memory of that morning's horrors swept over her like a tidal wave. Her heat missed a couple of beats at the realisation that Peter could be closing in. Without pausing to think she scurried commando-style through the opening, kicking the gate shut behind her with her good foot. Blinking, Helen raised a hand to her head; the fingers came away gleaming wet. How long had she been unconscious? She had no idea. It must have been no more than seconds, a couple of minutes at most, otherwise—

Helen clasped her head in her hands and squeezed her eyes shut. She couldn't go down that road. The terror inside her was so raw it was still bleeding. Thinking about what *could* have happened, had luck not been on her side, only made matters worse. It also distracted her from her most pressing need, which was to get inside the cottage. Once she had done that she could let it all out – the heartache, the fear, the revulsion, the whole fucking lot of it. But not before. Helen not only had to take care of herself; she had the baby to think of. With Peter gone, it was all she had left.

She slid along the path towards the back door, using her hands to drag herself forward. Her left leg provided extra propulsion; the right was now almost useless, a dangling mass of pain. From behind she heard a thud, as loud as last night's thunder. Something had struck the wooden gate a heavy blow. Helen groaned, knowing exactly what that something was. She did not have much time. The gate was old, its hinges rusting. It could not withstand many more assaults like that. A second report echoed round the silent garden. That was her cue to move, which she did with more speed than she had believed herself to be capable of. It was not enough. Helen was agonisingly close to the back door when there came a splintering sound, followed by a crash. She did not have to turn around to know the gate was no longer a barrier between her and the zombie. Looking around wildly, she spotted the pile of rubble that was all that remained of the crumbling shed Peter had demolished in spur-of-the-moment enthusiasm one day. Helen scrambled the short distance to it and rolled over until the mound was between her and the garden gate. Her heart was performing like a mad thing in her chest as she peered slowly around the edge, terrified she would see the creature lumbering straight at her.

But, thank God, Peter was following the path, pausing every now and then as if listening or trying to catch her scent. It did not even glance at the pile of rubble as it passed. Instead it continued heading towards the cottage, stumbling to a halt when it reached the gaping doorway of the log store. Helen watched it with unblinking eyes, not even daring to hope, as the creature made its way slowly to the entrance. Despite her caution, the adrenaline began to flow. She could feel it coursing through her system, flushing away the pain along with the doubts. Peter turned his head slowly from side to side, like an old man crossing a busy road, then stepped through the doorway. Helen did not hesitate. She leapt up and, barely feeling the myriad stabbing daggers of pain in her ankle, ran across the lawn to the storehouse. From inside came a series of crashes. In her mind's eye, she watched the creature toss the remaining logs out of its way as it searched for its prey. She'd been in there earlier; maybe it could smell her. Then all went silent. Helen slammed the door shut and leant against it with her left shoulder, her right hand fumbling with the bolt. A bomb exploded behind the door. Or at least that's how it felt. The force of it almost sent her flying. Seeing the door was being forced open, Helen yelled and threw herself against it, smashing it shut again. Her fingers found the bolt and slid the bar across into its socket. A second bomb detonated. This time the door stayed shut. Unlike the back gate it was new, and hopefully sturdy enough to withstand whatever the zombie threw at it. Helen stepped away cautiously, still half-expecting the wood to implode under the power of the blows being rained upon it. Fortunately it held while she made her way slowly to the cottage, the adrenaline having faded enough for her to feel every single ache and pain.

Once inside she locked the back door, then hobbled around each of the windows, making certain once more they were secure. She had no way of knowing how long the creature would be trapped in the storehouse. But, for the time being at least, she was safe. Suddenly the strength drained out of her and she grabbed hold of the back of the settee for support, lowering herself into it as shudders began to wrack her body. As soon as they eased the tears came, great big gulping cries which seemed to last an eternity. Finally even they stopped. Helen felt empty. Peter was dead. And yet he could not be dead. They'd not even been married five years and he was about to become a dad. How could he be dead? The words of a story she'd read somewhere came back to her. *Sometimes fate screws up, big time.* Wasn't that a fact.

Peter had died trying to ensure she lived. He'd gone back to the mainland, knowing the dangers, to get the medical supplies they would need for the birth. The Government warnings had made it clear; anyone bitten by one of those things would die within the hour, then return as one of them. Helen guessed Peter had been attacked yet had managed to survive long enough to make his way back to the island. Presumably the plague had fogged his dying brain, so that he did not realise that by returning, even with the supplies, he was putting her in danger. Yes, he'd died trying to make sure she lived. Now he was alive again, and trying to kill her. The irony was not lost on Helen. God had played enough practical jokes this year. What harm in one more?

The medical supplies were gone, too. She dared not leave the house to try to recover those she had dropped from the dune or those strewn around the wreckage of the boat, if the tide had not swept them away. The door that imprisoned Peter would not last for long. She did not want to be out in the open when it finally went.

Okay, so his shotgun was upstairs and Helen knew how to load it. But she was adamant she would not be able to shoot him should he break free, even knowing that *thing* was no longer her husband at all. It was a killing machine, as mindless and implacable in its pursuit of prey as a spider, and she would not hesitate squishing one of *those* should it come near her. Still... Peter may be dead but she still loved him. Maybe it would be better if she simply turned the shotgun on herself, ending her misery there and then before it could get any worse. Until now the baby had seemed the most important thing in the world. Protecting it as well as herself had been the instinct that spurred her on, made her fight to keep moving even when she thought death had her in its grasp. But the more Helen thought about it, the more she realised she had been fooling herself. How long could she live on the island with herself and the baby to feed? There was no means of reaching the mainland and certain death awaited them even if she somehow managed.

Cramp twisted her belly, fierce enough to make her gasp. *Must be shock. Think of what you've experienced today, all the exertions you've put your poor swollen body through. And you never ate any breakfast remember?* She sat still for a moment, gently massaging her belly. The first tendrils of panic began to infiltrate her. She hadn't felt the baby kick for ages. Sometimes it would lie unmoving for hours only to explode into furious motion the moment Helen became afraid for it, as if sensing its mother's concern. But this time was different. Even discounting the cramp, intuition, a sixth sense, whatever you wanted to call it, told her something was wrong. She pressed her distended stomach more firmly, trying desperately to elicit a response. Then a second cramp struck, much worse than the first, feeling as if her insides had been grabbed and mercilessly squeezed. Hot liquid surged from between her legs and for a moment she thought she had wet herself. When she noticed it didn't smell of piss the obvious alternative suggested itself. *No! Not for another six weeks!*.

But there was no denying the fact that, early or not, the contractions were starting in earnest. Helen tried to calm herself, breathing in deeply, exhaling slowly, trying to control her panic. Then she heard a banging from outside, almost in rhythm with the waves of pain. Peter must have broken free. She prayed to God the doors and windows of the cottage were as sturdy as she hoped. Not that she could do much about it if she was wrong. She had a child to deliver. That thought sliced straight through the panic and the self-denial, as effortlessly as a scalpel. Helen pushed herself up from the settee and staggered upstairs to the bedroom where she kept the few bits and pieces she had managed to accumulate. It was no substitute for a hospital, that was certain, but it was better than nothing.

A dark shape passed slowly by the frosted glass of the front door as she was halfway up. Helen froze. The thing smacked one hand against the pane with terrific force, but it held. The figure continued on its way, out of sight. Helen sighed with relief, then squealed as another contraction struck. It pinned her to the stairs, doubled up and gasping, for what seemed like an age before finally releasing her. She knew she should be timing the contractions, but that would have to wait. She made her way gingerly to the bathroom where she had stored soap, a plastic bowl, scissors, dressings and antiseptic cream, together with a pile of towels wrapped in plastic bags to keep them clean. She carried them in turn to the bedroom, where she arranged some of the towels next to a stack of pillows. Next she filled the bowl with scalding water from the hot tap and lugged that through. Finally she closed and bolted the bedroom door as a last line of defence before working off her soaking joggers and knickers. Then she lay on the bed and tried to keep herself from screaming at the ugliest contraction yet, not wanting the thing in the garden to hear.

Time passed slowly at first, only to accelerate rapidly as the intensity of the cramps increased. Helen, head and back raised by the pillows, legs wide open, each forming an inverted V, could do nothing but wait, trying her best to remember the breathing exercises they'd taught in the ante-natal classes. What she would not give to have her husband there, alive, holding her hand and whispering encouragement, sharing this most precious moment. She began to cry at the idea of it. Two savage cramps back-to-back made the tears flow even more freely. They passed like the others, but gradually the pain intensified, the gaps between contractions closed, until her body was a ball of white-hot agony with no room left for thought or reason. At one point her mind became coherent long enough for Helen to stuff a towel into her mouth, for she knew her screams were bellowing out unchecked. Pain regained control after that, taking her to new heights of suffering until Helen could not tell whether she was dead or just desperate to die. Finally, just as she reached the point where she knew, just knew, she could not take this any longer, her back arched and her lower half convulsed, sending a tiny blood-and-mucus encased figure sliding from her onto the bed. For a moment Helen stared at it, too numb to realise what it was.

Then recognition dawned. Even though her vagina stung and ached like hell, and though every muscle trembled, the worst of the pain inside had gone.

"My baby," she gasped, reaching out. But her hands faltered as they touched the infant. It was not cold, but it did not feel as warm as she'd expected. Neither was it moving. Babies didn't need to have their backsides slapped to start crying; most of them, she knew, simply arrived in the world bawling their heads off. Not this one. Not her baby. It was silent. Silent and unmoving and only lukewarm to the touch.

Stillborn.

No! Sobbing, she cradled it in her arms then shook it with as much force as she dared, frantically trying to get it to cry, to scream, to breathe, but all to no avail.

Stillborn. Dead.

Like his – and the tiny curled up fold of flesh between the baby's legs confirmed that, yes, it was a boy – like his dad.

Helen's sobs petered out as she finally gave up her attempts to resuscitate the infant, placing the body tenderly on the bed beside her. Then, ignoring the leaking fluids and the burning between her legs, she pushed the pillows away so she could lie down next to her son, turning to face him and giving him his first and last kiss, her lips brushing fleetingly against his forehead. There was no grief, no sense of loss, no fury with God or the unfairness of life, just a vacuum where her humanity used to be.

For a little while she slept. Occasionally she was disturbed by more cramps as her body expelled the placenta. When she woke the room was half-filled with shadows. Late evening, she guessed. The touch of something soft and cold against her skin made her look down. The baby, flesh grey, eyes wide and made of white, was wriggling frantically on the bed, toothless mouth opening and closing relentlessly. Helen gagged, and pushed herself away from it, only then noticing they were still joined by the umbilical cord that stretched from inside her. She grabbed the scissors from the bundle of supplies on the bedside table, and hastily cut through the cord. For one moment she was almost compelled to drive the twin blades straight into the tiny creature that writhed on the blood-soaked mattress alongside her. She even got as close as placing the points of the scissors against its flesh before she relented.

She could no more do that to her baby than she could turn the gun on Peter.

They were all she had left in the world.

Instead she turned the scissors on herself, piercing her left breast until blood bubbled and flowed. That done, she picked up the baby. Its body was rigid and this, coupled with its frantic movements, almost caused her to drop it. But she managed to retain her grip long enough to place it on her chest, one hand behind its head, gently pushing it down until its lips came into contact with the wound. Helen felt its hard gums gnaw at her skin, which immediately began to burn. *Now I'm infected too*, she thought, the prospect filling her with hope rather than dismay.

From downstairs she heard the sound of glass smashing.

Helen lay back, holding the infant even more tightly to her breast.

A slow smile of contentment spread across her lips.

Before long they would be a family again.

DEATH-CON 1

Sean Parker

(This is a work of fiction. Any resemblance to events, places or people is merely unfortunate)

Robert Neville found his first victim before he even reached the convention, while still on the train, forty or so miles from his destination. He had been trying to catch up on some reading from his portable slush pile, attempting to become interested in the tale of an inarticulate zombie (his tongue had rotted) and the apparently 'hot' former lesbian vampire that had inexplicably fallen in love with him. *'Don't say a word,' she breathed*, followed by a paragraph detailing the various movements of her breasts. *'We shall create our own special love, the eroticism of death...'* At which point, the woman sitting opposite him took out a mobile phone and began a conversation in a loud, scratchy voice, killing any chance of further reading. Probably for the best, he thought. Besides, the woman with the phone looked vaguely familiar.

"Yes, I'll be arriving in half an hour, it'll be great to see you again, I loved your story in *Attack of the Cthulhus*, chilling stuff... haha yes indeed, bye for now," she said, then dialled another number.

"Just to let you know I'll be arriving in half an hour or so, looking forward to seeing you, I adored your story in *Rednecks with Chainsaws*, frightening stuff... hehe oh yes, tata."

And another number:

"Oh hello, just thought I'd phone to say I'll be there in thirty minutes, dying to see you again, I am in awe of your story in *Abstract Tornadoes of the Mind*, thought-provoking stuff... ahem, indeed, bye!"

And another. Jesus Christ, thought Neville, poised to speak between this call and the next.

"Excuse me," he said, and the woman stopped in mid-dial

and threw him an inquiring look.

"Are you Tasmin Saylor, by any chance?" he continued.

She looked pleased. "Yes I am, how odd to be recognised. And—"

"I've read your recent collection, *Celtic Windtrap.*"

"Splendid, I do hope you enjoyed it. The old Celtic traditions are in danger of—"

"I'd like my money back."

Saylor's expression went from surprised to angry in the space of a second.

"And I would like the four hours of my life I spent reading it back. Can you provide that?"

Saylor made a move to gather up her bags and sit somewhere else. At the same moment they both realised that the carriage was, besides themselves, unoccupied. Oh good, thought Neville, story book perfect.

As if on cue, the train entered a tunnel. Neville grinned and Saylor gasped. The lights flickered and the sound of the tracks and the whoosh of air from a train passing in the opposite direction conspired to drown out the screams.

*

It took Neville a while to find the bed and breakfast where he had rented a room for the three days of the convention. It was a shabby building, off-white and peeling, much further from the centre of things than he had been led to believe by the owner, a fat balding man by the name of Chambers who sported glasses hanging from what looked like a plug chain around his neck and a tatty brown tank top.

As Neville signed the guest book, Chambers asked, "Are you here for the convention then?"

Neville looked up from the false name and address he was filling in and said, "What makes you think that?"

Chambers laughed. "Something in the eyes. We've got another one staying here; says he's a publisher. Mark Lewis.

Heard of him?"

Too good to be true, thought Neville, the owner of Voyeur Press. He shook his head and said, "No, I'm afraid I haven't."

After he had finished his business with Chambers, and left his bags in his dusty room, Neville ventured out in search of a do-it-yourself store, and later that afternoon, he paid a short, but exceedingly bloody, visit to Mr Lewis.

Neville had no time to relax. He spent a short time cleaning himself up, packing what he needed into a plastic shopping bag before heading out for a bite to eat at a quiet Thai restaurant. He'd had a busy day, and it was by no means over yet. He had to keep his strength up. As he ate, he read the typo-ridden story of a serial killer who kept body parts in his fridge and made wisecracks at inappropriate moments.

*

A small group of writers, editors, and fans had arranged to have a pre-con drink or two at a tiny, out of the way pub ten minutes staggering distance from their hotel. One of the fans lived in the area and decreed the ale to be of a reasonable quality here; so, via the marvels of the internet, here they now were.

And here, also, was Neville.

He was seated at the bar of the now nearly empty pub, nursing a double whisky back to health. All of the locals had cleared out *en masse* when a drunken editor had shouted, "Come on then, you filking bastard!" and another of their number had produced, as if from nowhere, a battered, slightly out of tune acoustic guitar, and proceeded to sing a song lamenting, at great length, the lack of computers in Asimov's 'Foundation' novels.

"Another?" asked the landlord, a seemingly aloof fellow called Grady, if the license displayed over the bar was to be believed. Neville nodded and Grady poured him another drink. Money changed hands, and Grady vanished for a while into the back of the pub. He reappeared holding a long butcher's knife covered with bits of lettuce and some sticky tomato seeds, which he placed on the bar within reach of Neville. It was impossible to tell if he gave Neville a pointed glance, or if the placing of the knife was mere coincidence. Grady had poured himself a large brandy and was now retreating back from the bar before Neville could think further on the matter. In the meantime a writer who was responsible for a fantasy novel which a reviewer in *Darker than Demonshit* had called '*the most important addition to the literature of the fantastic since the Gor novels*', had arrived at the bar, empty glasses in hand. Swifter than should be humanly possible, Neville snatched up the knife and stabbed the writer in the face with all his strength. Neville tugged the knife free, and the writer slumped onto a bar stool. Splayed out behind him, his legs twitched occasionally, and his glasses fell from his ruined face.

On hearing the shattering of glasses and the thud of presumably drunken flesh hitting the floor, the writer's companions cheered. The filker called out, "Lightweight! The night is young!" and grabbed an editor to help him return the fallen writer to his vertical position. Neville leaned forward as if to help them, taking the opportunity to take a slice out of the filkers vocal cords and stab the editor in the stomach. After that, things became a bit messy.

Neville charged across the room, knife held ahead of him like a lance, pausing only to extract his foot from the guitar that had splintered as he kicked at it as he passed. He was on the drunken group before they had even begun to extricate themselves from barstools and tables and each other. He slashed at anything that moved, and at things that had ceased to move.

The screams were terrible, but did not last too long. When they had faded, Grady returned to the bar, sipping his brandy and surveying the carnage. Neville tensed, but the barman merely turned towards him and asked, "Another drink?"

Neville nodded, and the barman poured him a whisky.

"This one is on the house. Drink up quickly though, I'm going to have to call the police. Damn shame I'm so short-sighted, I can hardly see a thing without my glasses." Grady smiled coldly as he spoke and sauntered down to the other end of the bar where the telephone sat. Neville slugged back his drink and gathered up his unused bag of tricks, and left with a small wave at the barman, who was by now too busy with his request for the assistance of two of the emergency services to notice.

Neville hoped the dark would hide the sight of his clothes. It did, and, shortly after arriving back at his room at the bed and breakfast, he fell asleep over a manuscript written by a well-respected author who had hit upon the idea of combining the style of William Burroughs with a plot centring on the activities of time-travelling werewolves from outer space.

*

Today would be the busiest day, and Neville spent several hours that morning readying himself for it. He ate a large breakfast, giving an uninterested response when Chambers asked if he had seen Lewis at all. Soon enough, it was time to get to the convention hotel. He wanted to catch a few slug-a-beds before the main events of the day. Walking quickly, he soon found a taxi rank, and got in the front vehicle. The taxi driver, old and wrinkled, smiled unpleasantly and said, "Just room for one more inside, sir."

Neville froze for a second, then shrugged, giving the driver his destination

As it happened, he only managed to cull one late riser, a hung-over American slipstream writer, who managed to vomit on Neville before he had time to use the nail gun from his bag of tricks. It produced an effect not unlike a particularly extravagant piercing, and it was quick.

With the writer dead, Neville searched the room for something to replace his vomit covered shirt with. He found a jumper and a jacket, changed quickly and left the room, careful not to leave any fingerprints on the little plastic sign hanging on the handle as he turned it to 'Do Not Disturb'.

At the side of the door to the main convention room Neville collected his dangly name-tag and filled it in. Apart from a long queue of people along the back wall, the room was sparsely filled. All were clutching manuscripts, and someone Neville recognised as an agent who specialised in splatterpunk sat at a table at the head of the line. Rage overcame Neville and he reached in his bag for his prize possession, a flick-knife with a blade as sharp as a razor. Starting at the back of the queue, he performed a twenty metre slicing motion which cut the throats of the entire line, each falling backwards like a blood fountaining domino. Neville nodded a brief hello to the agent, who returned it and went back to the now bloodstained manuscript in front of him.

Neville left, surprised that the burbling bloody pile of corpses and near-corpses hadn't attracted more attention, and headed for the dealers' room. He was looking forward to this.

Tables, books piled high here and there, magazines and artwork in amongst it all, accompanied by publishers and authors and artists and editors. Neville was at a loss amidst all these suitable victims. It took him a minute to notice how quiet the room had become, how still. Every single person in the place was staring directly straight at him, name tags swaying as they started to converge upon him, changing as they came.

Neville barely had time to scramble up onto a table, knocking paperbacks and plastic orcs flying, before they were upon him. An almost solid mass of tentacles, pale faces, sharpened teeth, mighty claws, denim dungarees, axes, chainsaws, unidentifiable limbs, eyes (within the confines of a face or without), gelatinous blobs, metallic devices of unclear purpose, pale girls in white with dark dark hair, wolves (half human or not), vampires old and new, dismembered body parts, crazed faces of mad professors, white coats of same, bleeping computers stationary in the background, merely observing with their mechanical unblinking recording devices, wisps of dangerous fog, devils, the uneasy dead, an underfoot crunching of rats, witches and witchfinders, a small sea of blood and a smattering of deranged clowns – this was the last thing Neville saw.

Eventually, the frenzy subsided, and the booksellers and browsers returned to human form. Somebody belched, somebody giggled nervously, and someone gagged at the sight of the bloody pile in the centre of the room. They'd have to clear it up, but later on would be fine. No time now, the raffle was due to start in a couple of minutes.

LIKE A BIRD

Mike Chinn

Connor dropped three euros onto the counter and lifted his beer. He cast a swift glance around the *Hotel Velhos Pássaros'* bar: apart from a barmaid and the Eagles singing quietly in the background about the girl from yesterday, he'd got the place to himself. From what he'd seen of the rest of the hotel – big, expensive, and empty – he was going to have a quiet few weeks. Not quite what he was expecting from the Azores – Maitland had made it sound like the Hawaii of the Atlantic. And Angie had always—

Angie...

He took a deep pull on his beer. That wasn't why he was here. So what if Angie's parents had been born on São Miguel – just up the road in Vila Franco do Campo. It was a coincidence. Life was full of them. Good and bad. Deal with it.

There was a small patio outside the bar. Five white tables – one of them with a sunshade still raised against a sun that had set over an hour ago – were placed at random on the concrete. Connor stepped out into the mild night air and dropped into the nearest seat. It was quiet, except for the sound of waves out in the dark somewhere. Not even the noise of holidaymakers. São Miguel didn't seem to have been discovered by most of Europe or the Japanese yet. Connor wondered how long that would last, with direct flights from Britain.

There was a sudden, bizarre sound out in the night. A brief stab of confused gabble. Like something that couldn't speak trying to form words. It came again. And again. Connor realised whatever it was, it was coming from above him. A creepy voice that was trying to tell him something; occasionally laughing when it realised Connor didn't understand him. A harsh, Mr Punch-like sound. A Mr Punch so drunk he could barely talk...

Getting quickly to his feet, Connor headed back into the bar.

It wasn't any fuller, the Eagles were bemoaning the loss of paradise, but someone had turned on a wide screen TV. A football match was playing silently to the empty room; Connor recognised only one team: Benfica. The girl was still tending the bar, though. She smiled at him – a huge, natural grin that warmed him through. He tried to read her name badge without looking obvious.

"Getting cold?" she asked. Oddly, her accent sounded more American than Portuguese.

Connor almost said: *No – I got freaked out by funny noises*, but stopped himself. He decided to nod instead. It was easier. "Could I have another large beer?" he asked, placing his empty glass on the bar top.

"Sure." She took the glass and dropped it into a bowl below the bar, pulled a clean one from a fridge and began to fill it.

"Do you serve food in the bar?" Connor asked. He was peckish – he never touched airline food, and he couldn't be bothered to try out the hotel's restaurant. Not tonight.

She half-turned her head and smiled again. "Sure. Sandwiches. Chicken or cheese salad." This time Connor couldn't help but notice how blue her eyes were; maybe you had to stand back a little to notice things like that. Her hair was shoulder-length, mid-brown and slightly waved. She was dressed in the plain white blouse and knee-length skirt that seemed to be the uniform for female staff. On her, they looked good.

"Could I have the chicken?"

She put the filled glass in front of him and began tapping out some private code on the cash register. She placed a printed receipt next to his beer and disappeared inside a small room at the rear of the bar. Connor heard the clatter of plates and cutlery. Obviously, she did everything in the bar.

When she reappeared with his sandwich, he got a better look at her badge. *Maria*, it read. He pulled out a ten-euro note, and he waved away the change. "Keep it," he said. Big spender. He was on expenses – and he felt like trying to impress her. If a three-euro tip was likely to impress an American-accented employee in this hotel.

"Those noises, outside," he said, after carefully chewing and swallowing his first bite of sandwich. "What are they? They sound pretty weird."

Her smile became a silent laugh. Connor found himself liking it very much – especially the way her eyes sparkled. "Those are birds. During the day they fly kilometres across the sea, but every night they return. They roost in the hills." She frowned. "What are they called…?"

"Albatrosses?" Connor suggested. It was the only seabird he could think of, other than gulls. And they didn't sound like any gulls he knew.

Maria shook her head. "No, no… *Shearwaters*… That is it. Shearwaters."

"Well, whatever…" He'd heard of shearwaters, but doubted he could pick one out of a line-up. He took another bite. "They still sound weird…"

"Like they are laughing at you? Or trying to speak?"

He washed the sandwich down with beer. "It's not just me, then?"

"Everyone says it – the first time they hear them. You get used to it." A telephone began to trill and Maria went to answer it. There followed a brief and – what sounded to Connor, anyway – heated conversation. But he thought Portuguese was one of those languages that sounded aggressive, anyway. For all he knew, she was swapping dirty suggestions with her boyfriend. Or husband.

Oh, I hope not, he found himself thinking. He finished his sandwich just as Maria put the receiver down.

"*Até logo*," she called back, deserting him and the bar. "See you later." Even the Eagles had gone quiet. Connor was left with just the silent football match. He drained his glass and headed for bed.

*

Connor leaned across the roof of his rental car, staring moodily down at the poetically christened *Lagoa do Fogo*. The Lake of Fire. That had been true once – the lake filled the crater of an extinct volcano – but the fire was long gone. All São Miguel had to show for its turbulent past were a few hot springs. And they'd been reduced to glorified steamers: cooking huge bundles of food for tourists.

He aimed his pocket digital camera at the lake, trying to be enthusiastic. Maitland wasn't paying him to be broody. But it was hard.

He hadn't dreamed about Angie for months. Last night she'd come back. Connor knew coming to the island would resurrect the memories. If he'd had the choice, he'd have passed up on the job; but work had been thin lately, and Maitland represented more than one job. Behind him were several travel companies, all eager to break new tourist ground. Look at it as a test: do a good job here, and who knows where he might be next. The Galapagos. The Antilles. The Falklands – God knows, that place could use the income.

He snapped off three shots in succession, not really looking at what he was taking. He could go through them tonight...

In the dream, Angie had been as he'd first known her: all wild light brown hair and eyes like sapphires. She'd been trying to say something... tell him something. She'd raised her arms imploringly, but instead of hands there'd been Punch and Judy puppets. Whatever Angie had been saying was drowned by their garbled shrieks and drunken, clotted laughter.

Connor's stomach growled warningly. He wished he'd actually had more to eat this morning – the hotel's buffet had certainly been a wide-ranging selection – but he hadn't felt up to much. After eyeing the attempt to appeal to all tastes – fry-ups and cereals bumping against croissants and cold meat – he'd just grabbed a glass of juice, dumped a few pieces of fruit on a plate and poured himself a cup of coffee. Sitting down, he'd looked around the mixture of staff and clients – the

107

former seemed to outnumber the latter – wondering if Maria would be there. He hadn't seen her and, after picking over the fruit with little enthusiasm and leaving the truly awful coffee, he'd gone back to his room to get his gear together.

As he'd left the hotel, one of the staff – a severe looking young woman with dark, scraped-back hair and tiny glasses – had given him such a hard look he'd wondered if he'd left his flies unzipped. But when he'd paused to look back, she'd gone.

Miss Danvers he'd dubbed her: the love child of the housekeeper from *Rebecca* and the butler from one of those Gothic black and white movies. *The Old Dark House*, something like that.

He turned away from Lagoa do Fogo and looked instead at the landscape around him. It wasn't anything special – just the ever-present hydrangeas spread across the fields. It was odd, seeing a bush that back home appeared singly in gardens, growing wild in huge numbers. The locals even seemed to use it as hedgerows. Typically, the blues and pinks were more vibrant than any he'd seen in England.

He took a couple more shots – even though he knew they wouldn't make it past the first sort – and got back in his car. He didn't have any plans for today – other than Lagoa do Fogo and the hot springs at Furnas; like all first days on every shoot he'd done, he was just going to drive and see what presented itself. Such as the aqueduct he'd passed earlier: that didn't seem to appear in many tourist guides. If he had anything to do with it, it would from now on.

His stomach muttered again. *Okay, you win*, he thought, starting the engine. Straight to Furnas and get something to eat. He was willing to bet there'd be at least one decent-sized cafe-bar there, overlooking the smelly, steaming pools.

*

That night, Connor sat in the bar with his laptop, digital

camera already docked, mobile at the ready. He sifted through the images he'd taken during the day, discarding the ones that showed nothing, or duplicated another shot. He was debating whether to tweak any with Photoshop – not sure if there was any point at this stage – when Maria spoke from the bar.

"Okay, I have to ask you. What are you doing?"

He glanced up. She was leaning over the bar, smiling that smile. Connor smiled back. Of course, he hadn't decided to work in the bar when he could have stayed in his room just because she was down here.

"I've been taking a few snaps of sites on the island," he said, rotating the laptop so she could see the screen. It was of a bunch of people standing around a steaming pool at Furnas. The composition reminded him of similar views of bonfire night – not that he expected Maria to see that. If she could actually see anything at that distance. He beckoned her closer. After the briefest of pauses, she came and sat on a chair opposite him.

"I'm working for a travel company," Connor explained. "They want to exploit the expanded Ponta Delgarda airport. I'm over here to take promotional shots."

She looked intently at the screen, then up at him. "Furnas. And you are reviewing them – selecting the best?"

She caught on quick, he gave her that. "Not these. I've just banged off a few with a digital camera – to give a feel for the place. I'll be e-mailing the images to Maitland – my contact – for his opinion..." he waved a finger at his mobile. "...see if he agrees with me which are the best sites."

"An electronic test-strip." She smiled again.

"Something like that." Connor admired the way she caught on. "You interested in photography?"

"My brother is. He works for an agency in New York. Some of it... rubbed off, I guess."

That explains the accent, Connor thought. Before he could ask, Maria started talking again.

"There is an old chapel outside, near the pool. It is the home of bats. Just before sundown, they fly out. Maybe you could take a shot of that?"

Connor nodded. Perhaps he could. It would require patience, and getting set up well before sundown. Wildlife photography wasn't his speciality, but he'd done some. And a beauty shot like that wouldn't be such a bad idea; mixed in with the usual scenery.

Maria stood up. "Can I get you another drink?"

"Yeah – okay. *Obrigado.*" He swivelled his laptop back and saved all the selected shots as small JPEGs. Maitland could make do with the raw snaps. As Maria returned to the bar for his beer, he opened up Outlook, typed out a quick message and attached all the selected shots. By the time she was back with his drink, the e-mail was almost half-sent.

"What time do you get off work?" he asked her before he had time to think about it.

She straightened up and looked hard at him for what felt like forever. "Depends," she replied eventually. "If the bar stays as busy as this, I could be here all night." The hard look dissolved into what was becoming a very familiar, and welcoming, smile.

"I'm serious. What time?"

"Midnight, I guess. Why?"

He picked up his beer and took a deep pull on it. "I wondered if I could buy you a drink, later."

"You could buy me one now…"

"Not the same."

She looked at him for another eternity. "Where were you thinking? There will be nowhere to go in Vila Franca."

He paused for a lifetime of his own. He felt light-headed, like he'd been drinking too fast. "My room's got a fully stocked mini-bar."

"Staff are not permitted to… fraternise… with guests you know."

Connor's light-headedness turned to nausea. He should have known…

Maria laughed: it was as delightful as her smile. "What is

your room number?"

*

Connor got wearily out of bed. It was still dark, but waves of heat were drifting in through the sliding doors out to the balcony. That and the creepy squawks from the hills. He shut the door, but the noises didn't quieten. Instead, they grew louder.

He moved cautiously along the wall. There was a vague memory of another window – not much bigger than a dormer – near the corner of the apartment. He tugged at the curtain that obscured the wall, trying to draw it aside. Outside the screeches were growing louder. Closer. There was an urgency to them now. A desperation – or order.

The curtain parted. The window was right in front of him, open by several inches. He reached to pull it shut – and something outside moved. A planter on the ledge shifted and fell. The window was wrenched out of Connor's fingers.

A moment later, an eye pressed up against the pane – large, black and cold as the glass. Something began to heave itself through the window – a formless shape, hard to see in the darkness. Connor ran to a nearby lamp, but it wouldn't light. He threw himself at the apartment's main light switch, but it clicked up and down uselessly.

The shape was almost through the window now. It shrieked and giggled; trying to form words – or speaking words he didn't understand. A huge beak snapped around each syllable. Its only visible eye glittered harsh and unreadable. The whole head loomed forward suddenly, pulling the rest of it into the room with a leathery flap—

Connor woke with a gasp. Somewhere the harsh sounds went on and on. He sat up, feeling as hot as he had in the dream, confused. It took a moment for his hearing to wake up too, and he realised the sounds he heard were coming from the bathroom. A shower.

The running water stopped. A few moments later, Maria stepped into the room, wrapped decorously in a white towel. She bent over Connor and kissed him lightly on the nose.

"*Bom dia*," she smiled, and stepped back, sorting through her discarded underclothes with a toe.

"What time is it?" he mumbled, trying to focus on his wristwatch.

She swept up the tiny pile of lingerie. "Five-thirty," she said over a shoulder, disappearing back into the bathroom.

"Jesus," Connor muttered to himself. "Early riser," he added, louder for Maria's benefit.

"I have to start work" she called.

"Shit..." Connor pulled himself from under the tangle of damp sheets. He felt obscurely guilty – he should have realised Maria had an early start. As he fumbled into a pair of shorts, she re-emerged from the bathroom. She was brushing at her blouse and skirt.

"Do they look too creased?" she was saying. "I hung them up while I showered – let the steam get to them."

"They look fine." He tried to pull her close, kiss her properly, but she sidestepped neatly.

"Not now," she said, waving a forefinger. "Now you are a guest again, and I am staff." She stepped in, kissed him lightly, and was away before he could grab her. "I will see you later." She unlocked the apartment door and drew it open.

"But..." This felt absurd.

She looked back once and smiled that smile. "Later, Con. *Adeus!*" The door shut itself behind her.

Connor stood, feeling stupid. He'd never had a one-night stand; he hadn't thought last night was one. Now he had his doubts. He'd been out of the game too long.

He opened the mini-bar and took out a bottle of sparkling water. As he opened it and took a deep, icy drink, he noticed all the beer and wine was gone. That was going to cost him. Or rather, cost Maitland.

He glanced at his watch. It was still only twenty to six. Far too early for breakfast, but he didn't see any point in going back to bed. Instead he followed Maria's example, and had a shower. Afterwards he pulled on his robe, made his way onto the balcony and sat watching the colour of the hills beyond slowly become more saturated as the daylight strengthened.

"Are you happy now, Angie?" he muttered to himself. He wanted to believe she was – laid to rest where her parents came from. Except they were still alive and living in Chelmsford.

Eventually he got up and wandered back into the room. Dressing slowly, his mind still on last night, he didn't see the thing on the floor until his naked foot stepped on it. He yelped – more in surprise than anything – and picked it up. It was a feather – a large one, the kind they always used in movies as quill pens, but black with white edges. Something Maria left behind? Not likely, he thought.

But it made him uneasy. He was about to toss it into the wastebasket when for some reason, he spun about and made for the balcony. He dropped the feather over the edge, watching it spiral down for a few moments. Before it hit the ground he slid the windows shut behind him and rushed down to breakfast.

The place was empty; well almost. Obviously no one wanted to get up this early – not on holiday. There were four waitresses – all nodded and wished him *Bom dia* as he walked in – nudging the food into more attractive displays. None of them was Maria.

Connor allowed himself breakfast this time. Starting with yoghurt and orange juice, and then piling his plate with eggs, sausage, and strips of bacon rigid as MDF. He tried the tea – not wanting to dare the coffee again – and found it was at least drinkable. Once he'd finished all that, he filled in any gaps with fruit.

Washing it all down with a second cup of tea, he took time to look around. A few more guests had arrived – they sounded Scandinavian – and all were making vast inroads into the cold meats. He also spotted the sharp-faced woman from yesterday – Miss Danvers. She had to be a supervisor – she did nothing except keep a harsh eye on the entire breakfast room. And the waitresses all seemed to be pointedly ignoring her. She gave Connor another brief, disapproving glance – or so it felt to him. He wondered if she'd found out about Maria.

A sudden burst of anger soured his throat. So what if she had? What the fuck had it got to do with her...?

The fury dropped. He knew perfectly well what it had to do with her – if this Miss Danvers character *was* some kind of manager. And if Maria hadn't been completely joking when she'd said guest and staff weren't supposed to – what had she said? – *Fraternise...*

When he looked again, the woman had gone. *Maybe she's just here to make me feel guilty*, he thought. If so, she was doing a bang up job so far.

He got up from his table. Time to check his e-mails – see if Maitland had come back with any comments yet – then get out there. And he thought he'd try photographing the bats Maria had told him about later.

As he left the room, he couldn't stop himself looking for the supervisor. Though what he thought he was going to say to her, he couldn't imagine.

*

Connor dropped his gadget bag on the floor. He collapsed back on his bed with an exasperated sigh. São Miguel, he decided, definitely had it in for him today. He'd used over two rolls of film, but knew from experience there wasn't a single decent shot on them. If he'd migrated to digital like so many of his colleagues, he'd simply have erased the duff images; but he was too much the traditionalist. He'd take film any day – regardless of the waste.

When he'd set off, the sun had been brilliant. By the time he'd reached the centre of the island, the clouds had come in.

Typical Azorean weather – all part of the joys of being on a mountain peak stuck out in the middle of the Atlantic. For a time a thick fog descended – actually low cloud sitting on the mountaintops – and Connor had been quite spooked. Everything had gone flat, and unreal. Sound didn't seem able to travel more than a few feet. Colours toned down to a universal grey – even the hydrangeas were muted.

It lifted after an hour or so, but Connor was no longer in the mood. After wasting his time and film, he'd called it a day and returned to the hotel – where the sun came back out again. So he'd tried shooting the bats.

Setting up as close to the tiny black and white chapel as he'd dared, he sat back to wait. When the bats had emerged – just like Maria had said, before the sun went down – he couldn't get a single one on camera. It wasn't particularly surprising – he wasn't a wildlife photographer, he didn't know all the tricks – but it had still pissed him off further.

In fact the most he'd done all day was leaf through all the background notes Maitland had given him before he'd flown out: a thick file of pages that read like a text book. He couldn't imagine why Maitland should think that he'd care. He was a photographer, not a historian.

Still, he was intrigued to learn that São Miguel was actually in two halves – two volcanoes, not so extinct, separated by geological ages. The oldest part had erupted from the sea floor millions of years ago; not up there with the dinosaurs, but pretty ancient. The other half was only a few thousand years old – new-born, almost. But you couldn't see the join: although far too young to have been eroded much, the baby half was masked by vegetation, identical to the rest. Only a geologist could spot the difference. Connor wasn't surprised to read that the Graham Hancocks and Von Danikens of the world had leapt on the last eruption to claim São Miguel was a remnant of ancient Atlantis.

"So why weren't they here to kick off the Portuguese?" Connor muttered aloud at his apartment in general. "All those flying saucers and death rays – could have seen off an army…"

He'd thought about Maria quite a bit, too. What she felt like, how she tasted – which was about all he knew. Except that her family had emigrated to America – like hundreds of Azoreans – to find a better life. Angie's parents had done the same – but gone the opposite way. Maria had returned to São Miguel last year – to visit or stay, she hadn't decided yet.

He glanced at his watch – it was almost nine. If he wanted to eat, he had to do it soon – the restaurant didn't stay open much later than ten.

Showering and changing quickly, his hair still wet, he rushed down to the lower ground floor. Luckily, the restaurant wasn't even half-full. He picked a small table and waited to be served.

He picked the *esparda* – spearfish – a local delicacy that lived around three thousand feet down. Judging by the way one had looked in a photograph Maitland showed him, the dark was the best place for them.

'With fried green bananas, Con,' Maitland had enthused. 'Can't beat it. Locals love 'em. Spearfish grow over three feet long – and you know, they've never brought up a young one…'

'Oh yes? So how do you know they *aren't* the young ones?' Connor had asked. Maitland hadn't seen the joke.

With the fish he ordered a bottle of white wine – local stuff he'd never heard of, but it was just dry enough for him and washed away the sweetness of the bananas. As he ate he watched the guests coming and going, unconsciously sizing them up for portraits. He knew Maria wouldn't be down here, but still couldn't stop himself checking every time a black and white uniform flickered across his vision.

After he'd finished he was nursing a final glass of wine, thoughts far away, when a shadow fell across him. Nudged from his reverie, he glanced up. It was Miss Danvers. The supervisor. She was staring at him strangely – as though she was sizing him up for something.

"Can I get you anything?" she asked. Her voice was as stern

as her face and, unlike Maria's, heavily accented.

"Er, no, thanks," he stuttered. "Just the bill, thanks… *obrigado*."

She turned stiffly away, and Connor almost felt relieved. *Jesus, what is it about her?* he wondered. She made him feel guilty just asking for his bill.

Ten minutes later, another waitress came and asked if he wanted anything else. He asked for the bill – again. She brought it over within a few moments. As he signed it, he couldn't help smiling to himself: the staff run around, yelling at each other louder than any self-important London chef, but they still never hurried themselves.

He strolled up to the bar. It was as empty as ever, the same Eagles' music playing in the background – but Maria wasn't there. A young boy was serving tonight – his chin dusted by a few downy whiskers. His English wasn't up to Connor's questions about Maria, and Connor hadn't mastered Portuguese. In the end the boy just shrugged, smiled apologetically, and went over to a couple at the far end of the bar who looked like they might actually want to buy a drink.

It felt like the ultimate betrayal. First São Miguel wasn't going to let him take any photographs, now it wasn't going to let him see one of its daughters, either.

Dejected, he went back to his room. It didn't even register that the light was on. Only when he saw Maria was already waiting for him, tucked in bed, that his brain caught up with the world.

"How did you get in?" he asked – not the brightest of questions.

She pouted. "Not a 'I have missed you'," she said. "Or just a simple 'Hello' would do…"

"Sorry…" Connor crossed the floor and half-threw himself onto the bed. Maria's arms were around him before he had his own around her. "Where've you been? I went to the bar…"

"Sorry. Sorry." She drew back a little and kissed him lightly on the tip of his nose. "It was my half day. I forgot to tell you.

117

Sorry."

"I thought you'd gone… or something." He was babbling, he knew. But at that moment he didn't care. "After the shitty day I've had…"

"Shhh…" Maria kissed him again… just a hint more passion this time. "Well now I am here to make it all better again…"

*

They made love slowly and tenderly. Connor didn't want it to end – didn't want to reach the climax that would leave him too sated and tired to continue. He wanted to explore Maria's body all night; he wanted her to stay with him – even when the morning came. He wanted her to feel just like he did.

For the first time in over a year, he wanted more than just sex.

When it did come, his climax racked his entire body. If he cried out, he couldn't tell – he was beyond almost all sensation.

As the final spasm relaxed its grip, Miss Danvers' face sprang into his mind: prim, disapproving. This time he was pretty sure he yelped.

Connor rolled off Maria and collapsed beside her. He was drenched with sweat, breathing hard – a little too hard. What did he expect? He wasn't a teenager any more. He probably had ten years on Maria.

She snuggled up to him. "I think you just woke up the entire hotel," she giggled.

He wrapped both arms around her, even now not wanting to let her go. "I'll claim you raped me," he murmured. Already sleep was dragging at him, but he was determined to hold on. He wasn't going to just roll over and pass out immediately like some thoughtless prat…

"Who is Angie?" she asked, quietly.

The drowsiness was gone in a moment. Connor half-propped himself on the arm Maria was lying across.

"Did I say that?" he said, knowing it was another stupid question.

She grunted something, wriggling closer. "Is she your wife?"

The sweat had turned icy cold, and Connor shivered. "She was. She died – two years ago."

Maria flinched back. "Con... I am sorry... I did not mean to—"

"No – that's okay." He kissed her hair; it smelled of shampoo but tasted of sweat. "I'm over it." Which was almost true – he was over her dying. It was her no longer living he was having trouble with.

"What happened?"

He was sure Maria didn't really want to know – it was the kind of reflex question people always asked. Besides, he didn't think he could tell her. It was a perfect post-coital topic: *My wife died two years ago because she had an ectopic pregnancy that went undetected until it was too late...*

Until she collapsed suddenly, bleeding heavily, at work. Even then, the surgeons should have been able to save her. But something went wrong – no one knew what, or weren't saying – and Angie died during surgery. Her and the embryo that had so fatally lost its way. The baby they'd been trying to have for years...

"Angie Furtado. Her family came from Vila Franca," he found himself saying. Just something to fill the silence – something other than the birds giggling and muttering outside. "She always claimed she was related to the singer. You know...?"

And when they'd brought her body back – to be buried in the ancestral soil – he hadn't been able to bring himself to accompany her.

Maria had raised herself up and was looking at him. "It is possible. Nelly Furtado's family came from there, too." It was too dark to read her expression, but something about the way she held her head made Connor want to sob. But he didn't want her pity... He didn't want—

And finally, he did begin to cry – deep and terrible. Tears ran down his face, flooded his throat. He thought he was going to drown in each sob. From a vast distance, he felt Maria holding him tight, rocking him like a child.

*

He awoke late. Maria had already gone. He wished he could have felt surprised. But after last night – the tearful, New Man purging – she'd have to have been pretty special to hang around. And Connor didn't want to delude himself she was looking for anything other than a bit of fun.

Hadn't he been doing just the same?

Breakfast was already over by the time he was showered and dressed. He loaded up the car and headed off, into the centre of the island. There'd be a bar or something where he could get a snack; and if not, so what? It wouldn't hurt to starve a little.

The day was bright and warm. And this time the weather held. He found some glorious scenes across Lagoa do Fogo, and out across the Atlantic. There wasn't a cloud to be seen. He returned to Furnas and shot a whole roll of film just of the pools; the sun bleached the clouds of steam a brilliant white. Even the crowds of tourists didn't detract from the scene; Connor could imagine the best image, reprinted in a brochure, yelling: *Come and join us!*

By the time he returned to the *Velhos Pássaros* he'd zigzagged across São Miguel, taking shot after shot, each one better than before. The hedgerows of hydrangeas began to look like cultivated shrubberies; the hilly fields more like New Zealand pasture. But the best was a series of shots he took of a scarecrow – no longer dapper, in last year's clothing – standing guard over an unused field, the rocky coast and azure sky a contrast to the ragged figure.

He quite forgot about eating, not remembering until he'd dropped his gear on the apartment floor and sat on the bed with a contented sigh. So unlike yesterday. Perhaps whatever he'd done to offend the island was forgiven, and today was São Miguel's attempt at restitution.

But he had to admit he was now starving, and whatever he'd thought this morning, there wasn't any delight in it. Getting showered, shaved and changed in record time, he made his way to the restaurant determined to stuff himself. He had the *esparda* again – he had to admit, Maitland had a point – this time with two bottles of wine, and a huge wedge of chocolate gateau for dessert. Miss Danvers didn't show up to ruin his mood; and he found himself flirting with his waitress – even if she wasn't Maria.

He returned to his room with the second, half-full bottle. His head spun a little, and he had some trouble making his key-card work, but he thought he deserved a little celebration. Today had been a good day. On the whole.

His light was on again, and he felt a small, warm surge against his heart.

"Maria?" he called. He walked unsteadily into the main apartment, grinning, arms wide to lift her up.

Sitting on the bed was Miss Danvers.

It was like a slap on the face. Connor's arms fell; he ignored the splash of wine that flew from the bottle. "This room's getting like Charing Cross station!" he muttered, slurring the words faintly. The bitterness of his tone surprised him almost as much as Miss Danvers' presence.

"I think you have been avoiding me, Mr Abrams," she said. She leaned back a little, resting on her arms, and crossed her legs. Connor hadn't realised they were so long, or shapely.

He put the wine bottle down on a table. "How the hell did you get in here?" he demanded.

"The same way as Maria – we all have access to keys..." She smiled at him. It was nothing like Maria's smile: this was predatory, self-satisfied.

"Where is Maria?" He took a step closer – then stepped back again, knowing the action looked menacing. "Is she in trouble?" *Because of me?* he added silently.

"Nothing that concerns you, Mr Abrams – or may I call you Con… like she did?" Again the smile. It was like being grinned at by some strange bird of prey. "She will probably come back. Everyone from São Miguel comes back."

Connor shook his head. She didn't seem to be making much sense – but that could be the wine. "Okay, so you're happy she's fucked off and left me, great. Now just piss off and leave me alone too, yeah?"

She stood and faced him. She was taller than he'd thought, almost eye to eye. He could smell her perfume – a musky scent he didn't recognise. Oddly, it reminded him of the sea. "You are a lonely man, Connor Abrams. Maria helped you with that loneliness for a while; now she is gone, I will do so."

Any other time, Connor would have rejoiced so many women seemed to want to get him into bed. Now, it creeped him out. "You're no Maria," he mumbled.

"I should hope not." She pulled at her hair and it fell loose in a long, black curtain. It softened her features. A moment later she removed her small glasses, and Connor felt like he was looking at an entirely different woman. Despite the wine, he was suddenly very, very aroused. "I am Dian," she said, her manner strangely formal.

She looped her arms slowly around him, pulling them closer. Her lips closed over his, her tongue – sharp and quick – slipped between his teeth.

They were in bed, naked. Connor didn't remember when it happened. Dian was all over his body, kissing, nipping, stroking. His erection was almost painful; more than anything he wanted to plunge it into her. He turned her onto her back, parting her legs – but she pushed him away easily.

"No," she whispered into his ear. "That you should not do. Maria will not like it."

"Then what?" he heard himself – he was almost begging. "I want—"

"There are many other ways to pleasure," she said, and

began to show him.

She used almost her entire body – hands, tongue, breasts, lips, feet... Countless times she took him to the edge of climax – and brought him back. It was frustrating and ultimately arousing... promises and teasing, yet always with the knowledge that finally, she would take him to the brink – and beyond—

But not just yet...

After what felt like hours of alternating stimulation and rejection, Dian finally allowed his climax. She leaned away as he came, leaving him to writhe like a dying chicken, coming all over his stomach. Once he was spent, she crouched over him, running a finger over the clots of semen, drawing ornate patterns on his body with a long sharp nail. Her eyes – harsh and glittering even without the glasses – stared at him through her fringe. Enjoying a private joke. The predatory smile flickered on and off almost before he saw it

"Better than her, yes?"

He took a deep breath and swallowed. "Different, yeah." How could it be better? Maria and he had enjoyed each other; what Dian had done with him was... Well, you couldn't even call it fucking...

She rolled off the bed and walked to the balcony doors. She knew Connor was watching her, and exaggerated every sway. As sleep crept up on him, he saw her slide the glass door open. Before his eyelids crashed down, the last thing he heard was a shearwater – chuckling sharply at the night.

*

Connor awoke abruptly, breath hitching in his throat in time to his lurching heartbeat. He could still feel himself falling – plunging down an endless tunnel. It was the nightmare which had awoken him, shaking and breathless. He sat up, his heart gradually slowing. What had they said when he was a kid? That if you didn't wake up before you hit the ground, you'd die?

He didn't need to worry about the ground in this version. He vaguely remembered the tunnel was lined with spikes, or claws. Or were they actually at the bottom, reaching up for him. It was fading already – but he could still feel their bite on his body.

Connor got out of bed, wincing. That pain wasn't anything to do with a dream – it was Dian's legacy. Even at that time of night it wasn't totally dark and he could see her signature – fine red traceries – all across his arms and body.

He paused at the balcony doors and looked back. Dian was sprawled across his bed, barely covered by a twisted sheet. What had he been thinking? Had he reached the point where he'd have any woman? Someone had told him once that a man would screw anything vaguely female – just as long as you put a bag over her head. He'd refused to believe it then; now he wasn't so sure.

Outside, the shearwaters burst into a brief, garbled chorus. Despite the door being open to the night, the room was still oppressive. As though all the heat and sweat they'd poured out had just hung around, no place to go. He stepped onto the balcony, careless of his nakedness; he didn't think the birds were likely to complain.

It was no cooler outside.

He leaned on the balcony rail, staring down. The shearwaters continued to mutter and giggle – maybe he had disturbed them. Whatever, he heard their strange, half-words from the black sky above him. Weren't they supposed to roost at night? Or perhaps the muggy air was keeping them awake too.

He went back into the room, and the cries followed him.

Dian was motionless on the bed. She could have been a corpse, laid out on her back, the creased sheet a ready-made shroud. But then she moved, and what little cover she'd had fell to the floor. Connor felt his breath catch. His eyes were drawn down her body to the small dark triangle between her thighs.

The mutterings and giggles seemed to intensify. It felt as though the room was filled with invisible, taunting birds, mocking him inarticulately. Sweat flowed down the sides of his face; he felt it pooling below his arms. He wiped his brow – but that only made it worse.

Dian moved again, arching her back and making a faint mewing sound. Her legs spread – just a little.

Connor was standing against the bed, his eyes locked on Dian's body. All around him the voices slurred their suggestions – but their meaning was becoming increasingly clear. Hell – why not? Where was the harm?

In a moment, he was on top of her, parting her legs. He forced himself inside, wanting to get that first moment over with; desperate to have her.

She awoke. Connor froze – suddenly unsure. Suddenly ashamed. She was going to scream – he knew it. But she laughed – at least, it sounded like a laugh – and clamped her legs tightly around him. She hissed something harsh in his ear; he didn't understand, but it sounded as taunting as the voices that still urged him on.

He didn't need any more urging.

Connor was brutal. He was selfish. He thrust himself into Dian with no regard. And all the while she clawed at him, cackling with derision at his efforts, pushing him to even greater violence…

Later, hunched in the shower, he felt sharp slivers of agony as the cold water ran down his shredded back. He was angry, humiliated, bewildered. He no longer recognised himself.

Dian stood in the bathroom doorway, watching him. She was dressed in her blouse and skirt again; hair pulled back and glasses in place. She was hard-faced Miss Danvers once more. Another time Connor might have marvelled at the transformation. She leaned carelessly against the doorframe, arms folded.

Connor turned the shower off and grabbed a towel.

Like a Bird

"You should not have done that," she said. It was the first lucid words she'd spoken for some time.

He scrubbed harshly at his damp body. Despite the cold shower, he still felt uncomfortably hot. "You seemed to enjoy it," he snapped back.

Dian unfolded her arms. "I did not say I did not want it," she said – as though explaining an obvious point to a dense child. "Only that you should not do it. Now I am afraid Maria will…" She tailed off, apparently unsure of how to continue. Then her sharp, cruel smile flashed for a moment. "Suffer," she finished.

Connor glared at her. "Don't you dare say anything!" he said, voice trembling as he choked back a yell.

"We are not exactly on speaking terms," Dian replied, that grin flashing on and off again. She half-turned. "I will see you later." She paused, and again Connor thought she was searching for the right words. "*Até logo…*"

With a fluid, sensuous grace that belied her prim exterior, Dian slipped out of the bathroom. Connor heard the apartment door open and shut quietly.

He wrapped the towel around his waist and walked heavily into the main room. Dawn was silhouetting the hills outside. Connor thought he saw narrow-winged shapes lifting off into the grey sky and streaming for the coast, but he guessed he was imagining it.

Just as he'd imagined all the gaunt black and white shapes perched on the balcony rail – the ones that had dived out of sight the moment he'd left the bathroom.

*

The fog was back with a vengeance. Connor had left the *Velhos Pássaros* early. He hadn't been able to face anyone; he couldn't bear the thought of seeing Dian at breakfast. And if he'd bumped into Maria…

Instead, he'd thrown all his gear into the car and headed up

126

into São Miguel's interior. He wondered what kind of photographs he'd produce in his present mood.

But the weather had dictated terms. Within half an hour of leaving the hotel, the cloud had begun to form around the peaks. It had only taken minutes to roll down; leaving Connor trapped in a cold, grey shroud. Visibility was so poor he'd turned the car off the road; he didn't want to risk running into something, or someone. Or just as likely, another car rearending his.

He took his gadget bag out of the boot and set off across a field. More in forlorn hope than any real expectation. But he thought maybe he'd come across something bleak and forbidding in the mist. He was just about up for that.

He was soaked within five minutes.

A grey shape congealed out of the fog in front of him. At first he thought it was someone coming towards him – another idiot out in lousy weather. Then he realised it was a scarecrow – or maybe the same one from yesterday: he was heading in much the same direction. He stopped to get his 35mm SLR out and fitted a 70-250mm zoom lens; this might make a good contrast to yesterday's scene. No good for brochures, but ideal for his portfolio.

He stepped closer, and realised it wasn't the same one after all. Yesterday's had been male – or at least the worn clothing had once belonged to a man. This was female, in a ragged skirt and a blouse that might have been white the day it was bought. Now all that remained was as ripped as the skirt, grey as the fog, and streaked with dirt.

Raising the camera he focussed on the sad shape, then zoomed in. The camera dropped from his numb hands; the strap wrenched at his neck.

It was Maria.

He lunged towards her, almost tripping over his gadget bag. He wasn't going mad – it *was* Maria. At first he thought her exposed arms and legs were as ripped as the clothing, but when he reached her, he saw her limbs were pocked with livid

127

circular marks. More like bites than anything else. Her brown hair was black with blood and rain and dirt. Her head was slumped forward, masking her face, and Connor had to force himself to raise it up. He didn't want to see her like this.

Maria's face was free of marks. In fact, it looked as though it had been washed clean of the dirt that smeared the rest of her. With his free hand, he gently touched a cheek.

Her eyes flickered, opening briefly.

Jesus! She was still alive!

Desperately, Connor tried to figure out how she'd been tied up. There was a simple cross shape behind her, driven into the ground, but it was so hard to find ropes or anything amongst the scraps of rag. His fingers were wet, slippery and rapidly growing numb.

He needed a knife.

Even though he was positive the car didn't have anything even remotely close, he started back for it. He'd gone a dozen steps when he saw another figure emerging from the cloud. A farmer? Perhaps he'd have a knife; something sharp, anyway…

It wasn't a farmer – or even a man. It was Dian. Smiling her sharp smile, naked once more, her loose hair lank in the damp air. Otherwise, she seemed oblivious to the chill.

"Hello, Connor," she said, almost casually. "You are early. Or am I late…?"

She sauntered past him, long legs carrying her across the wet, uneven ground easily. When she reached Maria, she examined her for a moment, head jerking from side to side.

"Almost time." She turned her back on the pitiful figure, watching Connor as he retraced his steps. "I told you Maria would have to suffer."

"Can't you get her down?" he begged. "For Christ's sake…!"

"For Christ's sake?" Dian frowned, her mouth pouting momentarily. "And why should I take her down? Do you think I did this?"

Connor didn't know what he thought. Clenching and

unclenching his fists, he stood uncertainly. Why the hell did he feel so helpless? Why didn't he just push Dian aside and tear down the cross… get Maria off it…?

"What is it?" he said. "Some kind of religious cult thing? Wicker man?"

Dian cocked her head again, staring at him with eyes he'd just realised never blinked. "We are returning home, Connor Abrams, that is all. No one leaves São Miguel forever: not your dead wife, not Maria's family, and not us. We have simply been away a little longer than most."

She's a fucking psycho! Connor thought, wishing for that knife again. "We?" he said, wondering if he kept her talking, maybe help might arrive.

"The natives of the island." She glanced back at Maria, as though she was expecting something to happen.

"The Azores have no natives." He remembered that much from Maitland's wad of notes. Then something struck him, and he started to laugh – but the sound was so shrill and unnatural, he forced himself to stop. "Unless you're Atlanteans…!"

The expression on Dian's face was unreadable. "It was the second upheaval," she said – so calm, so rational. "We all fled, believing the island would be destroyed. Instead, it was enlarged – twice the original size. And now, we are coming back."

Connor almost laughed again. Was she talking about the second volcanic eruption? That had been thousands of years ago. "So why has it taken so long for you to come back?"

"Not so long," she said, a dreaminess entering her voice. "I remember the times before the upheaval clearly – even though I was very young—" She broke off, turning back to look at Maria, and this time her entire body tensed. As though she was listening intently.

"Do you hear them?" she said, so softly that Connor barely caught the words, even in the fog-muffled quiet.

But he did hear something. Faint cries. The shearwaters? But there was something insistent, something urgent about these noises. It reminded Connor of—

Dian's hand seized his left arm. Her grip was so strong he winced. "You must see!"

She dragged him up to Maria's pitiful figure with no more effort than if he were made of paper. He looked wildly about – anywhere but at Maria, and what she'd become. The fog was smooth and inscrutable as Dian's face. He knew there'd be no help coming.

Dian squeezed his neck between the fingers of her free hand. They felt coarse and frozen. She forced him to his knees – as though he was praying.

"You must be there at the birth!" she breathed. He was enveloped in her strange, sea-breeze scent. "It is fair: as you eat our young – so they will eat you…!"

Each of the livid, circular marks on Maria's limbs was writhing – heaving up gradually with tiny, erratic jerks. Small, urgent cries were coming from them. Maria stirred feebly, and moaned – but her agonies were drowned by the rising squeals.

Connor tried to scream – to yell at Dian, plead with her, but all that escaped past her inexorable grip was a thin, pathetic whimper – like a dying gull.

The air grew darker. Thrashing shadows chased across the damp ground. *Clouds?* Connor wondered. No – not through the fog. His thoughts were becoming as shapeless as the grey mist.

Dian's frigid grasp relaxed, and Connor slumped bonelessly to the ground. He tried to focus his thoughts – force his brain back to rationality. But it was so hard. Gibberish rattled through his skull; his eyesight seemed to be dimming. Had she ruptured some vital blood vessel? Was his brain dying from oxygen starvation?

He could see Dian – a stark shape in the corner of his vision. He thought she'd dressed again. That made no sense, did it? But she was in white and black, and was that a belt dangling from her waist? It seemed to him that her long dark hair now reached halfway to the ground like a cloak, or wings…

Like a Bird

Pain speared up his neck, and he tasted blood. It really was growing darker – and colder. He could see Maria moving on the cross – wriggling to get free…! Christ – she was still alive!

But no, Maria wasn't moving, any more than Dian was really dressed in black and white. Any more than the giggling, hideous serpentine shapes were swooping around them, flapping long, impossibly thin wings. Any more than they rubbed lovingly against the bloody, ragged shape hanging from the cross – and the things wriggling from it.

As the chorus of shrieks reached a peak – no longer muffled – Dian spread wide her limbs, a great cruciform against the fog. A shrill babble of noise that could never have been words burst from her head – followed by a caw of greeting.

Before the light failed totally, Connor saw Dian's true mouth rear up, primed to strike – a hundred teeth already bared.

THE SPOON

John Mains

"Ladies and Gentlemen, Uri Geller!"

The audience went crazy as Uri walked towards the presenter, smiling and waving all the way. He sat down, made himself comfy and waited for the host's first question.

"Uri, I want to cut straight to the chase: can you do your famous spoon bending trick?"

The noise of the crowd just rose as the presenter brought a spoon out from the pocket of his finely tailored suit.

Uri grinned sheepishly.

"You know, I haven't performed this for many years. It might not work," he said, reluctantly reaching for the spoon and thinking about the shit fit he was going to throw when the interview was over.

Uri's fingers deftly plucked the spoon from the presenter's hand and he gently started to rub the spot where the bowl tapered into the handle. He closed his eyes and zoned out.

The audience looked at him expectantly.

All of a sudden, his eyes flew open and he let out a shriek of pain. He came off the chair and dropped to his knees, the spoon falling onto the floor with a clatter. He clutched at his face, and started to scream terribly. He turned a most horrible shade of purple and as the presenter was yelling out for a doctor, Uri's head popped off his shoulders and flew right into the lap of Mavis Treebuckle who had travelled all the way from Bristol for her eighty-third birthday. Her heart burst with a flourish.

As the audience started to scream and stampede, the spoon lay on the floor, quite content.

That's for getting my Uncle Frank, ya bastard, the spoon thought to itself.

132

THE LAKE

Franklin Marsh

1.

"It's around here somewhere."

"You've been saying that for the last twenty-five minutes."

Tom clenched his teeth, and gripped the steering wheel harder. As he slowed to negotiate a hairpin bend, he sneaked a look at Audrey out of the corner of his eye. The angry expression on her face confirmed Tom's suspicions.

"Nearly there," he muttered.

"This was supposed to be a nice day out. And you've ruined it. I've got to be back to pick the kids up from school at four."

Tom glanced at his watch: almost quarter past eleven. It's over, he thought. And I think she thinks that too. That's what this stupid picnic is all about.

The affair had lasted seven months. Tom hadn't seen it coming. Married for two years to Mo. Little Kayleigh coming up to a year. He'd always wanted to be married.

Was a little naïve to just how hard it would be. His wedding day was still the best day of his life. Looking sharp in a rented suit. Mo beautiful in white. Family and friends united.

All said they had a good day. No fights. Honeymoon in Corfu, paid for by her parents. Neither of them had been abroad before.

The sunshine and total culture shock had seemingly sealed their love. Mo had conceived during that week. Both sets of parents thrilled at the prospect of becoming grand – even his old man.

Much as he loved Kayleigh, that had been the beginning of the difficult times. Both too exhausted at the beginning to worry about each other, their lives filled with screaming, feeding and dirty nappies. He was working all hours as well.

Mo seemed happy looking after the baby and she seemed to

have grandiose plans for her daughter. Plans that involved Tom earning a lot more than he did as a painter and decorator.

In fact, from being the pre-marriage happy go lucky, take life as it comes girl he'd courted and married, she'd developed into a materialistic snob. And she had no interest in sex.

That was where Audrey came in. Tom, with co-workers Deano and Max, had landed a plum job on an upmarket housing estate.

Audrey seemed like the bored would-be raver housewife that you used to read about in the Sunday tabloids.

She'd flashed it at young Deano, who confided to Tom and Max that he would, but she reminded him of his Gran.

Unsuccessful there, she moved onto Tom, who never thought that something like this could happen to him.

Deano and Max had knocked off early one Friday and headed for the pub. Tom was finishing off (inevitably) the master bedroom, when Audrey had appeared in tears.

Her husband, Stefan, was a brute – and in Copenhagen on business. It just happened. Afterward, Tom had showered, then, racked with guilt, he'd headed home, stopping at the local garage on the way to pick up some flowers for Mo. She was so pathetically grateful that he'd made this uncalled for gesture, that he felt a thousand times worse.

Deano gave him a good natured ribbing on Monday, but the older Max was broodingly silent.

He cornered Tom later on.

"It's just a bit of fun; isn't it, Tom?"

"Yeah, course, Max. Don't worry."

"Don't get involved, Tommy boy. She's poison. You've got a kiddy to look after now. Don't forget that."

"Leave it out, Max. Anyway, it's my business, right?"

Max glared at him for what seemed a long time, then walked away. Tom felt guilty again, then angry at himself and Max for feeling that way.

He and Audrey enjoyed sex whenever and wherever they could. They started to meet for drinks at out of the way places.

The lying began. Mo didn't seem to mind. She seemed glad Tom was out of the way.

Then, about a month ago, Audrey started to get naggy, Finding fault. Criticising. I can get this at home, thought Tom. Several times, he nearly had a go and walked out but, perversely, he began to think that was what she wanted so decided to hang on.

When she proposed a picnic, he thought – this is it, goodbye. It's for the best. She suggested the coast. He thought of the Lake.

2.

"You're lost aren't you?"

"No, it's just been a while."

She sighed in exasperation, and glanced at her watch.

Piss off, thought Tom.

He made a sharp right and all of a sudden they were driving around a mobile home park.

"Oh, marvellous," sniped Audrey. "Have you booked a secret love nest? I'm getting angry, Tom."

So am I, he thought. Another turn and they were wending their way down a leafy lane, the trees crowding to the side of the road, leaning over the car, cutting out the sunlight.

They drove past a small picturesque church, and Tom knew where they were. He turned onto a dirt track and they bumped along for half a mile, Audrey's face a picture.

The car entered a small clearing. Tom parked and turned off the engine.

"We're here."

Audrey snorted. Tom got out of the car and walked to the boot. He opened up and took out Audrey's dainty wicker picnic basket and a blanket.

She remained motionless in the front passenger seat, arms folded, face like thunder.

He walked alongside the car and opened her door.

135

"Modom," he said, blanket folded over one arm, bowing like a *mâitre d'*. She forced a smile and climbed out of the car. It was dark in the clearing, and silent. She shivered.

"What is this place?"

"The Lake," he replied.

"I can't see any lake."

"It's just through there. Come on."

He led the way through the trees.

Tom leaned forward and held back a prickly shrub. Audrey crept through. He joined her. They were on a small patch of sand that sloped down to an expanse of black, rippling water.

Trees crowded around the waters' edge whichever way you looked. It felt oppressive.

"What a horrible place," snapped Audrey. "Why did you bring me here?"

"You wanted a picnic by the water," said Tom. "I thought of this place."

He wasn't quite sure why he'd brought her here. Probably because he thought this was the end of it, and wanted to unsettle her. Not give her the chance to dump him in a high-handed manner.

Although he didn't really care. He just wanted to get back to Mo. Try and make it up.

He thought back to his childhood. This place had always had a bad reputation. Kids dared one another to come here. They said birds didn't sing around the Lake.

He couldn't remember how the stories had started. It was back in Victorian times. A woman, or a girl. Drowned. Mums calling to the kids: 'Stay away from the Lake.' Which was like a red rag to a bull.

He turned to Audrey. She was shivering and looked thoroughly miserable. He thought of putting his arm around her. Perhaps that's why they had come here.

Like taking a first date to a horror film, hoping she'd hold on to you.

No, this was the end. He spread the blanket on the ground.

They sat down. Audrey opened the basket and removed plastic glasses, paper plates, and plastic knives and forks for them both.

She handed a chilled bottle of champagne to him.

"Not too much, you're driving," she admonished.

As Audrey doled out chicken salad from a large Tupperware bowl, Tom stood up and moved to the water's edge. He aimed the bottle out over the water.

The cork popped satisfyingly and sped out across the Lake. The champagne didn't fizz up, just a couple of wisps of white smoke.

He turned back and filled a glass, handing it to Audrey. He filled his own and said 'Cheers' smiling at her. She ate her salad silently, ignoring him. Bitch, he thought.

As he disconsolately picked at his food, it seemed to get darker. Neither of them spoke. The silence was becoming unbearable. Tension rose. He turned to see her glaring at him.

"You bastard," she said, quietly.

He chewed slowly, glowering back at her.

"You think you can just use me and then move on? Go back to your little wife?"

"Leave her out of this," Tom warned.

Audrey stood up and brushed herself down.

"Stefan is twice the man you are," she said.

Tom threw his plate, complete with the salad remains into the hamper. Audrey stared at it. Their eyes met. Her face screwed itself up as though in agony, and reddened.

Tom was slightly taken aback by the change. She screamed loudly startling him, then dived, hands reaching for his neck.

He grabbed her wrists, trying to keep her trembling clawed fingers away from him. She hissed and spat. Her knee thrust into his groin.

He screeched, and his grip weakened, enabling her to break free, and scratch her nails down his left cheek, drawing blood. His confused thoughts turned to his wife. How would he explain this to Mo?

Audrey backed away, breathing heavily. Tom heaved a sigh of relief and relaxed. As she bent over the picnic hamper, he moved forward, hand reaching out to touch her in a conciliatory gesture.

"Audrey, I…"

The champagne bottle hit him on the temple. He staggered back, dazed. She moved in again, the weight of the glass container making it awkward for her to wield.

He looked into her eyes and saw nothing. Not even hate. He was easily able to push her away, but realised that she was not going to stop.

Tom tried a punch to her chin, pulling it at the last moment. Audrey's teeth clicked together. She must have bitten her tongue as a rivulet of blood seeped from her lips.

She took a step backwards and tripped over the hamper, landing hard on her rump.

Tom leaned forward, hands on upper legs, gratefully drawing breath. Audrey sat there, eyes unfocused. The bottle slipped from her hands. She turned towards the Lake, and stared at the water.

"Aud…" Tom began.

She looked in his direction without seeing him. She fell forward onto her hands, and pushed herself upright, gaze once again directed to the middle of the body of water.

Absent-mindedly she brushed sand from her skirt and hands, then began to walk unsteadily towards the tiny waves touching the bottom of the slope.

"Audrey!" barked Tom, concern growing at her trance like state. She walked into the water.

"Come back!" Tom began to despair. There was no way he could follow her. He couldn't swim. He couldn't go home in wet clothes. What was wrong with her?

She was in up to her knees, still steadily walking forward, slower now because of the resistance of the liquid. If he really wanted to, he could still reach her and bring her back.

138

"Audrey," he whispered, watching in grim fascination.

The water reached her waist, and she glided forward, arms outstretched. As the water reached her shoulders, she kicked out with a splash, and began to swim, a strong crawl, to the middle of the Lake.

"AUDREY!" screamed Tom. What was she doing? He wrung his hands in helplessness, and looked around wildly.

What...? There was a man standing looking at him. About five hundred yards away. Standing in the trees behind the next little beach area.

He had blond hair and glasses. He was wearing some kind of camouflage gear. There was a tiny tent, also camouflage, behind him.

Tom saw the pole in his hands and understood. A fisherman! The man's head turned, and Tom realised that he was watching Audrey. Tom returned his gaze to the water.

Audrey was little more than a disembodied head, slowly moving away from the land, ripples emanating from her powerful swimming strokes. The head halted and began to revolve. It faced Tom.

"Audrey." It was more of a groan than anything.

The head slowly sank. It disappeared, under the water.

"NOOOO!" Tom couldn't believe it. He was shaking. Transfixed, he watched the surface of the Lake return to a mirror-like smoothness. Audrey might never have existed.

In desperation, he turned to look for the man. He wasn't there. Tom couldn't even make out the tent. Tears blinded his eyes. Mucous flowed down his nose.

He sobbed. Not knowing what else to do, he ran into the woods. Crashing through bushes, shrubs, sliced by thorns, grabbed at by branches, he ran full tilt, not knowing where he was going, or what he was doing, just trying to get away from that awful scene.

The acoustics of the wood played tricks with his hearing. He was being pursued. A wringing-wet, vengeful Audrey, Lake-weed clinging to her.

139

A wronged Stefan, threatening dire consequences. A spurned Mo, asking tearfully why? He turned to confront whichever nemesis was reaching out to touch him, and tripped over a tree-root.

He sprawled into thick undergrowth and lay there, lungs burning, fighting for breath.

Gradually, things calmed down. No one towered over him. As his breathing subsided, he could hear bird song. He laughed, tearfully grateful that he was away from the Lake. He closed his eyes.

Tom jerked to full wakefulness. Had he passed out? Fallen asleep? As thoughts tumbled around his mind, he heard again the sound that had woken him. Slow footsteps upon stone.

Looking around, he realised that they were coming from behind a screen of tall ferns. He eased himself through the green curtain.

Facing him was a large, arched gravestone. *Ambrose Pearson*, it read. *Poet And Tragedian. Faced Life's First Challenge August 2nd 1862. Succumbed To Fate's Whim December 24th 1895.*

As Tom began to wriggle towards the edge of the gravestone, he heard the voice.

"Bastard Satanists."

3.

Tom peered around the moss-covered gravestone. A portly, red-faced figure wearing a vicar's dog-collar was studying a chicken that had been nailed to the church door.

The fowl was upside-down, and had its wings widespread. The vicar was jacketless, and had his shirtsleeves rolled up. His attire from the waist down consisted of olive green army trousers and huge black boots.

"I can see you," he remarked, turning towards Ambrose Pearson's resting place. "Come out of there." His voice was mild.

Tom sheepishly emerged from behind the tilted stonework and shuffled forward.

The vicar frowned as he took in Tom's dishevelled appearance, including cuts and bruises.

"Been up at the Lake?"

"Y-yes," stuttered Tom.

The vicar's face became compassionate.

"Something frightened you?"

Tom couldn't reply. He found himself shaking.

"Come inside," said the vicar. "I'll just deal with our feathered friend. At least supper's taken care of tonight."

Tom watched as the vicar wrenched out the nails with his bare hands. He placed them in his trouser pocket, and held the chicken by its feet as he opened the church door.

Tom walked unsteadily into the dark, cool interior. The inside of the church was as tiny as the outside. Four pews stood to one side, the aisle running to the left of them.

A font, altar and pulpit were crammed into the end. Behind the altar stood a large wooden statue of Christ upon the cross.

The sun must have come out, as a multi-coloured mosaic from the stained glass windows decorated the stone floor.

Tom sank onto the front pew and put his head in his hands. He jumped violently as the vicar bellowed, "MRS BIGGINS!"

Tom felt a nudge, and saw a small silver hip flask proffered by the priest.

"Have a quick sip before Biggers gets here. Perk you up," whispered the vicar.

Tom took a hefty slug, and gasped for breath, his eyes watering. He felt the liquid burn its way down his oesophagus.

"What was that?" he wheezed, handing back the flask.

"Poteen," whispered the vicar, hiding the chicken behind his back like a guilty schoolboy as a figure that matched his in size and shape appeared from a door behind the pulpit.

"Ah, Mrs Biggins. Tea, please."

"Company, Gordon? I…" the woman stopped in mid comment as her gaze fell upon Tom. Her enquiring expression became one of disapproval.

"He's been up at the Lake," she muttered, turning on a heel and disappearing back through the door.

"Good old Biggers," laughed the vicar. "Her tea is the equal of my poteen; you'll see."

He stuffed the chicken under a pew and held out a hand to Tom.

"Bluett," he said.

Blew it? Thought Tom, bewildered.

"Gordon Bluett. Vicar of this parish, for my sins."

Tom received a firm, but rather damp handshake. He remained silent.

"Apologies for the... er... language, and my abruptness earlier on. I thought you might be one of the witches."

"Witches?"

"Yes. We've a practising coven, apparently. I'm new here, you see. See myself as a bit of new broom. Wanted to make an impression.

"Someone tipped me the wink. I made a few enquiries, but couldn't trace anyone involved. Suspected it might be a few idiots who like to prance around in the buff, you know, that sort of thing.

"So I thought I'd come over as a bit fire and brimstone. Had a bit of a rant in the parish mag. Some Johnny at the local rag saw fit to reprint it.

"And now I've some jokers nailing chickens to my door! Well, Biggers and I will enjoy a spot of *coq au vin* tonight, I can tell you.

"Take more than that to put the wind up me. Ex-army, you know. Chaplain in the Greenjackets."

He gestured, and Tom looked around. On the end of the pew he saw a folded newspaper. The headline trumpeted: '*SCOURGE OF SATAN VICAR.*'

Bluett had paused, as though waiting for Tom to comment. Tom remained silent, returning his gaze to the vicar.

"Care to talk about it?" said Bluett.

He was interrupted by the return of Mrs Biggins with a tea tray. She slapped it down on the pew, gave Tom a filthy look, and once again retreated.

Bluett poured two cups of tea, adding a belt from the hip-flask to his. Tom shook his head.

"What do you know about the Lake?" asked Bluett, casually.

"A woman drowned herself," blurted out Tom, warmed by the strong tea.

"Violet Carrington," supplied Bluett. "She's the one most seen. You know the story?"

"Vaguely," answered Tom.

"Back in Victoria's day. There used to be a big house, you know, mansion, near here. It's a caravan park now. Mobile homes. But back then it was The Big House as they used to say.

"Violet worked below stairs. Married an under-footman. Albert Smithee. Didn't have a clue he was a philanderer. Until he impregnated one of the other maids.

"They were both dismissed. She ran to the Lake and threw herself in. Body never recovered. He took to drink. Hanged himself up there in the woods."

Tom was thinking. His mother had told him a variant of this story, he felt sure.

"So, she haunts the place?" he asked.

The vicar shifted, as though uncomfortable.

"Not exactly. People say they've seen a woman up there. No definite identification though. It seems she was the first."

Tom frowned, not following.

"What do you mean?"

"Well, the place has become a kind of Lover's Leap. All sorts of people, wronged in love or what have you, go up there and do themselves in. The Lake must be full of 'em. During doubleyew-doubleyew two the big house was a military hospital. For those with shellshock, you know, psychiatric problems. Well, what with a war on, young lads being shipped back to the front, young girls not knowing what would become

143

of their fiancés and the like, there was an awful lot of bed-hopping. Any amount of boys and girls took themselves off to the Lake and disappeared. Unrequited love, rape, losing one's loved one. One chap went off his head and got hold of his service pistol. Absolute slaughter. He got away from the military police and apparently ended up in the Lake. But Violet was the first... *cause célèbre*. The first newspaper case."

Bluett paused again, and poured two more cups of tea. He then spoke again.

"Every now and again we hear of another tragedy. The last one was a local angler. Fished at the Lake almost every weekend. Returned home early one Saturday and caught his wife *in flagrante* with her lover. He strangled them with his fishing wire. Brought the bodies back up here to dispose of them in the Lake. Accidently drowned whilst trying to commit that ghastly task. The three bodies washed up together, entwined."

Bluett stood up.

"You know, I thought I was being put out to grass here. But what with the Lake, and these *devil worship wallahs*, I feel that I'm fighting real evil."

He smiled, and glanced at his watch.

"Good Lord, ten to four. Must crack on."

He retrieved the chicken from under the pew.

"Let's see if I can sneak this chap into the pot without Biggers noticing."

He looked at Tom, and said gently, "Take as long as you like. You're safe here," before moving off, to vanish through the door at the back.

Tom clutched his mug. He looked up at Jesus in agony. Whose sins did you die for? he thought. Mine?

Ten to four. Audrey's children would be coming out of school soon. Ryan and Sophie. Waiting, watching as friends were picked up by their mums and dads. You shouldn't be alone at that age. At any age. Tears came. He looked after

Bluett, and was surprised to notice wet footprints, rapidly drying, leading to the door. After a few seconds they were gone. He realised that there was nothing in his hands, no tea tray on the pew. The light faded outside, darkening the interior of the church. Tom looked around, taking in the neglected aura. Dust everywhere. Weeds poking through the stone floor.

He saw the newspaper. It was yellowed. He picked it up and watched it fall open, revealing the complete headline. '*SCOURGE OF SATAN VICAR IN LOVE TRYST WITH HOUSEKEEPER. Watery grave for Holy adulterers.*'

He let it fall, and wandered to the open doorway.

The graveyard was terribly overgrown, grass waist high, obscuring most of the stones.

Tom shivered, and looked into the woods. The scratches on his cheek throbbed. He found himself pushing his way through the dense undergrowth. A deathly silence fell. He burst through into the open. He was standing in the little bay just down from where he had last seen Audrey. He strained his eyes, and thought he could just make out the picnic basket. Looking around, he thought he saw the tattered remains of what might have been a small tent.

It seemed to be growing colder. He edged forward, halting at the water's edge. Tiny ripples broke against his trainers. He stared at his slightly shimmering reflection, trying to see beyond it, into the depths.

'To DT - with grateful thanks'

SYNCHRONICITY

Craig Herbertson

"Synchronicity,"

"Pardon?"

It amused me to watch Peters, the class intellectual, utilise a word that contained more than two syllables, in the presence of Dermott, the class philistine, whose vocabulary extended as far as immediate needs.

The others hadn't remarked Dermott's baffled exclamation, their faces buried in the menu in urbane contemplation of the starter.

"Synchronicity," repeated Peters, never one to let go of conversation when it was he who spoke. "The conjunction of events. Why we are all here at this time and place."

"Not 'invitation' then," said Campbell caustically. "Nothing to do with all being forty-eight years old and this date marking our departure from Bellport High?"

"Not all forty-eight," said Peters weakly. Despite his intellect, he had never been quicker than Campbell in riposte. "The ladies, the good wives and our venerable teacher of Mathematics, Mr Weasel." Peters indicated the aged figure of Weasel whose much-mimicked hand movements, were illustrating to Mrs Chalmers, wife of the head boy, how to square a hypotenuse.

"Poor Chalmers," muttered Mulholland. "You'd think Weasel would be able to leave the subject behind after twenty-five years of retirement."

I contemplated Mulholland for a moment. He had been immediately recognisable outside the Dome Restaurant. The ancient steps of the converted bank building had lent his spare figure a certain grandeur. He was clad in tweeds, plus fours, a hunting cap pulled down to shade one side of his face. In short, Mulholand's anachronistic clothes were a far cry from the scruffy, ripped and smelling garments of his youth. He

146

looked almost elegant between the colonnades of the posh Italian restaurant: An utter contrast to the gauche, bullied teenager who had cowered through the corridors of Bellport High.

How did I recognise him? The missing eye did the trick; frozen in an eternal wink that lurked beneath the cap with a kind of raw, sexual ugliness. I was surprised he hadn't covered it with a patch but then his whole demeanour surprised me. Thirty years had clearly wrought a remarkable change in Mulholland. Time had dealt less severely with him than the rest of us, I supposed.

He spoke again "I always understood synchronicity to mean our experience of events that occur in a meaningful manner, but which are causally unrelated. If Campbell wrote a merry little poem and I were to produce the same lyric, at the same time but in a different place, that would be synchronous."

I looked at Mulholland in some astonishment, recalling a day at school, over thirty years before, where I had found him hiding in a stock cupboard. He had been unable to speak for tears. Thankfully, he appeared now to have grown where others had shrunk. Peters for example, whose hair was thinner, his bulbous head shining luminous between the strands like one of those Scandinavian lamps: his voice still betraying the same irritating tones. A voice that was certainly irritating Dermott who understood very little beyond food and drink.

Nothing much changed there. Not even his trim waistline or penchant for tight pants. Campbell was still cracking jokes, mostly with Dermott's attractive wife. Nothing *whatsoever* changed there on the surface. But looking down the line of all the old school leavers was like attending a Warhol exhibition of 'Dorian Grays'. Aristotle would have had a field day demonstrating how depravity and apathy had left their marks.

I supposed I looked as decrepit as the rest. Perhaps I held a unique position. I seemed to be the only one who would have to select between the rent money and this ridiculously priced italian meal. I became even more conscious of the ragged edges of my cuffs and collar.

At least I hadn't married. Half the company seemed to be saddled with dull wives all of whom were contemplating Ravioli with *academia barilla pecorino gran cru* as a main meal. Must be herd instinct, I reflected, wincing at their varied incompetence in pronunciation. I glanced at the incomprehensible menu, written only in Italian. As with the tables, everything sparse as though simplicity and elegance were a fair substitute for sumptuous excess. For this price, naked, dancing ladies wouldn't be unfair.

I could avoid a starter but then I had no doubt that, if I did, we would end up mucking in. Dermott would steer us in that direction if he had a starter and several beers. If he had no starter and went light on the alcohol, he'd somehow engineer that we pay separately. That was always his skill at school: the art of justifying everything he did.

Compromise. What was the cheapest? Prawn cocktail? Do they still do that? What's it called in Italian? I glanced up. Hopefully, someone across the other side would give some kind of culinary clues. Chalmers was talking a little too loudly in Italian just to show he could do it. Good old headboy. Campbell had left off his wife and was eyeing the table to the left, which seemed to have commandeered most of the remaining single women. You could see that he was reflecting on past triumphs. Slim pickings there my boy: mostly divorced with three kids or exceptionally obvious reasons for still being single.

Mr Weasel tried to catch my eye across the two empty chairs. I managed to feign interest in the menu. It's amazing how heinous crimes seem to fade into playful mischievousness after the passage of years. That tottering old bastard, who looked like someone's favourite grandfather, had whupped us liberally with the tawse. Sore hands for months afterwards. And his habit of strolling the corridors swishing dawdling arses with his hickory cane. It must have been illegal even then, but he got away with it. Interesting that he wasn't keen to sit with the ladies. I established to myself that I hated him as much now as I did then. There was only one person from Bellport High who I could possibly hate more than Weasel but fortunately, he hadn't turned up.

I couldn't imagine school reunions held much appeal for Gray. Gray was an orphan. He'd arrived from somewhere else having been expelled for something awful. Bellport High seemed to be the natural dumping ground for maniacs.

I once speculated that *Gray* had killed his parents or *they* had run away from home. I kept that speculation to myself then, as you didn't want to draw unwelcome attention from Gray. He wasn't a big lad or particularly strong but one glance at his eyes was enough to shake you. He was utterly immoral; unpredictable, quick, inhuman; worse still, a creative sadist with an inventive collection of tortures that would have shamed De Sade. Eighteen years old... it seemed incredible looking around the faces around the table... these empty chairs would probably have been filled if Gray hadn't shortened the life span of half the school.

"Anyone know what happened to Gray?" The words had spilled unwilling from my mouth.

"Ask him," said Campbell with a smile. I sensed a shadow, an aura, something behind me, and looked up.

Have you ever experienced it? You stick your head down a rabbit hole and something with eyes springs out; you turn around while walking, and when you look back, your face hits a lamppost. Or maybe one of those tricks at school where they stick a worm in your hand. It was partly the unexpected, the shock of seeing his face above me as I had seen it so many times before: Peters' claptrap about synchronicity. But then it was also the fact that the face had changed so much in thirty years.

Gray wasn't leering down with anticipation. His face was still darkly handsome but it was careworn, chiselled with lines that lent his fine cheekbones a sort of tired elegance. Remarkably, the eyes had changed: Where hate and glee had battled for supremacy there was only a kind of haunted stillness. "Sorry I'm late," he said. He removed his expensive German great coat and his dark eyes swept the table with a view to sitting.

I confess I laughed. It was shock, relief, absurdity. Gray and 'sorry'. Like Hitler saying, 'I didn't mean to upset people'. I managed to kind of smother it into a welcome and indicated the empty chairs opposite.

Gray's entrance silenced us. Chalmers, the one boy who had tried to stand up to him at school, and that, only because his position demanded it, gave a kind of frozen nod to the empty chair at his side. The wives were giving him the once over as they would any handsome stranger. Peters, Campbell and Dermott had all been drawn into his perverse circle in varying degrees of complicity. Still they said nothing. Only Dermott, incapable of guilt, gave a slight nod. Mulholland, whose lost eye was a victim of one of Gray's sportive exploits, pursed his lips and looked back at the menu.

It was Weasel, a teacher after all, and a sadist to boot, who broke the silence. "Gunney? Geld? I'm terribly sorry but…"

"Gray, it's quite understandable. I wasn't in your class, sir…"

"Gray," said Weasel half to himself, liking the 'sir'. Gray had always avoided being beaten at school so Weasel was unlikely to remember him. I had a gut feeling that Weasel's nights were spent in sweaty dreams consumed by the pain-filled features of young boys. Now two of the school's old monsters shared a table with us like camp commandants partying with their prisoners.

Time heals, they say. So, we were all going to be civilised under the rococo lights, with the piped Domingo, over some fancy meal whose name I would never master. After some Friuli wine, we would doubtless recount the old horrors with a laugh and a smile. I looked at Mulholland's disfigured face and wondered how he felt behind that impassive mask. Probably like me, faintly sick.

"Mind if we order, Gray?" said Chalmers. He was trying to establish himself. Strange after all these years the same old predatory instincts surfaced. Gray's simple acquiescence drew an undisguised relaxation from Chalmers.

I thought back to their numerous confrontations. That time in Physics when Gray had electrified some water and was forcing that poor sap... what was his name... Angel, that was it, Angel. He was forcing Angel's hand into the water. Angel was screaming piteously as he always did. Chalmers came through and ordered him to stop. Then Gray with his glee-filled eyes said 'Stop what? This?' Without hesitation, he had placed his own hand in the electrified water and simply held it there. Chalmers, not for the first or last time, looked like a sanctimonious fool. Then the bucket of water over the door; only Gray had not used water but a single glass of beer, which left Chalmers, its unhappy victim, with some ridiculous explanations to do later.

But these were innocuous bagatelles. How many times had I walked into the form room to see Mulholland upside down in a wastepaper basket while the others looked and laughed and hit? Or that skinny fellow, Angel, undoubtedly the school wimp, pants at ankles, tied to a post in the playground. Once he had tattooed Angel's back and stomach with a Biro: 'front' and 'back' only in Gray's peculiar world of humour the words were in the wrong position. That poor kid... man now... must still bear the scars.

"And what do you do nowadays, Gray?" Weasel was still placing Gray. The name must surely have filtered through the staffroom at some point. You couldn't hold the entire student body in thrall without a flame from the inferno disturbing the pipe smoke.

"Offshore Banking," said Gray. "I think I'll miss the starter and try this ravioli with the ladies. I believe it's especially good here." He had caught their choice in their muted table talk and seemed to relax a little. He looked composed, sat in his expensive French shirt, sporting gold cufflinks and a

151

conservative tie. Still, there was just a faint echo of the driven boy emerging with his laconic voice. And the voice, the taunting, teasing voice of the torturer as he forced poor Angel to eat a spit-covered sweet, Mulholland to drink the lav water, me to whistle while he pinched my nipple. Better not dwell on the voice, I reflected. Might as well try to enjoy this Italian extravaganza before facing the financial music next month.

"What's your line, Chalmers?"

Chalmers hesitated a fraction, "Insurance," he said quietly.

"Oh, now I recall. I met... oh, I forget... but he said our head boy was a clerk with..." Gray drummed his fingers on the table.

Did I see a familiar light in his eyes? It was the way he had voiced 'clerk', just a bare hint of contempt. Not enough to be rude, not enough for anyone inattentive to really hear; only that apparently haphazard conjunction of the words 'boy' and 'clerk' to make Chalmers uneasy. Now, observing Chalmers, I could see that he had saved for this meal whereas Gray looked every inch the man who could buy and sell the restaurant.

Dermott piped up. In anyone else, it would have been an attempt to steer the conversation to safer waters. Dermott simply wanted to know.

"What's this synchronicity you're blabbing about, Peters?"

"Well, I was just going to point out... what a perfect example. We're all wondering what happened to Gray? And there he stands, just at that moment. It's a Jungian concept, the conjunction of events all melding together in one instant."

Dermott's face took on the solid mask of indifference; immediately dismissing 'synchronicity' as something that could be neither bought nor sold.

Mulholland quietly interjected. "I think I just mentioned that it refers to our experience of events that occur in a meaningful manner, but which have no causal relation. An historical example is that Lincoln dreamed of his assassination just before he actually was..."

Peters was off expounding his genius to the table behind.

Mulholland raised his eyebrows in a dismissive gesture.

"I'm somewhat famished," croaked Weasel, for once gauging the mood. Campbell and the other men sought the attention of a waiter. I didn't bother. I had tried on numerous unsuccessful occasions to effect that trick. Gray's hands were up in an instant. His compelling personality drew a waiter as easily as an angler plays a caught salmon.

The waiter came up. "We're all, I believe ready to order," said Gray competently. "Ladies?" There was brief flurry. "Starters: *Bruschetta* for me, a prawn cocktail, two *Carpaccio*, one *Prosciutto Bruschetta Fegatini*, that's that toast with chicken liver... let me see." He continued the order with the assurance of a seasoned epicure. The waiter was having difficulty keeping up as he pushed on to the main menu: Ravioli for the girls and the rest; Mulholland, the veal. Me? I settled, optimistically, for poor man's spaghetti bolognaise.

Gray was quietly ordering the most expensive champagne in the house when there was a sudden gasp from Chalmers.

"Angel," he said.

The waiter stiffened. It was only then that we all looked up. Waiters are just waiters aren't they? Even on a busy night, their job is to blend into the background. Like dodgems, they weave around you. On a successful night, you would hardly remember they were there, never mind a face. But Chalmers had remembered. All of thirty years and here was Angel, beggar at the feast, and our head boy had recognised him.

I vividly recall Mulholland's expression in that moment. Angel had saved Mulholland from being the most contemptible boy in the school. Both had been the victims of endless torture, the human canvas for Gray's Machiavellian art. Mulholland's single eye reflected what we all thought. Here was Angel, at the age of forty-eight, a menial waiter, still offering his humble services to his old classmates. Physical torture was passé. Now Angel would spend the evening serving our expensive culinary wants like some despised Southern Slave. I speculated what we should tip him.

Gray was the first to react. "Sit down, Angel, won't you."

Angel shook his head quickly. "Can't... working".

That was the problem with Angel. I was just thankful that I had been a decent enough bloke at school. I don't think there was anyone throughout the filled tables of the restaurant who hadn't participated in, or at least gained vicarious pleasure from, Angel's career of humiliation. Mulholland, dressed behind his lordly façade, perhaps understood better than most that Angel's deferential obsequiousness had brought the pain to his own door. Weakness is like a magnet. It attracts bullies and Angel had been unfortunate in encountering the worst of them all.

"Drink?" said Campbell.

"Synchronicity," this before Angel had a chance to refuse. Peters, a man with a chasm where others had social sense, betrayed his delight. "Angel here, serving the very boy who..." What he would have carried on to say is anyone's guess. Chalmers managed to ejaculate something about stopping for a drink after and Angel began to take the order. His hands shook. His distress was utterly painful. He made several mistakes. You could tell that seasoned epicures like Gray and Campbell would have made mince of him in other circumstances. By about the fourth effort Angel had somehow interpreted our needs and was slinking off to the kitchen. We all seemed to be getting our starters and the spaghetti, veal, ravioli and, most importantly, Champagne was hopefully *en route*. I needed a drink to numb the pain.

"Not a very happy boy," said Weasel absentmindedly. I restrained the impulse to mention that his state of mind might have been improved with even a little help from those responsible for his protection. What was the point? All water under the bridge. Then Mulholland said. "Not a very happy school."

I suppose you don't say this kind of thing at a school reunion. Jolly, cheery remarks like 'I remember when you had hair' or 'putting on a bit around the middle' filled the bill.

Synchronicity

Mulholland had broken a rule beyond old school rules but, as I said earlier, he seemed to have grown with the passing years and looked well able to forge a new set.

"How do you mean?" said Weasel.

"The petty torture, the beatings, the sadistic boys and masters."

Jesus! Mulholland wasn't beating about the bush. I got that sudden vertigo, almost like the precipitation of an LSD rush, where the whole evening seemed about to be swept away like a conjurer doing the plates and tablecloth trick.

"Come," said Weasel, next to Gray the last person to have the right to comment. "The old school was a super environment for young minds."

As if to illustrate the point Angel returned. He spilled part of my prawn cocktail on my sleeve, dropped Gray's *Bruschetta* and failed to open the champagne. Everybody tried to minimise his misadventures and Gray finally took the bottle and opened it with a flourish. Perhaps it was Gray's nature. Perhaps he was simply born to torture others even had he wished otherwise. Angel stood for a moment. There was a terrible silence.

I tried. "Angel, is there a cigarette machine here?" I didn't smoke. I was just putting enough words together to make any conceivable sentence.

"No," said Angel. He hovered.

"My *Bruschetta*?" said Gray. I felt then that I had hit the nail on the head. Gray and Angel were like some ill-fated duo. An eternity could come and go and Angel would still be the mouse to his cat. Angel stood, lost for a second. I felt he might be confused about his role: old school wimp or incompetent waiter. Finally, he left for the kitchen to an immediate lightening of the atmosphere.

Mulholland, however, had had no interest in a lightened atmosphere. "There's an example of our beneficent school system," he said, toying with his crab.

"Well," said Dermott getting down to brass tacks, "you

155

don't seem to have done so badly out of it. Nor the rest of us for that matter." He indicated the crowd of us, slouched in the comfy chairs, picking at our *hors d'oeuvre* and sipping champagne.

"Despite rather than because of Bellport High," said Mulholland.

"Oh come, come," said Weasel.

"A place of petty torture and sadistic bullying. You were there, Mr Weasel when I lost my eye. Do you recall the incident?"

Angel had returned with a second bottle of champagne. He hovered on the edge of the crowd, seemingly indecisive as to whether he should attempt to open the bottle or surrender to Gray's surer hand.

"Yes, vaguely." It was the wrong thing to say but of course, Mulholland had broken every code in the book.

"You'll remember though, Gray?" The table went silent.

Gray eased back in the chair a little. He eyed Mulholland with something like respect. "It was the last day at school. We dangled you from the sixth floor stairwell. Campbell, Dermott and I. You were upside down screaming, a stupid schoolboy prank, which I intensely regret now. There was some confusion afterwards. In the struggle, you might have hit your head on the banister or something of the sort. Poked out your eye. Very regrettable."

"Yes, I recall very well now," said Weasel. I was on corridor duty and was on hand to give you first aid. Regrettable accident, horseplay and the like and very fortunate I was immediately on hand. Such, sadly, is life…"

"Regrettable, yes, unfortunate, yes," said Mulholland. "Not so regrettable that Gray didn't manage to make it to the dining room for lunch, neatly covering his tracks. And unfortunate that you were never able to establish who was to blame. Nice to find out after all these years."

"Yes," said Weasel, not listening, "a regrettable and unfortunate incident. But time heals all. Now we can sit together like old chums and laugh about it all."

Angel had contrived to remove the starters. He had given up with the champagne and the bottle lay conveniently within Gray's reach. He took it deliberately. An uncomfortable silence followed the popped cork. Angel laid out the main courses and stood just behind me facing Gray with Weasel on his right. The dishes looked surprisingly good, although bigger portions would have suited me and as always with sod's law, the others' ravioli looked a lot better than my miserable portion of spaghetti.

Gray began to pour the wine. I gripped Angel's arm and whispered. "Have a drink with us." He kind of hovered but didn't pick up a glass. I'd done my best.

Nobody seemed inclined to start. Then Peters guffawed. "Why, synchronicity! All this ravioli. Precisely the meal we had for lunch on our last day."

"How jolly," said Mulholland with heavy irony. "That fine example of conjunctive events has fairly cheered my soul."

"I have a better." said Angel suddenly.

We paused, forks raised. Even the tables beyond us hushed.

"I was on the corridor at the time Mulholland was injured," said Angel quietly. "Mr Weasel lashed at me with his cane. He missed. At the same instant you were being lowered down the stairwell by your legs. Gray and his crew had done that to me so many times it was almost fun to watch it happen to someone else. Except that when Mr Weasel struck out with his hickory cane he caught your eye."

Mulholland quailed for a moment. Pursed his lips and determinedly, poured himself a large glass.

The silence deepened into something dreadful.

"I saw Gray run." Angel continued with enthusiasm. "He was obviously after an alibi." He looked at me with a beaming smile. "He elbowed you out of your seat at the dining table."

Angel looked at the air above his old classmates, following an imagined parabola. He said: "I watched that eye hurtle through the air like a comet, out of the corridor, through the open door of the dining room and splash! Straight into a plate of ravioli. Your ravioli, Gray."

Angel smiled, realising perhaps, that the unusual circumstances had encouraged him to overstep the boundary between customer and waiter.

In the ensuing silence, he coughed and said politely. "Enjoy your meal."

Mulholland gave me a queer look and we both picked up our knives. "That," he said, piercing a glistering sliver of veal, "is what *I* would call synchronicity."

IN THE THICKET

Paul Finch

It was in the summer of 1909 when the Reverend Littlefellow and his nephew, Fred, took a train from Cambridge to Stratford-upon-Avon, and from there a pony and trap to the quiet village of Bulfratton.

The Reverend Littlefellow did not quite match his name. He stood a good six feet three inches tall, though he wasn't especially broad at the shoulder or thick around the waist. During his student days, the nickname 'Beanpole' had accurately, if somewhat uncharitably, described his appearance, and now, twenty years on, there wasn't a great deal of difference. He was a cheerful-looking chap for all that; of handsome, smiling countenance, and with a full head of bright, reddish curls, currently hidden beneath a white, wide-brimmed sunhat, which contrasted rather sharply with his black clerical garb. Beside him on the trap, his nephew was less easy to read. A little on the plump side, though well turned-out in a matching jacket, cap and knee-breeches, he wore a blank expression on his broad, pale face, which one might easily expect to turn pugnacious. His mousy-brown hair was combed and cut very smartly, he sat upright, and listened politely as his uncle chattered. Yet it might have struck anyone who paid close attention to the passing twosome, that the younger fellow may just – just – have his mind on other, less edifying things.

He hadn't, after all, been expelled from Harrow for nothing.

"What amazes me more than anything," the reverend gentleman was saying, "is that any church left over from the Saxon era has not already been fully excavated and documented."

His nephew nodded, as though this was a puzzle to him as well.

Littlefellow elaborated: "The original Saxon church, St. Tidfrith's, closed some time in the early eighth century. I'm

159

not exactly sure when or why. That's what we're hoping to find out this weekend. What I do know is that over three hundred years later, shortly after the Norman conquest, another church was built about a mile to the west. This one also was called St. Tidfrith's, so it was clearly intended to be a direct replacement. That's where my friend Carmichael is now the rector, though of course the Norman church has itself been rebuilt several times since then. Later on, a medieval village sprang up around this latter church, which eventually became Bulfratton. I don't know whether there was an earlier village than that – a Saxon village maybe, that was served by the original Saxon St. Tidfrith's, but that may also be something we can discover. As I say, the ruins of the first church are now about a mile out of Bulfratton, in the middle of a small wood that the locals call 'the Thicket'. It's all very exciting."

Littlefellow's nephew looked as though he was about to respond to this, but in the end said nothing.

*

Ernest Carmichael and Winston Littlefellow had been friends since their student days.

At the end of their respective courses, both had taken up positions in the clergy. Carmichael had eventually married (though his wife, Abigail, later passed on with pneumonia), and now, in 1909, had been rector at St. Tidfrith's in south Warwickshire for thirteen years. A corpulent, always jovial man, he'd become a popular figure in his parish, and was as regular a visitor to the oak-beamed bar in the Ditch-Digger's Arms as he was the host of services on Sunday morning, and as good a fellow to share a pipe and chinwag with over a few late-evening whiskies as he was a shoulder to cry on for the spiritually distressed. He'd never lost touch however, with his old friend Littlefellow, who, contrastingly, had remained a bachelor and had pursued his own vocation in the closeted, academic environs of St. Cecilia's College, Cambridge, where he was now chaplain.

The main reason Littlefellow hadn't married was that the short time he spent away from his duties was occupied by his other great interest in life – the study of historic Church architecture. His was a leisurely, uncomplicated existence, so it hadn't been an easy thing for him when, unexpectedly that May, he'd received into his care fourteen-year-old Fred, for reasons not yet fully understood.

In his letter, the headmaster at Harrow had underlined a number of specified offences, none of which on their own seemed particularly heinous to Littlefellow, though he supposed that when placed in the context of one occurrence following another, at speed, for several months, it made the matter slightly more serious. Either way, for the moment the boy was his and his alone. Fred's father, Jerome, and his new American wife, Sonja, were currently sailing the Mediterranean in a yacht, and out of contact. Fred had been due to join them in Nice at the beginning of July. And he still would, though now, with a copy of both the Harrow headmaster's letter and one written by his uncle in his pocket, it wasn't likely to be the joyful reunion that either father or son had been expecting when they'd parted company last January.

Still that wouldn't be any of Littlefellow's concern. Come the arrival of mid-summer, he'd doubtless be off on another of his antiquarian jaunts, as indeed he was now. The end-of-term examinations, when college chaps seldom appeared for air let alone to take religious counselling, was always too good an opportunity to miss.

"What an imposing structure," he said, as they arrived at the front door of St. Tidfrith's rectory.

It was a rambling old building, possibly Georgian, all red brick with luxuriant green ivy hanging thick over its mullioned windows. Behind it, flat farmland rolled off into a hazy distance, now turning crimson as the evening descended. To the fore, a dusty track wound past a flower-filled garden, then around the village green, where it adjoined a small market-square, the centrepiece of which was a tall cross of weathered stone. The cottages for the most part were either timbered or thatched. It all made for a pleasant rural scene.

"Carmichael's cable tells me the key can be found under the left-hand plant pot," Littlefellow remarked. "His housekeeper was under orders to leave us a cold collation before departing for the evening."

Young Fred hopped down to search for the key, while his uncle took the trap around to the rear of the building, where apparently a man from the village would act as stable-boy for the duration of their stay. Carmichael himself would not be in attendance. This had lowered Littlefellow's spirits briefly, when he'd first heard; his normally reliable old friend was apparently in another part of the country seeing to an ailing relative – but the house was theirs for the weekend, so long as they promised not to 'raze it to the ground' during their 'revels'.

As Littlefellow handed the reins to the stable-boy, he noted for the first time the village church. It stood behind a high wall, so that all he could really see of it were its octagonal twin towers. Shaking his head in despair at the absurdity of the Gothic revivalists, he went into the house.

*

Carmichael's housekeeper had been as good as her employer's word.

Once Littlefellow and his nephew had made themselves comfortable in their respective bedrooms, they came downstairs to the dining room, and found an excellent repast awaiting them – ham, beef, eggs, buttered crusty bread, a jug of milk for the boy and a bottle of wine for his uncle. There was also a note from Carmichael, which was propped up against a vase in the hall. It stated that Mrs Marlcroft, the housekeeper, kept a tidy house and had strict rules. She set breakfast at eight and dinner at nine. She'd take it as a politeness if guests who'd been out tramping in the countryside would remove their muddy boots before coming indoors.

The place was not atypical of country vicarages, in that it was spacious and gloomy. Its few furnishings did not complement its large rooms. Though it contained ornaments here and there, mainly statuettes, and the occasional painting, the décor in general had faded, creating a sombre impression that the house's best times had gone. A large fire had been made up in the parlour, which gave the room a cheerful atmosphere but also rendered it uncomfortably warm. It being June, the temptation was immediately to damp the fire down and then open a window or two.

Littlefellow was determined not to let any of this sour his spirits. More fine weather was forecast for the following day, and he was now slipping into that relaxed and amiable mood that he always felt on the first night of a holiday.

"So, how do you feel?" he asked his nephew.

Fred pursed his lips and nodded, as though everything was to his liking, though yet again his demeanour in general was somewhat inscrutable.

"The place is ours for the next four days," the reverend added. "So we should make the best of it. The rules of the house seem pretty straightforward."

He glanced again at Carmichael's note. There was a postscript beneath the advice regarding Mrs Marlcroft, which he hadn't noticed previously:

Winston, old boy, before you go rooting around in the Thicket, there are a couple of volumes in my library that you might want to peruse. Anecdotes of the Dark Ages – P. Regis, and Parish Records, 1770-1820. I've marked the appropriate pages. Enjoy Bulfratton. I hope you find something interesting. Just be sensible.

Littlefellow went straight to the library, which was more the size of a large study and located at the rear of the house. He searched among its shelves, but though everything appeared to be arranged in alphabetical order, there was no sign of either of the two books that his friend had recommended.

*

The weather the following day was as fine as Littlefellow could have hoped for, and he walked into the village with high spirits, stripped to his shirtsleeves, wearing his sunhat and carrying his camera, notebooks and such in a large satchel. Fred, also in shirtsleeves, accompanied him.

Not knowing the geography of the area, they strolled around the village green to the square and called at the Ditch-Digger's Arms, a large, brick-built hostelry with a steeply pitched slate roof and a shield over its front door, which bore the image of a spade crossed by what looked like a wooden crucifix. Inside the tap-room, the landlord, who had clearly just opened for the day, was behind his counter, polishing a glass tankard. He was a thickset countryman with lush, white side-whiskers. He beamed when they entered.

"Morning gentlemen. Anything I can get for you?"

"No thank you," Littlefellow replied, though Fred eyed the row of brass beer-pumps with more than a little interest.

"Just directions, if it's convenient," the reverend added. "We're seeking the Thicket."

The landlord's welcoming smile faded a little. At the end of the counter, an aged man sitting wreathed in pipe-smoke, turned and looked at them.

"The Thicket?" the landlord said.

"I understand that's where the ruins are of the old Saxon church?" Littlefellow added. "The original St. Tidfrith's?"

"Don't know anything about a church. There's a broken arch there, a few stumps of old stone."

"That's what I was led to believe. Can you possibly direct us?"

"I can." The landlord seemed in no great rush, however. He

carefully hung the tankard from an overhead beam. "There isn't a great deal left of it, mind. It's all overgrown."

Littlefellow rubbed his hands. "All to the good. There are few better subjects for photography than ancient stonework wrapped in foliage."

"Very well, sir. Seeing as you're bent on it."

And, somewhat reluctantly, the landlord gave them the necessary directions, which were fairly simple and to the point. As they left the establishment, Littlefellow fancied he heard some mumbled words from the man at the end of the bar. They sounded something like: 'Wouldn't believe you anyway.'

Once outside, they crossed the market square and took a small road, which led out of the village – according to a lichen-covered signpost, in the direction of somewhere called Long Compton. After several hundred yards, a shady lane branched away to the left. They took this and, though it terminated at the entrance to a field, on the right-hand side there was a stile. They climbed through it, and saw a path running in a straight line across a large meadow. At the far end of this, maybe five minutes' walk away, a dusty green mass fringed the horizon. Evidently, this was the celebrated Thicket.

At which point Fred spoke.

It was such a rare occurrence that Littlefellow was startled.

"Uncle, I need to return to the rectory," the boy said.

"I – er, I beg your pardon?"

"I'm afraid I've left your camera-stand."

For the first time the Littlefellow noticed that the boy hadn't been carrying the fold-away tripod, as he'd been asked to.

"Do you need it?" Fred wondered. "Is it immensely important?"

"It – well, yes, it is."

"Then as I say, I'll go back and get it."

Littlefellow eyed the lad speculatively. This was already the longest conversation they'd had together. For his age and shape, Fred's voice was rather weak, even querulous. Though like everything else about him, it could be deceptive.

"It was the only thing you had to carry," the reverend said, ostensibly as an admonishment, but mainly because he suddenly felt a need to know more. Had the lad left the camera-stand deliberately? Was something else afoot? Given Fred's history of untrustworthiness, and the enigmatic blandness of his expression, it was increasingly difficult to judge.

"I know, but let me make it up to you," Fred pleaded, with such apparent remorse that it was difficult to deny him. "I shan't be long, I promise."

"Very well," the reverend grunted – he couldn't see that any real harm would come from this. "But hurry. The light is excellent. I don't want to lose it if clouds come over."

Fred wandered off in the opposite direction and Littlefellow proceeded alone, wafting at bumblebees and horseflies, and making sure to stick to the meadow path, which wasn't as well trodden as he'd expected. When he finally reached the far end of it, though he was only a mile from the village as the crow flew, he had the odd impression he'd come considerably further. Behind him lay open pasture, largely empty of life – even cattle were absent from it. In front, on the other side of a low ditch, was the Thicket. It was, as he'd imagined, a small wood or spinney; he'd been advised that it was only two or three hundred yards across, though at present it was thick with leaf and filled with greenish shadows. There was also a quietness about it, an unusual stillness – but it didn't look particularly out of the ordinary. Where the path ended at the ditch, a small footbridge allowed easy access to the other side.

Littlefellow walked over, his footfalls on the timber sounding curiously loud.

That was when he had his first real surprise of the day.

At first he only noticed from the corner of his eye, but then he turned and stared.

What initially he'd taken for the remnants of an old fence running along the bottom of the ditch, he now realised was a line of crucifixes.

He peered down at them perplexed.

The ditch was only a couple of feet deep and completely dry. It ran along the edge of the Thicket for as far as he could see in either direction. But without any doubt, crucifixes – albeit crude ones, just pieces of wood fastened together with twine – had been placed along the foot of it, at regular intervals of ten yards or so. There was one right alongside the footbridge itself.

"Bless my soul," the reverend muttered.

He glanced again into the Thicket, as if the answer lay there. Still there was no movement. For the most part, its trees were of the standard deciduous variety – alder, willow, hornbeam, silver birch. But there was much vegetation filling the spaces between them. And now that he considered it, it *did* look a little deeper and more tangled than the average stretch of shire-country woodland. Ridiculously, he felt a twinge of unease.

He stayed where he was for a moment, not stepping off the bridge, unsure what to do next. For no reason he could ascertain, going any further suddenly seemed unwise. He shielded his eyes and glanced overhead. The sun was still high, the sky still clear and powder-blue. The day was fine, but of course there was no guarantee it would remain that way, and he *did* want to take some photographs. At length, writing the crucifixes off as some innocent but obscure country practise, that he – a cloistered academic – was unaware of, he shrugged and went on in.

As soon as he entered the Thicket, that brief discomfort he'd felt seemed absurd. There was no path, but a natural avenue seemed to open up for him – gaps and breaks in the foliage, which he was able to slip through with ease. After only a few minutes, he came upon the object of his interest.

The landlord's description had been uncannily accurate.

No buildings remained, though the chancel arch was still present, and the main body of the church – perhaps forty yards long – could be identified because its footings were visible. Various items of fallen debris could also be seen: pieces of masonry; a section of pillar that maybe once stood to the side of the entrance door. And all of it was swamped with greenery. In fact, only glimpses of stonework could be had through the profusion of leaves and creeper. Ivy clad the chancel arch entirely, so that it resembled topiary rather than architecture. A great, knotted hummock of briars occupied what had once been the nave. Not that Littlefellow was put off by any of this. In fact, he was enthused. The entire ruin basked in a sun-dappled glow that was most photogenic. He longed to set up his camera immediately and record his findings, but for the present had to content himself with plodding around and making feverish notes.

On the west side lay what looked like the remains of a graveyard: a broken-down boundary wall encircled it and horizontal slabs peeked out from its deep herbage.

Littlefellow stopped when he saw this.

He could scarcely believe it.

An Anglo-Saxon graveyard? With intact tombs?

And no-one had made a study of the place?

For a second it seemed too unlikely to be true. Then he clambered excitedly over the wall and waded forward through the undergrowth. The first slab bore carved characters, but they were so faint that he couldn't make them out properly. They *might* be Old English, he supposed. But they might just as easily be of more recent date.

Uncertainty set in.

This surely could not be an original Dark Age cemetery? Not sitting here like this, untouched, unexcavated. Carmichael must be wrong. This site *had* to date from a later period. Why, it didn't even feature in the manuals or guidebooks. Most probably the church itself was Saxon, and the graveyard had continued to be used. But then...

He blundered around some more. Further carved characters were visible on the next tombstone, but on this one there were patterns as well: vinescroll decorations in the corners, and across the bottom a row of featureless men wearing helmets and holding spears. By Jove, it certainly *looked* Saxon.

Then the reverend gentleman heard a whisper.

He looked up and glanced around.

The sun continued to dapple the ruins and their raiment of leaves. It shone in shafts between the trunks of the encircling wood. But still there was no movement; no sign that anyone else was present.

The silence in that place was suddenly quite noticeable.

For the first time, it struck Littlefellow how odd it was that on a fine June day like this, not a single bird seemed to be singing.

*

Fred had ordered his fourth pint of ale when he was finally shown out of the inn.

He'd just placed another threepence on the counter and was watching the foaming brew be drawn, when a comely young barmaid in a short-sleeved summer blouse arrived to help with the lunchtime custom. Fred openly leered at her, then made a crude comment about 'melons in lace'.

"Here, that's enough of that!" the landlord said, immediately emptying the tankard.

He'd been eyeing the young fellow suspiciously for the last fifteen minutes, and now pushed his coins back across the bar-top to him. Fred ignored them; they weren't his anyway – he'd filched a handful of coppers from his uncle's purse first thing that morning. He glared dully back.

"I won't have talk like that in here," the landlord added. "Take yourself elsewhere."

"Do you know who my father is?" the boy replied, in his most haughty Harrow accent.

The landlord leaned forward, red-faced. "I don't care if it's His Royal Highness King Edward the bloody Seventh. I don't like your attitude and I want you out."

"You'll regret this."

169

"The only thing I regret is serving you at all. I don't know who that parson chap is you were with, but if I see him, I'll fix it he knows he isn't welcome anywhere round here so long as he's with you."

"You think I care what *he* says? I'll go and find him. I'll bring him straight here."

"Get out, you young scoundrel! Before I throw you out!"

Realising that further conversation with this peasant ignoramus was futile, Fred waved a warning finger at him, then turned and walked stiffly to the door. Once he was outside, he stood blinking in the bright sunlight. He knew he was supposed to have collected something, but he wasn't sure what. Anyway, where was his wretched uncle now? Ah yes, the so-called Thicket. He began to roam vaguely in that direction.

After only three mugs of beer he wasn't greatly inebriated, despite his tender age, and as he strolled, the warm sun and country air did much to clear his head. Soon he was able to balance properly and focus again. Finally he remembered that he was supposed to have brought the camera-stand. Too late now, he decided – he'd reached the signpost to Little Compton. There was no going back from here. Not a second time. Not that he'd ever intended to go all the way back to the rectory in the first place, of course.

*

In truth, only a handful of tombstones were on view in the graveyard. The rest, if there'd been any others – only village notaries would have been buried so grandly after all – were either lost in the foliage or had been removed during subsequent centuries. Doubtless there were other graves here somewhere, though most would have been unmarked; after all, generations of ordinary villagers would also have been laid to rest in this place. Now however, Littlefellow had found something more interesting.

Beyond the chancel, considerable portions remained of what

looked like a small outbuilding. It might well have been the priest's house: it was square-shaped, maybe twenty yards by twenty. For the most part only its lower sections remained, and its interior had been inundated by vegetation. But pieces of its left-hand wall stood to nearly six feet tall, and a window was still visible; it was a basic triangular opening, typical of the early Saxon style. This pleased Littlefellow no end, as did another find a minute later: at the next corner of the building was a fine example of what archaeologists referred to as 'long and short work' – the alternate use of horizontal and vertical stones. This was vintage Saxon craftsmanship, sure proof that at least the majority of this site was as ancient as Carmichael had claimed.

It again begged the question: why had the place been left alone for so long?

Littlefellow glanced around, watching the encircling trees. The silence that lay between them was intense; distracting if not exactly disquieting.

Eventually he got back to work. The whisper he thought he'd heard, he'd put down to a breeze sighing through the leaves. But it was more difficult a moment later to explain a sudden *crack*, which sounded like a branch being forcefully snapped.

Littlefellow jumped. He turned sharply. Yet again, verdant depths were all that met his eye. Here and there, on the odd patch of forest floor, shadows stirred – reflections of the boughs overhead. But there was no other movement. Dismissing it, he took out a pad and pencil and began to sketch the 'long and short work'. He'd do the window next.

Unfortunately, he now couldn't shake off the suspicion that he wasn't quite alone.

He glanced over his shoulder continually. It crossed his mind that Fred might be lurking about somewhere, playing a childish game. Heaven knew, the boy ought to have been back some time ago. Realising that he wasn't getting anywhere, Littlefellow broke off from his sketching and peered hard into the Thicket, in the direction where he thought he'd heard that *crack*.

And was disconcerted to hear a sound from another direction.

In fact, from exactly the opposite direction.

He swung around.

This one had sounded like movement amid undergrowth: a brief rustling of twigs.

The clergyman felt his first genuine pang of unease.

Whoever was out there, was he circling the site? Or was there more than one of him?

It could be a deer of course, but Littlefellow didn't think it was.

Suddenly the pencil in his hand felt greasy with sweat. He looked back at the tell-tale stonework. It was beautiful, so well preserved. But he no longer had the enthusiasm to do it justice in his sketchbook.

And then he heard another sound.

He jerked around sharply.

This had been much closer; several feet away at the most. Littlefellow strained his eyes to penetrate the trees, again seeing nothing suspicious. Yet this one had been the most distinctive so far, and the most sinister. It had sounded like a titter; like a low, dry-throated chuckle.

Overhead, the much-anticipated clouds had now stolen up, and the sun suddenly vanished. A fog-like shadow spread among the silent trunks.

Littlefellow now *knew* that he was being observed, and that whoever was doing it was getting bolder, coming steadily closer.

"All right," he said aloud, packing his pencil and pad away. "I'm leaving. But this isn't funny, I advise you. When I return, and I *will* return, I'll have assistance."

It was probably some bored local element, he told himself; most likely children. Still, he wasn't being made a fool of. He snapped his satchel closed, slung it over his shoulder and, with as much dignity as he could muster, strode away.

And only then did it strike him that he wasn't sure how to get back.

He halted again. There were no distinguishing features in the trees, so he had no reference points. Had he come into the Thicket from the north or the east? He wasn't entirely sure, and in any case it was still mid-day, so the sun was directly overhead – or at least it would be if he could see it. He tried to remember which side of the ruined church he'd emerged next to: the chancel? The priest's house? The graveyard?

Then he heard foliage start to *crackle*. And continue crackling.

It was coming from the other side of the site, but it seemed to be moving in this direction, and it was loud – unashamedly loud, as if the person who was doing it was no longer concerned to conceal his presence. Littlefellow didn't even look. In fact the next thing he knew, he was walking quickly away. All right, he didn't know the route back, but he could find it easily enough. The Thicket was only a few hundred yards deep. At some point soon he'd come to its perimeter.

It wasn't an easy journey however. Whereas a natural pathway had aided him before, now the reverse was true. Suddenly the undergrowth was waist-high and thickly meshed, so he had to kick and stomp his way through it. With the sun gone, he found himself in an odd emerald twilight, where shadows seemed to move in his peripheral vision, where thorns plucked at his clothes like fingers. A low, claw-like bough raked off his sunhat; he ignored it, pressing determinedly on. He told himself repeatedly that there was nobody behind him; that the sounds he could hear, he was making himself.

When daylight finally reappeared some thirty yards ahead he all but shouted with relief. As the woodland thinned, he ran the remaining distance, gasping for breath as he burst out onto the edge of open farmland again. He tottered forward, and then the ground gave way and he dropped onto his knees. He landed heavily, winding himself and ripping holes in his trouser-legs... and, to his shock, finding that he was in the ditch with the crucifixes.

As before, it led away in both directions for as far as he could see.

Littlefellow stood up. At first he wondered if he'd unconsciously found his way back to the point where he'd started, but no – there was no sign of the footbridge. Instead, his directional instinct suggested that he'd come out of the Thicket on its far side.

Which meant that this ditch entirely surrounded it. Hemmed it in.

That wasn't a pleasant thought, and he hurried to scramble up the slope and into the field, now dabbing sweat from his brow.

He stared back at the mass of trees, half-expecting to see something from a fairy tale: nightmarish trunks, twisted and bent like tortured bodies; naked, leafless branches; black moss; wads of loathsome fungus. But in actual fact the Thicket seemed peaceful and healthy again. The sun broke out overhead, embossing the vibrant green of its foliage, sending golden shafts into its leafy heart.

*

The reappearance of the sun made Fred feel sleepy.

A couple of minutes earlier he'd climbed through the stile, and now he was half way across the meadow. He yawned as the heat oppressed him, but pushed on doggedly. It would be nice to lie down right here and have a snooze, but the old boy would only make a fuss if he didn't return. There'd be difficulty enough explaining why he hadn't brought the tripod for the camera. Fred had decided to say that he hadn't been able to find the thing, but that could prove awkward if, when they got back to the rectory, it turned out to be standing in the hall or somewhere obvious like that. Still, being chastised was not exactly a new experience for him, and he sincerely doubted his Uncle Winston would be as deft a hand with the willow wand as the masters back at Harrow, even in the unlikely event that he was willing to employ such punishment. So what did it really matter?

The Thicket was now about thirty yards ahead. Fred saw that a small footbridge gave access to it. Beyond the outer bulwark of trees lay a dull, greenish gloom.

*

When Littlefellow got back to the rectory, he was in a dishevelled state. He'd removed his clerical collar, and his black shirt was unbuttoned at the throat. He was also dusty, sweaty and breathing heavily. Immediately on entering the building, he saw Mrs Marlcroft, a formidable, four-square lady of advanced years, who wore her steel-grey hair in a tight bun on the very top of her head.

She started. "Good gracious, Mr Littlefellow! Has there been an accident?"

"I, er... pardon me, Mrs Marlcroft. I've just walked a considerable distance over brook and field."

She glanced down and saw that his shoes and the cuffs of his trousers were wet, muddy and dotted with leaf-matter. She raised an imperious eyebrow.

Oblivious to this, he added: "However, it's most important that I locate my nephew. I believe he came back here to collect a camera-stand?"

"Well he certainly isn't here now," she said stiffly.

She didn't mind admitting that the tall, red-haired cleric had disappointed her. When she'd first met him that morning at breakfast, he'd seemed a polite, mild-mannered man. But to have broken her most cardinal rule at this early instance was a grave discourtesy. On top of that, he hadn't paid any heed to the two books she'd gone to great lengths to leave out for him on the hall dresser. She wasted no time in drawing his attention to this.

"I'm sorry?" he said, looking preoccupied, "I beg your pardon?"

"These books, sir," she replied. "I understood they were of some importance to you. I looked in the library specially. I left them here for you yesterday, before I went home."

Still wondering where Fred might have got to, Littlefellow – muddy shoes and all – walked absently across the polished hall floor, and gazed down at the volumes in question. What on earth was the woman talking about? He hadn't requested that any books be left out.

Both were venerable items, by the looks of them; bound in dark leather, but musty and worn. The title of the one on top was printed in gold leaf. It read: *Anecdotes of the Dark Ages*.

Immediately Littlefellow realised what had happened. These were the two books that Carmichael had advised he consult with regard to the Thicket. Mrs Marlcroft had obviously seen the note, and thinking to help, had gone to fetch them herself. No wonder Littlefellow hadn't been able to find them in the library.

"It's very kind of you, dear lady," he said. "But at this moment it's imperative that I look for my neph…"

And then another thought struck him.

Carmichael's note had specifically suggested he consult these books *before* he visit the Thicket.

Without another word, he picked them up and clumped through to the drawing-room, leaving the housekeeper glaring after him, unable to believe his audacity.

He dumped his satchel, and slumped down into an armchair. The first of the two books, as he'd seen, was *Anecdotes of the Dark Ages*. The second was the much older tome, *Parish Records, 1770-1820*. This latter one was virtually desiccated with age; its inside leaves were yellow and brittle and looked set to fall out *en masse*. Not wishing to cause more damage than was necessary, Littlefellow laid that one aside and took up the first, which, though according to its imprint, had been published over thirty years ago, was in much better condition.

In the Thicket

He opened it.

It quickly became apparent that its author, a chap called Philip Regis, was given to flowery prose, though this wasn't necessarily unsuited to his choice of subject-matter. His book was basically an assessment of fables and apocrypha of the Anglo-Saxon age. Its first proper page, for instance, bore a lurid illustration of Harold Godwinson's epic but semi-mythical encounter with the Viking berserker at the start of the battle of Stamford Bridge. Likewise, a glimpse of the Table of Contents showed entire chapters devoted to Havelok the Dane and Hereward the Wake, though almost nothing factual was known about either.

Littlefellow skimmed his way in, feeling increasingly as though he was wasting his time. Only when he suddenly spotted a corner of blue card did he remember that Carmichael had promised to 'mark the relevant page'. He turned to it, and found a body of text, the central paragraphs of which Carmichael had been good enough to run a pencil rule alongside. Littlefellow read through them:

Much has been made, of course, of the great missionary, Saint Augustine of Canterbury's journeys through early England, then a patchwork of small, fledgling kingdoms.

Many wondrous stories concern the personal powers of Saint Augustine, not least those detailing his long fireside conversations with the warlike King Ethelbert of Kent, a committed pagan who was so fearful the eloquent visitor would enthral him with magic that he insisted they only ever meet out of doors. At length, so impressed was Ethelbert by the arguments of Augustine, that he embraced Christianity of his own free will.

Perhaps the most remarkable of all these tales, however, comes to us from the year 604 AD and describes the arrival of the saint at a place now called Bulfratton in modern-day Warwickshire, where he intended to say Mass and preach a sermon. Before commencing, Augustine insisted that no person under excommunication could hear the holy service. At once, or so the legend asserts, a number of dead people, both men and women, climbed from their graves and left the churchyard, vanishing into the surrounding wood...

Though a chaplain by trade, Littlefellow was also a modern man, educated and well-informed. He didn't normally attach any significance to tales of the supernatural. As he reached for the second of these two books, however, the hair was prickling at the nape of his neck.

*

Fred had been wandering through the trees for ten minutes or so, and was getting increasingly puzzled as to where he was supposed to be going, when he suddenly spotted the girl.

She was about fifteen yards ahead and following a meandering path, which, though it was invisible to him, was clearly well-known to her. He stopped, fascinated. Where she might have come from, he didn't know. Were there cottages in the Thicket, or maybe round to the other side of it?

He could only see the girl from behind, but it was a pleasant view all the same. She wore rough country-garb, but had very long flaxen hair hanging down almost to the small of her back. She walked slowly, idly, but with a gentle, sensual sway to her hips.

Instinctively, the boy started to follow her. He didn't immediately intend to catch her up. He would see where she went to first. But all thoughts of locating the ruined church and his uncle were now forgotten.

*

"Er, hello – I don't suppose you've seen my nephew?" Littlefellow stammered.

178

As he'd passed the rear gate to the Ditch-Digger's Arms, the landlord had appeared carrying a beer-cask.

"The boy I was with earlier," the reverend added. "I seem to have lost track of him."

"Yes, I've seen him," the landlord said gruffly. He loaded the cask onto the back of a cart, then rubbed his hands on his apron. "I sent him on his way if you want to know the truth, sir."

"On his way?"

"I'm afraid he cheeked one of my bar-staff."

"On his way to where?"

The landlord hooked his thumbs into his belt, shocked that this pleasant-seeming gentleman didn't express embarrassment or even surprise at such a revelation.

"Please?" Littlefellow asked him. "It's quite important."

"He said he was going looking for you."

"I see."

With mounting trepidation, Littlefellow continued on his way, hurrying across the market-square and taking the road to Long Compton.

The reference in the second book, *Parish Records, 1770-1820,* had been almost nothing; little more than a sentence half-concealed amid reams of irrelevant minutiae. But even so Carmichael had thought to underline it with his pencil – twice.

It had been a December entry, dating from the year 1773; a quick memo to Mr Henry Salister, apparently the incumbent at St. Tidfrith's at the time, from his churchwarden:

To offer special prayers over the festive tide for the goodly folk of Bulfratton, and protection against those still dwelling in the Thicket...

*

Fred was growing in confidence as he followed the girl deeper into the trees.

The little minx knew he was trailing her, of that he was sure.

She was walking far too slowly to be otherwise, and was much too relaxed about it. Unable to avert his eyes from the easy, side-to-side motion of her bottom, he increased his pace. She was teasing him, he told himself, taunting him. Just like Jennifer, the groundskeeper's daughter back at school – the *real* reason for his expulsion, of course, though thankfully her father hadn't wished any of the details to be made public.

Fred licked the palm of his hand and brushed his hair flat as he gained ground.

"Hello there," he said. "Can you wait up a moment?"

If the girl heard him, she didn't respond; just continued to walk ahead.

He closed the gap on her. "I say?"

And then she passed through a patch of sunlight, and for a very brief moment he was startled. Her lustrous long hair was flaxen-gold, or so he'd first assumed in the dimness of the wood. But just then it had looked – well, *white*.

Surely that couldn't be right?

Had his eyes been playing tricks on him?

"I say, I'm talking to you!" he called, now racing to catch her up.

One way or another, he'd have an answer.

*

Littlefellow was feeling his forty years as he dashed along the path across the meadow. Thanks to his exhaustive ramblings earlier, it now seemed much longer and more arduous than he remembered. He was panting and stumbling when he finally came to the footbridge. He halted to get his breath, then peered across it into the shadows of the Thicket.

Yet again, the temptation was to hold his ground here, to find some reason not to go further. But insisting to himself that this was all stuff and nonsense, he pressed on across and strode boldly beneath the branches.

If nothing else, he was sure that he could find his way quickly to the ruin. It was roughly in the centre, and Fred had to be around there somewhere. It occurred to Littlefellow to call out. That would be the obvious thing to do; Fred couldn't be too far away, wherever he was. Yet some sixth sense prevented the clergyman from doing this. He tried to convince himself that it had nothing to do with not wanting to announce his presence, yet he couldn't deny it: twenty yards in and already he felt as though he was being watched.

He glanced from side to side as he progressed: low-hanging branches, leafy dells, deeper shades of green now the afternoon was advancing. He inwardly flinched as the sun went in again and shadows fell over him. It was nothing, he reassured himself; merely a cloud.

How quiet it was, though.

Shouldn't there be some sound at least?

He was now pushing through waist-high ferns. The tree-trunks nearby were layered with ivy. There was almost a jungle atmosphere. He didn't remember this part of the Thicket. He must have veered away from the path he'd taken before. Of course, previously it was as though that path had appeared for him, as though he'd been guided. But that was ludicrous. *Guided?* What utter and complete tosh.

"Fred!" he called out, though still not at the top of his voice. "Fred, where are you?"

There was no immediate reply, but then Littlefellow thought he heard movement to his left – a furtive scuttling sound. He spun around, and saw a mass of rhododendron bushes quivering, as though someone had just burrowed through them.

"Fred, is that you?"

Gradually, the bushes became still.

The reverend glanced behind him. He could no longer see the meadow. How far had he come in? Forty yards, maybe fifty? He continued to pivot around until he'd made a full circle, scanning the woodland on all sides. Was it his imagination, or was it actually growing darker in here? And whereas it had been cool before, now it felt positively *cold*. He tried to suppress a shudder, but failed.

And something touched his shoulder.

Littlefellow froze.

Very slowly, he turned his head.

It would be a leaf or twig that had fallen. What else could it be?

But when he saw the pallid hand – long, limp and lifeless – draped on his black shirt like a huge dead spider, he gave a loud, inarticulate squawk, and tore himself away. He blundered headlong for twenty yards, before swinging around and stumbling backwards.

And to his astonishment, seeing Fred.

The boy stood there looking rather lost. His hand was still in the air, as though he hadn't yet realised that his uncle's shoulder had moved.

"Good Heavens!" the reverend exclaimed, hastily recovering himself. "Fred! What on earth...?" But his words tailed off, because now he saw the blood on his nephew's shirt. He hurried back over. "What happened?"

The boy seemed uncertain. His expression was vaguely startled, his eyes puffy as though he'd just been woken from sleep. "I – I'm not sure. Think I must've hit my head."

"Quickly!" His uncle took him by the wrist. "Let's get you back to the village."

The boy complied meekly.

Littlefellow was determined not to get lost this time. He strode defiantly back the way he had come, crashing through undergrowth regardless of who might hear, determinedly closing his ears to any imagined sounds of pursuit. He hauled Fred along behind him like a piece of baggage. The boy remained in a bewildered state, but as the footbridge came in sight he slowed to a halt.

"Where are we going?" he asked, sounding uneasy.

"Back to the rectory, where I can get a doctor to look you over."

Fred walked on a few more yards, but when they reached the very edge of the ditch, he stopped again. "Uncle, I won't go any further."

Littlefellow looked at him askance. "What do you mean?"

The boy shook his head. He pulled his arm loose and backed up a couple of steps. His face was sallow, haggard. His eyes had widened; they'd become quite glassy.

"Fred," his uncle said, "we need to get medical assistance for you."

"I can't leave."

"What do you mean you *can't*?"

"I just can't."

And now, at last, Littlefellow saw why.

If it was possible for the reverend gentleman to pale on that bright summer's day, he did. If it was possible for his skin to goose-pimple all over, it did.

Slowly, without a word, he retreated across the footbridge until he'd reached the other side, where he halted, gazing mutely. He wanted to speak, but no words were possible. He wanted to pray, but weirdly it seemed inappropriate. In all things, he realised, he was helpless. He spent several minutes simply staring into the harrowed eyes of his nephew, before turning and, with an attitude of combined shock and horror, marching stiffly away across the meadow.

Fred – who had leaked blood onto his shirt not from a gash on his head, but from a small wound at the side of his throat – slunk back into the shadows.

JOHN & JENNY AND THE LUMP: A CAUTIONARY TALE

John Llewellyn Probert

See Jenny. Jenny is a lady. She has a lump. It is right in the middle of her tummy.

"How strange" she says. "It was not here yesterday."

She shows John. John is her husband.

"How strange," John says also. "Does it hurt?"

"No," says Jenny. "Would you like to touch it?"

John touches the lump. It feels like a plum.

The lump can move up.

The lump can move down.

The lump can move from side to side (a little bit).

"You should see the doctor," says John.

"I do not wish to see the doctor," says Jenny. "I expect the lump will go away on its own."

The next day the lump is as big as an orange.

"Does it hurt now?" asks John.

"No," says Jenny, "and the little bumps that are new do not hurt either."

There are eight new little bumps – four on each side. Can you count to eight?

"You must see the doctor now," says John.

John rings the doctor on the telephone.

The doctor comes quickly. He looks at the lump. He presses the lump and its eight little bumps.

The lump moves up.

The lump moves down.

The lump moves from side to side (a little bit).

The doctor is worried. He rings for an ambulance.

The ambulance goes woo-woo. Can you make a noise like that?

See Jenny. She is in the hospital. She is in bed. Jenny is going to have an operation.

John & Jenny and the Lump

John goes to have a drink. He has coffee from a machine. He likes coffee. He drinks it quickly and goes back to Jenny.

Jenny is very quiet.

The lump has gone.

Jenny has a hole in her tummy where the lump was.

John is very upset.

John rings for the nurse.

The lump is sitting on the table by the bed.

It has eight legs and two big claws at the front and lots of tiny tiny eyes and it is as big as a big red grapefruit.

Do you like grapefruit? The juice of a grapefruit is sharp.

The claws of the lump are sharp as well, but in a different way.

The lump is on John. The lump likes John. John does not like the lump.

"Get off, lump," he cries.

See John hit the lump.

See the lump fall on the floor.

See the lump upside-down. Its legs wiggle in the air. It looks funny.

John stamps on it.

Stamp. Stamp. Stamp.

See the gooey mess on the floor.

John needs to wash his hands. They are all red.

The nurse comes in.

See the nurse see John with his red hands and the mess on the floor and Jenny all quiet in the bed.

See the nurse scream.

Hear the nurse scream.

"Ahhhhhhhhhhhhhhhhhhhhhhhhhhhhhh!"

See John. John is in prison.

John has a lump.

See the nurse. The nurse is on the ward. The nurse has a lump.

See the doctor. The doctor is at home. The doctor has a lump.

185

The lumps move up.
The lumps move down.
The lumps move from side to side (a little bit).
Can you guess what they are?
Have you got one yet?

IN AN OLD OVERCOAT

Frank Nicholas

Some people just make it too easy, Raymond half smirked and half sighed to himself. He slipped into a seat in the almost empty train coach and listened to the fitful snoring from directly behind him. It was a combination of a whisper and a groan and it rose above the clatter of the wheels on the track. There was no other sound in the coach, whose only other occupants were a bored looking blonde at the far end, her nose in a celebrity magazine, and the fat Goth halfway down the aisle with his headphones in. That left only Raymond and the sleeping old man in the seat behind him. The old man with the coat.

It had been a good enough day, all in all, for Raymond. A few purses and wallets at the station, an iPod and a decent mobile that might fetch a few notes if Barry was in a generous mood. Which he usually was, providing the pigs were flying low under a bright blue moon.

Raymond was still mildly hacked off that the bloke in the suit, Briefcase Guy with the mobile and the voice, hadn't been carrying more than a fiver and some change. Forty minutes he'd sat behind him and his phone and his voice, having to listen to his ceaseless bragging about this trip to Paris and that jaunt to New York and how he'd dropped a grand at the roulette wheel and picked up double at the card tables. You know the thing, real wanker talk. Raymond didn't know who Briefcase was trying to impress down the other end of the call but the sighing, fidgeting and irritated glances from any passenger within a twenty seat radius made it clear that none of the passive recipients of the news were bowled over by it. And, when he'd finally got off, minus his wallet, there was a visible relaxing all around.

Raymond had moved through to the next carriage as soon as the crowds had thinned out. It was getting gloomy outside.

The suburban rush-hour commuters would already be home or off to the pub or wherever else they were headed. The only ones left were those whose journeys took them to farther flung destinations. Like the old man with the coat.

It was quite an expensive coat. Raymond had been able to tell from halfway down the coach. A heavy, black overcoat, the edges sharp, in good shape. It was sitting up, almost to attention, where it had been left in the empty seat next to the old man. His wrinkled face was resting against the window and Raymond had heard his snores as he got within a few rows of him.

Just too bloody easy.

The toilets were at this end of the coach. All Raymond needed to do was get up as if he was going for a pee. As he passed the coat, a quick in and out. No mess. No fuss. Here goes...

Bollocks! Some fin-headed lanky streak from the next coach had just gone into the toilet. And Raymond was halfway to his feet and his nerve was up. A quick turn of the head. Magazine Blonde was texting someone. Fat Goth – how much must he be sweating in all that black and under that make-up? – had his eyes closed. That voice in Raymond's head, the instinct voice that had grown strong after years of picking just the right moment, said, 'Now!' And he knew to trust that voice. It had kept him right so far. So, 'Now!' it was!

He swiveled in his seat, reaching out a hand. If anyone came by, that hand would be tapping the sleeping old guy's shoulder and he'd be asking him if he had the right time. But no-one was coming past, so he reached for the coat, nudged the lapel to give him a look inside for pockets. The material parted, a glimpse of dark silk inside. A soft yielding under his fingertips, like touching a cobweb. A shifting greyness, all sticky strands. And a glare from the eyes that opened at the centre of it, burning back at him, wetly and yellowly.

What? thought Raymond. His fingers were already well within the folds of cloth before he registered what he was

188

seeing. Christ, what was seeing him! Round, yellowed eyes that even now were glaring at him from within the lined and wrinkled folds of a shrunken, greyish face. From inside this empty old overcoat, a face was looking at him.

His cry was swiftly transformed into a cough and he turned his head quickly enough to see that he was being ignored. The old man made a whimpering sound. It might have been fear or excitement, depending on what kind of dream he was having. Raymond tried to will his heart to beat quieter, but the old man didn't budge, not even when a thin line of drool began making its way from the sagging mouth toward his shoulder. And when Raymond turned his eyes back to the coat, when he forced them to look, there was nothing there except a dark blue silk lining.

Then the lights came, moving steadily into view as the train slowed. There was a muffled rushing noise then the snap of the lock in the toilet. People were waiting outside on the oncoming platform. The toilet door was opening. And there was Raymond with his hand inside someone else's coat. The instinct voice yelled, 'Move!'

His fingers closed on leather. Before he knew it, he'd grabbed the wallet and it was in his own pocket and he was on his feet, backing away, still looking, searching, for some wizened thing lurking in the dark folds.

An arm coiled round him, sudden and unexpected. He turned, jolted, and there was a face bearing down on him. Raymond blinked quickly, wiping away the image of greying, shriveled features. What they were replaced with was the pink and pissed off face of the guy who was just trying to get past him and into the coach when Raymond had backed into him. He mumbled an apology and squeezed past, making for the exit.

He could still hear the old man's whimpering breathing. Did he know about... whatever it was? Should he tell him? "By the way, mate, I couldn't help noticing, when I was picking your pocket, that there's something horrible living inside your overcoat." Yeah, so that when they nicked him, he could plead diminished responsibility? Best leave it!

Then the door was hissing closed. Raymond jabbed at the button so hard he nearly broke his finger. He swore, then jabbed again. Somebody was sure to have noticed that he was acting a bit... well, wrong and he didn't want to be on the train when they put two and two together. He also didn't want to be on the train with him! With the old man with the coat.

The doors hissed open before he could damage his fingers irreparably. And, let's face it, Raymond's nimble fingers were his livelihood. He more fell than leapt onto the platform, winding himself, just to add to the hammering heart he'd already got from the lift, from the collision in the aisle, from the... From the thing that wasn't there! He decided that, there and then, under the buzzing yellow lights on the empty platform, as the train shunted off out of view. It was not, could not have been, definitely was not there. Adrenaline, a trick of the light, stop bloody thinking about it, would you?

There was a bench. If he could just make it to that and get his breath back. He could feel the leather gripped tightly in his pocket. God, he hoped there was more in it than Briefcase's haul after all this. Was he giggling? Then he felt his wrist tightening. There was a tingling racing up his arm. Which one was that, a heart attack or a stroke?

The bench was really three metal seats on a single support, so he was half lying, half crushed against the arm rest when he started to retch, He saw the mulched remains of his Prêt A Manger sandwich again before closing his eyes and trying to decide if the God he wasn't sure he even believed in would be offended if he picked now to start praying.

Minutes passed. A wind was blowing down the manmade, brick-lined valley around the station. Raymond had already thought of masks and monkeys and intensely horrible faces of crumpled linen. Linen? A vague memory of some creepy story he'd read as a kid. But the lining was silk, surely? A mask was possible, but creepy. Why would an old man like that be carrying a mask around? And a monkey was less plausible but potentially even creepier.

Oh, to hell with it! He needed to get home. Twenty minutes and he'd be through the door, into the fridge and halfway through a can of lager, with the oven on to heat up. The thought distracted him cheerily, so much so that he nearly didn't notice he was at completely the wrong station and well over twenty minutes from home.

He strode toward the timetable board expecting to be disappointed and was. Nothing for an hour. He was cold and, after losing his lunch, hungry, and his arm ached, though he checked his reflection in the station window and guessed that he didn't look like he'd had a stroke.

There was a payphone and where there was a payphone, bingo, there were taxi numbers. Raymond wasn't bothered about the fare, he just wanted home. Anyway, that had looked like an expensive coat. He could only hope the old man's wallet confirmed his professional appraisal.

His hand came out of his pocket, still clenched shut, but empty. He looked at it dumbly for a few seconds, almost as if it was someone else's hand, then he thrust it back into the pocket. The iPod and mobile were still there but there sure as hell wasn't any wallet.

Bollocks! He must have dropped it when he smacked into that guy in the aisle. Or it had fallen out when he'd done his *Fall Guy* leap from the stationary train. All that for nothing!

Between the purses and wallets he'd managed not to drop like a twat, plus Briefcase's fiver, he guessed he should have enough to at least get him to the right town. It was only when he was getting into the cab that he remembered the feel of leathery hide between his fingers as he'd lain across the seats. It hadn't fallen on the ground there. He'd checked twice before calling the taxi and once after. So what did that leave? Had he maybe passed out and some chancer had wandered down, clocked him and ripped him off? Robbing a sleeping man? How bloody small could some people get?

At home, later and less hungry than he'd expected, he crawled off to bed and slept. Or he would have done but, every time he closed his eyes, in the darkness that waited behind his lids, another pair of yellow eyes opened.

The eyes went away and Raymond did sleep, finally, but only after most of the second six-pack. And, when he woke up, mouth like a desert and bladder struggling to contain an ocean, he couldn't remember what he had dreamt about. But, for some uncomfortable reason, he felt he should be glad that he couldn't remember.

The face that squinted back at him from the bathroom mirror was a greener shade of pale and the bags under the eyes and the furrows in the brow matched the general description of a man suffering from whatever was going on in his head right then. Maybe, once he'd showered, scraped his chin and his tongue and had a cup of coffee, he might just pass as a corpse. Still, he consoled himself that he looked better than Barry. Barry was the master of pained expressions, particularly whenever anyone tried to get him to part with a few extra quid. Which was something Raymond had to look forward to in a few hours time.

"Barry had to give up dipping because of his affliction," Sam told him later. "When you're as tight fisted as him, you can't get your fingers apart to lift a wallet, can you?" She'd come round for dinner that night, like she did every Thursday and, after the usual pleasantries, "You look crap, you been out on the sauce?" she'd curled up next to Raymond for pizza and some chat.

Raymond had once joked that he'd gone after Samantha's handbag and ended up stealing her heart instead. And, when she'd finished telling him what a twat he was for even thinking up a line like that, let alone saying it aloud, and had wiped the tears of laughter from her eyes, he'd sworn silently never to use the line again. Actually, when Sam eventually did find out that he'd genuinely been after her handbag that night he'd approached her in the club, they'd split up, for a while but not for good. For Sam was the kind of girl who knew when she was onto a good thing and, until one came along, she reckoned she might as well still see Raymond for a few laughs and what have you.

Not that there were many laughs that night and Sam was beginning to think what-have-you might be off the menu. "So, Dodgy Barry ripped you off on the phone? He rips everyone off. That's why they call him Dodgy Barry. You knew he was going to, so stop looking so grim, would you?"

Raymond, who hadn't realised he was looking grim, nodded and smiled. He hadn't realised because he'd drifted away from his own complaining about the fat fence and had been having some kind of daydream. When he'd snapped back to attention under Sam's annoyed yet concerned gaze, the details of the dream flew apart like a cobweb in a gale. There was just that sensation of helplessness, as if the world, or his part of it at least, was getting so much bigger. Too big for him, at any rate.

"You're right," he said, groping for the last words of Sam's to have registered with him. "I should have gone to Scrupulously Fair Barry, just along the road, but he was out helping kittens across the road and rescuing old ladies from trees."

"Ha, ha, funny," Sam smirked.

He kissed her then and, when their lips parted, he said, "Does that taste funny to you?"

And, from there, it was a quick four-legged shuffle from the sofa to the bedroom, where three out of four Thursdays, as well as the odd Tuesday and Saturday, usually ended up.

Samantha grinned as she tugged Raymond's pullover over his head and began to do the same with his sweatshirt. "How many layers have you got on?" she asked when she saw the hem of his T-shirt poking out.

"Feeling the cold," was the gist of the muffled words that escaped the folds of sweatshirt.

She ran her fingers up his back, making him shiver with what she took for pleasurable anticipation, and was about to say something about soon warming him up when she stopped and quickly pulled her hand away.

"What's up?"

"Turn around."

Raymond's face was halfway into a grin when he spotted the look in Sam's wide eyes. What the hell was that, revulsion? "What? What is it?"

"What's that?" she said. "On your back. Like, I don't know, like leather. And there was something wet. Let me see."

He was already at the full length wardrobe mirror, twisting and turning, trying to get a better glimpse of the patch of wrinkled skin behind his shoulder blade. But the more he twisted, the more his skin folded and flexed. And then Sam was in the way, her shadow stopping him from getting a decent look. Was it grey, that uneven patch? He reached around, angling his hand to scratch it.

"Don't," Sam protested, grabbing his hand away. "You don't want it bleeding. It might spread. Have you seen a doctor about that? It might be skin cancer."

"Thanks for leaping straight to that conclusion," Raymond muttered.

"Sorry." Sam kissed him, softly, mouth closed. "But it looks really, well, horrible."

He tried to return the kiss but her mouth remained tight. "Sorry," she said again, "but I've gone off the idea." And, as he pulled his T-shirt back on, feeling confused by the fact that he was more relieved than angry, she urged him, "You should get that seen to."

And that, though neither of them knew it at the time, was the end of Samantha and Raymond. She left early that night, didn't come round on Saturday and, when Thursday came around again, he made no move toward the bedroom and she didn't insist. She could tell, without asking, that he hadn't done anything about getting it seen to, even though it was clearly playing on his mind. He looked paler, which only made the rings under his eyes look all the darker. As she kissed him on her way out to the taxi, she said, "Get some sleep. And get an appointment."

Raymond smiled at the closed door. Sleep would be good. Should be good. If it wasn't for the things that came with sleep lately. The feelings and the dreams. Something scuttling and spidery and cold under his skin that made him shiver and itch and curl in on himself under layers of duvet that didn't keep the cold out. But how could they, when the cold came from inside?

He wanted to scratch and claw, not just at his back but every inch of his skin. He found himself fantasising at one point about taking one of the kitchen knives and stabbing it into the places where he felt that shifting within his flesh, as if there was a living thing in there he could kill, something black and spiny that he could draw out, twitching, on the point of the blade.

The subcutaneous scuttling only seemed to calm down when he was in his cocoon, wrapped as warm as he could make himself. The washing machine was in use almost constantly, churning round replacement bedding that hung and steamed before radiators that were switched on round the clock. The flat soon took on the humid air of a swamp. And still Raymond wondered how he could sweat so much and still be cold.

The mound of bedding upset him strangely, as if he might crawl inside the heap and find a detached human face, skin like leather, nestling amongst the folds. But he was too cold to resist their embrace for long. If he could just sleep, he knew, the sensations of being invaded from within would cease.

But the dreams, when he did sleep, were worse. He wasn't there in his dreams, at least not as the Raymond he recognised. There were only strangers there. Like the Widow.

He is somewhere dark and warm. In the dreams he is always somewhere dark and warm. The Widow looks in at him, framed in a sudden rectangle of bright light, her face taut, severe. She has an armful of clothes which she hangs mechanically, coat hangers muffled as they clatter together on either side of him. How does he know she is a widow? Because she is dressed in black? Because her face is carefully scrubbed of all make-up? Then she moves aside and he sees the wooden box on the bed. Is that it? No. He'd known before he saw the coffin that this woman, this unknown but naggingly familiar woman, was a widow. It isn't the box, though that brings a pang of longing from somewhere unexpected. If he could just move, just step out of the warmth and darkness. If he could see who is in the box. If he could clamber into it, out of the warmth and darkness, into the cold hardness.

There are others in the room now, shuffling figures in black that block out the drab wallpaper. Whispered words of condolence, clasped hands and stiff embraces. The figures shuffle in and out but the Widow remains. And one other. A man in a well-cut suit whose eyes rarely stray from the black-clad woman. At moments, when he knows no-one is looking, his hangdog expression betrays a flicker of a smile. Not the wistful smile of someone remembering times never to return; the type Raymond remembers his mother breaking into between the sobs after his old man's third and final heart attack. No, these are secret, gloating, thin-lipped smiles, meant for no-one. Unless, perhaps, the smiling man knows Raymond is there, in the warm, dark space in the corner of the room.

There is something familiar too, about that secretly smiling man. He is dark and vaguely handsome and well maintained. The type of man you'd remember meeting. Yet Raymond can't put his finger on where he's seen him. Hah! He isn't even sure he has fingers to put on anything. He can see or feel no part of his body, as though he is just a face, hanging there in the darkness.

And then a voice whispers, in his ear or in his mind, that of course he knows his own brother. It is a new voice. Not the instinct voice that he knows so well. It is softer, subtler, yet more dangerous. And Raymond feels those yellow eyes burning somewhere nearby even as he screws his own eyes up tightly and forces himself to remember that he doesn't have a brother. And, when he opens them again, the mourners are gone, leaving only the Widow and the Secret Smiler. And, of course, whoever is in the box. And the smiles are no longer secret. They are there on display, vicious and triumphant, as they look down on the late lamented. And the embrace that follows is not one of the bereaved comforting the bereaved. It is tight and passionate, as if pent-up from years of being furtive and hidden. The greedy, jealous bastard! He'd always suspected something was going on with her but not with his own...

"I don't have a brother, I don't have a brother, I don't know these people!" But before he can convince himself of something he's never questioned before, the Widow is reaching into the dark beside him, grabbing rustling bundles and throwing them into a pile. All fake grief and genuine passion gone, determined and businesslike. Then a word from the man who is NOT his brother. Smiling again, holding garments to himself, checking to see if they fit. To see if he can slip into them as comfortably as he's slipped into my bed and into my...

No, no wife! No brother! No!

Everything has taken on a yellowish tinge, as if Raymond is watching things unfold through thickening, oily liquid. And, when the smiling man, an approving, avaricious smile on his lips, the same one he'd shown when regarding the Widow, moves forward and reaches out and causes the warm darkness to bunch and rustle around Raymond, he sees, finally, something he recognises about the face. Something he recalls from his own life outside the dream. Just for a second, he sees the face loll and sag and a trickle of drool run from the corner of the slack mouth. Though the dribbling and the greyness of the skin are only a flash, the mouth remains slack, startled, and Raymond sees that when his smiling betrayer had reached into the darkness, Raymond had reached out to him, gripping his wrist. And, no, he now sees, he doesn't have fingers after all.

Then the darkness closed in and rolled out again and

Raymond was back in his nest of sodden duvets, gasping and heaving and sick with his own stink.

He clawed his way to the shower, stumbling over dropped clothes and God alone knew what else. The warm water began to drain away what felt like a thickening second skin of built up sweat grease. He felt different in some difficult to fathom way. Not better, exactly, but as if some sort of fever had broken.

The face in the mirror was drained and grey and shadowed, though he told himself the thick growth of stubble had something to do with that. But it wasn't his face that told the most vivid tale of how ill he had been, it was his body. While he'd never been one for the gym, he'd always kept himself in shape. After all, he never knew when he was going to need to do a runner and, if he wasn't fast enough, when he was going to have to fight his way out of trouble. Wiry was the word. Though it wasn't the word he'd use to describe what he saw when he looked down at his own naked body. Scrawny. Shrivelled. With his stick-thin arms and distended belly, spidery seemed apt.

He wiped more steam from the mirror, staring hard at his own reflected form. He blinked twice. First time in surprise, then in relief. He recognised himself in his reflection. A bit flabbier round the edges but, then, he'd been in bed for... Christ, how long was it? He examined himself for long moments. His eyes must have been playing tricks before. A mild hallucination, probably, brought on by the fever. Just like the dreams. He'd never been so ill before. Maybe it was some kind of flu. It wouldn't have surprised him. You never know what you're going to pick up on public transport, do you?

Turning, inspecting his ribs and back, he saw himself shiver, his shoulders tensing in the glass, as the unbidden image of a shrivelled face scuttled to mind and opened its yellow eyes. As he tried to shrug off the image, he saw the yellow eyes still there in the mirror.

He span round so fast he tumbled over and nearly cracked

his head on the bath, remembering too late that he was ill and weakened. The eyes were gone. Not that they had ever been there. Because, if they had been, he realised, they would have been peering out from the shadow of his shoulder blade.

The skin around his shoulder still felt odd and patchy, but no matter how he angled himself, he couldn't see any change. A rash or something to do with the illness. Then he was suddenly aware of how cold he was, the steam filling the bathroom having turned chilly and misty.

Clothed again, he stumbled back through the debris of his sitting room toward the wreckage of the kitchen. His stomach practically screamed at him as he lurched to the fridge in search of something to fill himself again. Whatever food he had bought before his confinement could no longer answer to that description and he nearly gagged at the stink when he opened the fridge door.

In fact the entire flat stank to high heavens and, after he turned off the oppressive heating, he was soon opening windows in every room to let out the moist and humid fug and let in some of the noise from the outside world.

Moving as quickly as he could while still maintaining his balance, Raymond hauled bundles of damp laundry from the washer and thrust more sweat-soiled clothing inside in its place, switching the machine on even when he realised he'd long since run out of washing powder. The sink was quickly piled with dishes, though he could scarcely force himself to look at the plates and figure out what the blue-furred lumps had once been. Bin bags overflowed with snatched up rubbish. If Sam was to see the place like this…

He remembered, then, and the warmth of the tears that sprang to his eyes took him by surprise. How long had it been since he'd seen her? His mobile phone lay on the sofa, battery run flat. He would have to wait for it to charge up before he could even check if she'd called.

From the pile of mail, the letters nearer the top increasingly red-lettered and angry looking, he guessed that the door hadn't been opened in the last few weeks; at least no further than the space it takes to pass a takeaway meal through. This was confirmed by the heap of discarded wallets he'd clearly ploughed through to find the money for each forgotten meal.

He sat for a while, his eyes flicking between the slowly expanding power bar on the phone and the pile of mail. He twice, three times, reached out to pluck up an envelope and open it, but something about them scared him. They came from Out There, somewhere, and he was not up to dealing with Out There yet. After waiting still and patient for hours for the phone to power up, he still paused when the bar hit full and waited some more.

The traffic noise outside had become deafening. And there were voices in the street, loud and harsh. He closed the windows, trembling in the slight coolness of the draught, then grabbed another jumper from the pile that was next in line for the washing machine, rubbing absently at what might have been an egg stain down the front of it as he went to switch on the heating again.

He trembled again when he finally lifted the phone and was told he had over a dozen missed calls, only three of which were the usual junk from his network provider. Sam's calls went from worried that he wasn't answering to angry to worried again to a tearful, furious, lengthy 'Screw you' that he cut off before the end. Barry's, on the other hand, started off with his usual jovial insults, though the joviality became a lot more transparent as the calls went on.

Raymond was going to have to go to work. Not because he was scared of Dodgy Barry. The fat misanthrope was all crude bluster and only resorted to violence if it was unavoidable, and if he could find someone stupid or psychotic enough to con into perpetrating it. The idea of going Out There, though, made his stomach coil up into so many knots that he barely made it to the bathroom in time.

When he finally left the flat, telling himself that a stack of empty wallets wasn't going to refill his stomach, he already knew it was a mistake. He was in no state to run if he had to get away sharpish and, given that he could barely carry the weight of the various layers he was wearing, he certainly wasn't up to scrapping his way out of bother. Still, if he did get caught with his hand in the wrong pocket, he reckoned his shambling appearance would convince anyone he was just a confused wino and he'd probably get off with a minor kicking.

The walk to the station was colder than he'd expected and the chill in the air was clearly affecting the moods of those people he was forced to share the street with. Bull-necked men and acid-faced women glowered all around him. Even those who laughed and chatted seemed to be hiding a depth of anger behind a brittle surface as they loomed past him.

Raymond was glad to get into the coach, past the throng of seething strangers. He just wanted to get a seat to himself where he could huddle and gather his strength. Perhaps at the end of the carriage, just past the old man. The one with the coat. The one who slumped there, undisturbed after all this time, his feet anchored in a slowly growing mound of drained paper cups, discarded newspapers, plastic sandwich wrappers and uncollected tickets. His grey skin was all the greyer for the dust that clung to it. His gaping mouth, the drool now dried and flaking, was spanned by a mass of cobwebs. But it wasn't the old man that made Raymond whimper in the back of his throat. It was the coat, which was propped up beside him, warm and dark. And empty!

Empty. Just like the seat. There was no old man, no coat, and Raymond was glad to drop into the space before his legs gave out from under him. At least the carriage was warm. He closed his eyes, willing the image of that web-coated cavernous mouth to fade.

The old chest is warm and he feels snug in its dark confines. Or he does until the sky opens up above him and two pink circles gaze down at him from the light with wide, bright eyes. Round and pink and so alike they can only be brothers. The smaller one looking anxiously around, beseeching the older,

201

panicking in case they are caught, "Daddy always said not to—"

"Daddy's not well, he can't stop us, look, a shiny medal, wouldn't you want one of these?" The older boy coaxing, teasing the smile out that was always hiding behind the youngster's solemn expression. "It's just a game, Daddy won't know."

The younger sibling stretches in, so far he almost looks set to topple into the wooden chest where Daddy... where Raymond lies. A huge grin and a cry of, "I want to wear this one," brings a frown to his brother's face that is less out of fear of being discovered and more out of annoyance that this little upstart has made first pick.

"I'm taking it," his tone is final, it's not for discussion. "You'll have to choose again." There are the beginnings of sobs in the young brother's voice as he pleads, but the older of the two is stone faced. "You always want what I have, well you're not getting this." And, as the youngster stomps off, jealous, threatening to tell Mummy and Daddy, the older brother defiantly reaches into the chest, safe in the knowledge that fear will stop him telling Daddy how they were playing where they were forbidden.

Oh, but Daddy knows. Daddy sees you, Out There, outside the warmth and darkness. Daddy sees you through his yellow eyes. And Daddy's got you!

The air explodes. The sky is on fire while the earth below is a freezing mass of mud and limbs and blood. With all the explosions above and all around, the terrified, ragged breath of the young soldier is heard only by Raymond, as the young man delves into the darkness beside him, hauling and jostling, his face hardened with desperation. His hands come out and there is blood on them. He wipes dark smears onto his already filthy uniform before returning to his task, pulling out the lifeless mass that Raymond has shared the darkness with.

The young soldier shivers constantly, through fear or cold, Raymond doesn't know. But he is welcome to join him in the warm darkness. The sky explodes again and the young man sees into the dark folds that he has struggled to retrieve from the fallen foe, and screams as Raymond reaches out to beckon him in.

"Are you okay, mate?"

Raymond tried to speak as the uniformed man gently prodded his shoulder. The words that came out were not what he expected.

The uniformed man, who Raymond eventually saw as a ticket collector, not an enemy soldier, shook his head, not understanding. Raymond spoke again, slowly, deliberately, his own voice and his own language this time. He explained that he'd been having a daydream and, yes, he had a ticket and, yes, he knew he didn't look at all well and, yes, he knew he should get home to his bed.

What the hell was that? He'd never fallen asleep while working before, even in his partying days. If he was that out of it he wasn't going to risk a fumbled dip. The only thing was to get home as quickly as possible, before the peak times with all those impatient, snarling strangers, with their various odours that he had never noticed before; acrid, greasy, sickly, the smell of things decaying while still living. He could maybe try again tomorrow and just get himself home and call Sam tonight. Should he call her? Perhaps it would help to talk to someone. He could always talk to Sam.

As it turned out, he couldn't talk to Sam at all. At first, he was cheered when he heard the obvious relief in her voice that he'd called. But, when the relief changed gear rapidly into suspicion and then anger, he grew suddenly more scared of her than he had been of all the unhappy people Out There in the cold.

Where were the words? He always had words. Sometimes they were the wrong words, stupid, glib, nonsensical words that sometimes made Sam laugh for their sheer ridiculousness. But, when all she wanted him to do was talk to her, explain things to her, he had no words left. The only words that were in his head were in a voice that he was only recently becoming accustomed to. It was a voice that used its words to tell him that Sam was, after all, just another one from Out There, in the cold, and could he really trust her? Of course he could trust her, Raymond protested, inwardly, helplessly, silently. And, after minutes of his silence, Sam had no words left for him and he sat, looking at the dead phone, that other voice having stilled now, leaving him very alone.

It was another two days before the increasingly painful hunger forced him out of the flat again. There was enough money in his account to buy food for the next week or two. After that, though, he would have to think of something. He'd even, in his desperation, thought about asking Barry for a loan. But a petty thief who'd lost his nerve was going to be as much use to Dodgy Barry as a hook to hang his scruples on. So he'd finally phoned his mum, safe in the knowledge that she was several cities away so wouldn't feel the urge to rush round and bring the traces of Out There into his sanctuary. He knew that he was in for that unspoken but ever-present tone of disappointment and disapproval, so he kept the call short, just long enough to be sure that she really would put some cash into his account, just till he had found his feet again. He wasn't convinced that he'd pulled off the optimism he'd strived for in this claim, but he didn't give her long enough to question it.

In those two days, the world Out There had done something very strange. It had shifted and grown out of proportion, the buildings looming more and more menacingly around and above him, in the same way that he now noticed all people seemed to do. The streets between his flat and the nearest shop with a cash machine had grown longer, more packed with scowling outsiders and growling cars. He was horribly aware that the in-built camera at the cash machine was examining him minutely as he fumbled over his PIN, but he couldn't muster up the courage to glare defiantly back at it in case he found it was watching him through a single yellow eye.

The bright lighting in the shop hummed with an intense

whine and had a white, icy glare to it that made him shudder. And he was convinced that the scruffy-haired student-type at the check-out was watching him with a glaring intensity, as if he could see whatever it was that was growing inside Raymond. The beeping of the barcode scanner was a barely disguised scream of electronic disgust and the boy snatched the note and dropped the change into his trembling hand, careful not to make contact. And, when he got back to the security of the flat and realised he'd either forgotten or left behind half the things he wanted or needed, the thought of venturing out once more into that icy cavern, with its jostling, impatient denizens, reduced him to a tearful ball on the floor.

There were more fitful dreams over the next night. Or nights. Raymond had lost the concept of time somewhere or had it stolen from him. In amongst the fragments of increasingly dim and foggy scenes that unfolded, he retained memories... of a snatched cloak from a crumpled form in dismal, ordure-stinking alleyway... of a robe that unfurls and divulges some horror that causes its pious would-be wearer to recant his God... a rough sack cloth that drags its occupant into its own, coarse depths... a ragged fur, matted and reeking of odours both animal and human, but warm, so very warm, in the dark at the back of the cave...

But, more vivid than these snared, yellow-tinged dream snatches, he sees a man, young and wiry, smug faced, eyes darting slyly, leaning in closer, extending a greedy hand forward, deftly plucking the folds of surrounding, silky darkness back, so that Raymond's yellow gaze can fall more fully upon him. So familiar and recent yet so oddly alien when witnessed from this angle. Then the look of surprised, revolted horror as the wiry man, no longer smug, pulls his hand from the folds and finds it withered and skeletal, as if layers of skin have been peeled away, leaving his every nerve exposed to the cold outer world. He turns grey, his wiry frame collapsing in on itself, leaving a rumpled pile of clothing in the aisle, apparently empty, until something inside it squirms.

The world outside, as overgrown and overcrowded and overawing as it was, had to be better than crawling into the dark with these dreams as his only company and, as soon as the strength returned to Raymond's limbs, he dragged himself down the stairs and into the street below.

Oh, but it was cold and the dreams were so warm and no-one could touch him there. Not until he was ready to touch them. To change them and reduce them and show them the world they wandered through in its starkness.

Raymond closed the door to the street for the last time. Did he drop the key? He didn't think to search for it. He wasn't going back in there, back to the whispering dreams. If he could just keep warm. Just keep moving. That was it. Just keep moving and keep himself awake.

It was only after he'd passed a figure in the street that a flicker of recognition he'd felt grew to include a name. Samantha? It was Sam. Sam, with her bright eyes and warm smell. Sam, who he could always talk to, even though she was from Out There! Sam! He thought to turn back, reach out to her, to say her name. But the thought that she wouldn't know him, wouldn't see him, was there. After all, she hadn't even spared him a second glance as he'd shuffled past. His mouth opened to form the name, hung wordlessly, then closed again. Avoid looking at people, something told him. Avoid touching them. Just keep moving.

He'd found the coat... where? In a doorway, discarded by a tramp who had more pride than to wear it? Stolen from somewhere? No, it was the nice woman in the little shop full of old clothes who had insisted he take it, he looked so cold, even on such a lovely day. Nice lady? She was trying to trick him. It was freezing. He could see the lying, angry giant lurking behind the pretence of concern in those eyes, waiting to burst through. He wouldn't let her touch him, though, when she handed him the garment. She didn't deserve to be infected. To be touched by the truth. She hadn't earned it.

Where had he got the coat? Was it even the same coat?

None of his clothes seemed like his anymore. Nothing seemed to fit. He got so confused these days. It had to be the cold. His skin seemed so thin and blue and his veins showed through so clearly, grey, wriggling and twitching under the surface.

Raymond... Was that his name? It sounded right but he couldn't be sure of anything, could he? Couldn't trust anything, not even his own memories. Particularly since he wasn't convinced they actually were his own memories anyway, these dreams that reached back ever further into a rustling, warm darkness.

The coat bothered him. It wasn't his, he didn't think. It was too big and it smelled of old, old men. He shrugged himself out of it easily as he shifted on the park bench and looked up at the sun and wondered why its heat wasn't reaching him. Perhaps it had forgotten him, just like he had, himself.

He sat like that for a long time, the rough looking, wiry man on the bench. The man with the coat. The man who was once someone called Raymond but was no more, since who and what he was had crawled out, perhaps out of his yawning, spittle flecked mouth, and had gone to find a place of warmth. The rough looking, wiry man was empty and, soon enough, would be found and taken away.

But, in an old overcoat, something that contained a trace of Raymond was waiting, knowing that eventually, as they always did, someone from Out There would reach into the folds and he could invite them to join him in the warm darkness.

THE LOOKER

Julia Lufford

Friday night and the moon was full. And Johnny Vallance was hunting.

A new town, a new hunting ground. Somewhere where Johnny was unknown, somewhere where his reputation hadn't preceded him.

Loud music, flashing lights. The club was full of pretty girls, and even more blokes trying to get in their hot pants. Plenty of competition for Johnny, but he was confident; his charms never failed him. He knew he could have any girl there. But he didn't want just any girl, he wanted the right girl.

He bought a drink and leaned nonchalantly against the bar, surveying the crowd.

Blondes, brunettes, redheads. Tall, short, slim, curvy. Yes, lots of girls. Some were already eyeing him up. But none of them were what he was looking for.

He bought another pint and went on the prowl. Moving among the gyrating dancers, looking for the right girl.

It was the summer of love, and love could be had for free, but finding the right girl was getting harder. Especially in a club like this. He could have looked elsewhere, there were plenty of girls who would fulfil part of his needs. But that wasn't good enough – she had to be a looker, too.

Suddenly: there! There she was – a dolly bird wearing a black and white PVC mini-dress and Kinky Boots – dancing around a handbag with a couple of her friends. Aged about eighteen, long blonde hair, blue eyes, pretty face, nice figure. Oh, she was a looker, all right.

The song came to an end, and the girl and her friends decided they weren't going to dance to the next record. They began to make their way towards the bar. Johnny took a deep breath – yes, she was the one – satisfied, he moved in for the kill.

"Got a light?" he asked stepping into her path and separating her from her two friends.

"Oh, yeah, sure."

The girl rummaged in her bag, and produced a lighter.

"Want one?" Johnny offered.

"Mmm, please."

Cigarettes lit, Johnny asked, "Can I buy you a drink?" A simple opening, he knew he didn't need to use a cheesy chat-up line.

The girl quickly appraised his handsome features – very dishy, she thought. "Oh, yes, go on then, I'll have a Babycham, please."

Johnny ordered her drink and another pint for himself.

"Thanks," she said. "It's groovy here, isn't it?"

Johnny grinned. "It sure is, babe."

"I haven't seen you at the Love Inn before."

"No, I'm new in town. The name's Johnny."

"Hi Johnny. I'm Carol."

"Pleased to meet you, Carol."

"New, hey? Maybe I could show you the sights sometime."

"I'd like that." Johnny grinned, eyeing the swell of her breasts.

"Oi! Cheeky." Carol laughed.

A new tune started up. "Ooh, this is one of my favourites," Carol said.

"Well come on then, let's dance." Johnny said, leading her onto the dance floor.

"Whoo, I'm all about go-goed out." Carol giggled.

"Let's get another drink. Same again?"

"Please."

Back at the bar, Carol asked, "So what do you do with yourself, Johnny?"

"I'm an artist."

"Oh wow, cool!"

"What about you?"

"I work in a boutique."

"I was thinking maybe you could model for me sometime."

"I only do nude," Carol said, straight-faced, and then burst out laughing.

"Funny that," Johnny grinned, "so do I!"

"Would you like to come back to mine?" Her voice was a little breathless.

"Yeah, babe. I'd like that very much."

"Well, this is it."

"Nice pad."

"Sorry about the mess. My flatmate Lucy designs and makes clothes," Carol explained. "She's always leaving material and stuff lying around." She picked up a large pair of scissors that had been left on the couch.

"It's cool. To be honest I didn't come to check out the décor. And anyway, I'm sure your bedroom is much tidier."

Smiling, Carol took his hand. "It's through here."

In the glow of a lava lamp, their clothes were soon shed, and together they fell onto the bed.

"Be gentle – it's my first time."

"Don't worry, baby, I'll never hurt you; I love you."

"I love you too, Johnny."

As he entered her, Carol gave a whimper and then a cry. But as he moved within her, Carol was soon gasping and crying in pleasure.

The next morning, as she got dressed, Carol complained, "I wish I didn't have to go to work. Will I see you tonight?"

"Sorry, babe," Johnny shrugged, sitting up in bed.

"Oh." Disappointed, Carol asked, "How about tomorrow, then? We could spend all of Sunday together."

"We could, but we're not going to," Johnny said callously.

"Oh, are you painting or something?"

Johnny sighed. "Come on, babe. We've had some fun, but

that's all it was."

"What!?" Carol was incredulous.

Johnny lit a cigarette. "It was a one night stand, nothing more."

"Is that all it was for you?"

"Of course."

"But you said you loved me."

"And I did, like no other man before. But that's your lot. Why would I want to be tied down at my age?"

Carol was crying now. "I thought you'd marry me."

"You stupid cow!" Johnny's laugh was full of scorn. "Marry you? Why would I want to marry you? I never want to see you again."

"But..." Carol seemed lost for words. "But you said you loved me."

"Look, you're a pretty girl but you've lost your appeal."

"Lost my appeal? What do you mean?"

"Talk about dumb blondes!" Johnny was up out of bed now, pulling on his clothes. "I'll spell it out shall I?" He threw aside the bedcovers to reveal the sheet stained with blood. "Your virginity. I like shagging virgins!"

"You bastard!" Carol yelled.

"Oh come on, you enjoyed it as much as I did. 'Oh, Johnny. Oh yeah, Johnny. Yes, Johnny,'" Johnny mocked. He began to cry and gasp, mimicking the cries she had made in the throes of passion.

"Bastard!"

"I don't suppose you're on the pill, are you? Better make sure you take one, or you could end up with a little bastard of your own." Sneering, Johnny bent to pull on his boots.

Carol seized a vase; and struck him a blow to the back of his head. "Bastard!"

When Johnny regained consciousness he found he was securely tied to a chair. "What is this? Let me go!"

"I'm sorry if I hurt you, Johnny," Carol said.

Johnny struggled to free himself. "Why the hell did you...?"

"You hurt me with the things you said earlier. But I still love you, and I forgive you."

"Come on, babe, let me go and I'll forgive you too."

"We can still be together, we don't even have to get married," Carol continued, seemingly unaware that Johnny had spoken.

The ropes had been tied tight. Johnny was unable to loosen them.

"Sure, sure. Just untie me, now."

"I love you, Johnny."

"And I love you, too!"

"Really, Johnny?"

"Yeah, babe. Just cut me loose and I'll show you how much I love you."

Carol had picked up her flatmate's scissors.

"Good idea, babe. Cut me free," he urged.

Carol moved closer. She bent and kissed his eyes.

"Hey, what are you doing?"

"This way we can be together."

"You're crazy! Let me go!" Johnny suddenly yelled, struggling violently to escape.

"Together forever," Carol murmured.

Carol's hand moved closer, the scissors getting inexorably nearer. "And you won't even have to see me ever again."

"Please, nooo!" Johnny whimpered; his vision filled with the approaching silver blades. Realising they would be the last thing he would ever see he began to scream.

As the points of the scissors penetrated his eyes, Johnny's tears were red, and his cries did not change to ones of pleasure.

WHAT WE CANNOT RECALL

Gary Fry

That morning everything changed. His mum roused him roughly.

"Come on, Colin. Look sharp. You're going to spend some time with nana."

It was the first he had heard. Yawning, he sat up in the sheets, his pyjamas shielding him from the autumn chill. Daylight poured through the window that had been stripped of curtains, revealing the townscape of housing, mills and grime. Suddenly his clothing was thrown at him.

What was this? *Not* his school uniform. There must be some mistake – mum had gone doolally or something. In his haze Colin remembered something about nana.

"Where'm I going?" he managed, only now seeing his bedroom with a full pair of eyes.

"I just told you," mum snapped back. She was cramming more of his garments from the wardrobe into one of dad's fishing bags. "Nana's waiting for you."

"And granddad?"

"Yes." A pause, then, "Well, he's sick in bed, and you might not get to see him today, but if you're good…"

Mum always left the promise of a treat unelaborated. Colin was only eleven, but he was certain she did this so that he couldn't hold her to her word. She was smart, his mum. Yet so was he.

"Can I take my diary and some stories?"

"Yes. Everything you can fit in the top of here." She turned the bag his way, slapping the space between the ragged lips of its mouth. "We don't want your education to suffer."

As mum left for the rest of the house, Colin clambered into shirt and pants. Whatever the problem was, he determined not to be a hindrance. More bombing, he feared. They'd been warned in assembly yesterday. It might get worse, and for some reason Coventry was a popular target, though perhaps 'popular' wasn't quite the word. Gathering his books he attempted to produce an alternative and then carried his luggage to the lounge. It was a big old house with its own garden. Dad was always telling them how lucky they were, but there was little chance of that today.

Mum was rescuing keys from the bureau. She whirled at the sound of his footsteps. "All set?" she asked, the tails of her coat settling.

"*Unfortunate*," Colin concluded, lost momentarily in thought.

"I beg your pardon?"

He repaired successfully with, "Why do the Germans want to bomb *us*?"

She came across, ruffled his hair. "It's a changing world, son. Everything that seemed natural… just isn't any more."

That meant she didn't understand it, either. But human contact was enough for Colin. He smiled his usual smile, the one that often reassured his mum that everything was fine. She kissed him, and he her back. Then they were ready.

The journey by car was through hectic streets. People rushed around – women, children. Not everybody was lucky enough to have their own transport and it was with a tempered relief that he and mum finally reached the suburbs, the great majority of which was smouldering dust from an attack the previous week. Colin put his head down to address a page; some of his friends had lived in these flattened houses.

Mum must have detected the sullenness of his bearing, because she was asking, "What're you writing, sweetheart?"

He hoisted the open diary for inspection.

"Can't you see I'm driving? Sorry. Temper's not allowed. Read it out to me, would you?"

"It says, 'The world will end soon'," Colin proclaimed in an uncertain voice.

"Is all the spelling correct?" Mum was clearly uneasy with the sentiment, but she played the game well. "Have you

214

checked your dictionary?"

"Yes. And no errors."

"Good." Another pause, clearly in preparation for, "So why dwell on *that* one?"

"I'm not sure if I should add a full stop," finished Colin, and then there was silence. Was mum also wondering?

Buildings gave way to the countryside. Birds, the first he had seen in months, clattered out of trees and the canal paced the road, its murky surface reflecting drab sky. There would be black specks in that water before long, the roar of the combined assault of the Luftwaffe. He hoped his dad was doing as much to frighten the children in Germany, though maybe nothing like this should happen in any nation. It was enough to make Colin cry, as much in anger as in fear or misery.

The car had reached Widen Wye, the tiny village in which nana and granddad lived. After a moment on the single lane flanked by shops, Mum said in a queer voice, "Why don't you write 'ghost town'. Can you spell the first word? Gee, aitch –"

Of course he could: it was only on the cover of his favourite book! This morning, however, the frights had escaped the page. Where was everybody? The pavements had been abandoned. Doors were shut, windows darkened. Of course the news would have travelled by wireless, but what danger was there here? Wasn't that why mum had brought him?

"Let's ask nana and granddad," he said.

"I imagine we'll have to."

The secluded former farmhouse lay beyond woods, of which Colin was secretly afraid. There were altogether too many shadows among the dense accumulation of elm. Entities shifted audibly, and whatever their identity proved to be, it would surely be too late to flee once they grew visible. It wasn't nice even to pass by in the safe car and in the company of mum. He could remember arriving with dad a few years ago: that had been better, but there was no use thinking that way.

Nana was waiting at the front door as the brakes protested.

She was a large cuddly lady whom Colin of course loved, yet who often irritated him by treating him too childishly. Here she came now with her plump arms smothering, the smell of home cooking – the good part! – stamped into her enormous dress. She was on his mum's side of the family. Dad's parents were dead.

"Here's a shiny shilling for my treasure!"

The coin was dropped into Colin's free hand. Had it not occurred to her that with the shops closed, there was nowhere to spend the money? The notion prompted his enquiry.

"Nana, why is the village so empty?"

"What's that?" the older woman asked Colin's mum, as though the boy were incapable of proper explanation. Or maybe she hoped an elder might be less prone to fantasy. There was certainly an element of unrest in her tone. "What are you saying about Widen Wye?"

"Well, there's the curfew and lights out, I realise – but that's later. There's nobody at all about. It seemed very strange when we drove in. Mum, mum, are you all right?"

Nana had clapped one palm to her mouth. She appeared genuinely shaken. "I'm sorry, my – my dear. It's all these rumours of what *they* might have."

"*They?*"

"The Hun. There's talk of such weapons, that do terrible things to your bod—"

"It's just propaganda, mum. You mustn't listen. Our boys know precisely what they're doing."

"No. Yes. Oh, I mean I *don't know*. Something hit the woods last week. Your father went to investigate with several of the other leftover chaps, and he hasn't been right since."

"*Right*? I'd assumed it was just a bug. May I see?"

"Probably best not to disturb him. He's been sleeping in the spare room these past few days. I keep putting my ear to the door – it sounds like a pig in there! Dreadful rough. It's probably nothing, but it worries me. I haven't seen him at all today. I'm reluctant to go in. You know what's he's like."

"A proud man. And not the only one in – from England."

"Oh, here's me prattling on about my woes, when you have… Do *you* have any – *news*?"

Colin had the impression that the grownups were talking around him, because mum answered with renewed purpose. "Not a word. I need to be home in case. I'll visit in a few days. Look after him, won't you? He's missing his…"

"Dee ay dee. Of course he must be."

Their vocal shorthand meant that dad might be alive or dead, that mum was leaving, and that nana had a licence to baby him to her heart's content. He felt angry on all three counts, though mostly because they believed he could be fooled. Before the car raced off, he offered a perfunctory kiss to his mum, and then hefted his bag inside.

Nana had prepared a pie that cheered him while eating. Nevertheless as he washed down the pastry with fresh lemonade he was still out of sorts. He removed his book and set to reading at table, though he knew he wouldn't get far without interruption.

"The ghost stories of Mister James."

"Em Are, nana," he replied, a match for her earlier obliqueness, but then explaining, "Montague Rhodes. He was a professor at a university."

"I'm all in favour of doing well at school, but do you think that kind of material is suitable for a child?"

"These are great stories."

"I'm not sure reading's good for anyone. I mean, look what the so-called educated classes are doing to our planet. Words mess with your head."

"And language is what separates us from the beasts," Colin claimed, having no idea from where he'd derived the statement. In any case he stood and strode to the back door, shutting himself out with 'The Ash-Tree'. Not suitable material! What horrors could the fine writer possibly offer to challenge those of the actual world? More recently Colin had read as a necessary form of escape.

It wasn't long, however, before James's unsettling prose forced him to glance up. The disused farmyard was deserted. Here were the remnants of wooden pens where pigs, long since slaughtered and served as breakfast, had once grunted and squealed. But his gaze was solicited at a further remove – by the woods. In the midday light the shadows therein writhed.

Suddenly the tale seemed rather less appealing. Leaving his collection on the doorstep Colin hurried around the one-storey house, halting unplanned at the curtained window of the spare room. He put an ear to the glass, concentrating. Whatever was wrong with granddad it had affected his nose. His breath came in great wheezing groans. Maybe his mouth had been contaminated, too. At least he wasn't in the second bedroom, where Colin always slept. The condition might be contagious. Nana shouldn't be blamed for not checking on him.

But she'd annoyed Colin in another sense. How could she say that about books? More likely the global conflict was related to the likes of the coin she had given him. Colin fished it from his pocket. Very well: if that were her idea of how the world should go, he would honour it. Surely one of the shops in the village had opened by now. He fled the front yard and charged along the road until he was well out of sight of the house.

There was a shorter route through the woods (dad had walked it with him on a previous visit, in happier times that now seemed only a dream) but Colin was scared. He marched headlong, staring purposefully forwards, the darkness in the peripheries not stirring, not sprawling, not reaching out for him. When he drew abreast a metal signpost announcing WIDEN WYE he exhaled lengthily, his heart rate steadying. He would be with other people soon.

Or would he? How else to assess the peculiar emptiness of the village, the absence of anything other than birdsong, and even that at a wary distance? As he wandered up the street robbed even of transport, he could see his reflection in the blank glass of the facades on either side. It was as if everybody had gone out of business simultaneously. But – was there movement inside the greengrocers? Colin stepped up to the handle, and the door creaked open at his pressure.

There was an aged man standing at the till-point. He was extraordinarily ugly, the lower half of his face protruding, his flesh pinker than a young child's painting of a human to which he less than comfortably bore a resemblance. He wore a white overcoat, and at the ends of the baggy arms, hands worked clumsily together. Was he writing in pen on his left palm? Mum sometimes did that in order not to forget anything important. He appeared to be mumbling the words too, with what little he could summon by way of a voice. It sounded more like the communication of an animal.

Suddenly the parody of a shopkeeper looked across at Colin. The eyes were not the normal shape. The hands went up immediately, the pen flying. There was something wrong with his fingers.

The door had somehow locked – no, it was a puller, and not a pusher. Was the man screeching in his wake? It would be foolish to stop and turn. Colin surged on, taking a left after the bank of shops to enter a residential area. There he hid behind the hedge of the first of a row of terraced houses. These seemed every bit as lifeless, though that was to his advantage: no threat as he anticipated pursuit from the ghoul. But nothing came, and he was free to examine the property.

Was there a face in the upstairs window of the third house up? There must be something wrong with the glass, since the skin appeared to be covered in words. Perhaps they'd had newspaper up as curtains, and the print had been transferred. Whatever the case, he was able to determine that the figure was an old bald man. It must be the beginnings of a beard that made his jaw stick out like that.

Colin edged through the small gardens of the block, thinking hard. Wasn't it likely that all the men he might see would be elderly? Any male able to fight had been conscripted. But that left women and children, and there were none to be seen. The lane bore no vehicles, either. Could Widen Wye have been evacuated without the chaps knowing? And what of nana and grandd—

A hand dropped onto his shoulder. Colin jerked, pulling away. But the fingers retained their grip. He looked down, panic fogging his vision. There were inked words around the knuckles: did one phrase read ONCE WE ALL CARED, and another COMMUNITY AND PEACE GOING – ? The lines formed an elaborate weave upon the hairy pink tissue, though his attention was rather captured elsewhere. In lieu of the standard five, there were *seven* meaty digits.

He shrieked, breaking free on the back of sheer horror. On this occasion he did look back – he had to – and saw a hideous shape leaning out of an opened window. Diminishing daylight lent the man a sallow hue; he scarcely resembled a man at all. He was in a dark suit torn at the neck. His head was that of a pig, cross-fertilised with human stock. The snout was stunted, the eye-sockets oval, the ears thick and pointed. Stiff tufts of hair wired the scalp. Although most of it was misshapen fabric, every visible portion of flesh had been covered with handwritten text. He or it was screaming in either pain or rage – or might that be a call for similar others?

Colin was across the lane before he might make any such discovery. There was no property opposite, just a field that plunged to a black-ragged fringe of trees. To avoid the restless village, there was only this route home to his grandparents. Suddenly he wasn't thinking about his aversion to the woods, nor about his grievance with nana; all he wanted was to be safe, to make sure they were safe, to tell them what he had seen. Without further hesitation he darted into the shadows.

The secret was, dad had explained, to keep straight on. No matter what obstacles lie in your path – dips, hillocks, fallen trunks – never deviate. Above the spiny bones of the interlocking treetops there was sufficient sunlight, however cloud-cloaked, to enable him to orientate. Unseen creatures scuttled upon a bed of dead leaves; insects bombed and

220

whined; the scent of bark was pungent. But Colin wasn't distracted. Even if he were being pursued, he wouldn't be caught.

He'd tramped for long minutes, maybe an hour of them, before he began to suspect, with something like terror, that he was lost. The pattern of the trees was complex and monotonous, the darkness of the late-afternoon lessening his visual range. He attempted to waylay panic by recalling anything useful he had once read. He might follow the path of a stream, but there was no stream. Then tracks, maybe. Certainly the ground appeared to have been navigated recently.

Time passed, the early evening pressing down into the woods, as he trailed a meandering sequence of contours in the soil. Had these been left by animals? Evidently the prints had been made barefoot, though what in the natural world was so burdened by toes? Each step seemed to have double the ordinary count. He was in the process of giving up this hunt – none of the marks could have been left by granddad – when he heard the savage festivities.

He'd come to a clearing in which, to his initial relief, a collection of motorcars was parked. A first silver sliver of moonlight glinted on the bonnets, a welcome respite from the pervasive shadows. *Humans*, thought Colin, and charged forwards, brambles clawing at his shirt. The surface of the space was all shale and wood-chippings, each of the vehicles unoccupied. There must be a gathering on the far side, back inside the woods, for the sounds had grown louder with his movement. Suddenly it wasn't possible to sustain his earlier optimism.

He had crept into undergrowth in front of the transport. Now he could see a dim region whose inhabitants were vaguely illuminated by the perishing embers of a campfire. The odour of charred meat carried on the breeze, though perhaps the roasting was over. Each of the figures – there were perhaps a dozen – was seated on debris and gnawing at gnarled fragments that resembled, yet couldn't be, branches. These were the pink pig-like creatures, one member of which he'd already been introduced to. Baldish, wrinkled, in men's clothes, they slavered over the food, snorting repulsively. All of the flesh on view was covered in microscopic inscriptions. Even from afar, Colin knew these were chaotically penned words.

Had the beasts formerly been the remaining men, those too old for combat, of Widen Wye? It seemed plausible, but what had caused them to become this way and why had they written all over themselves? Colin sensed his head whirling, though a solution to the latter puzzle occurred to him. What with rationing, perhaps the fellows had lacked paper on which to inscribe their final recognisably human reflections, the better to recall what they had once believed. That made satisfactory, if disturbing sense, and yet a more vital question remained.

Where were all the women and children?

One of the monsters was raising a blackened chunk to its snout. Although the texture was nondescript, Colin could see at the end of it a splayed hand no larger than his own.

He screamed. He couldn't help himself. His heart drummed wildly.

Here was another of the brutes casting aside, with one seven fingered appendage, a broad pelvic bone from which it had gobbled a last morsel of nourishment. Mum always called them childbearing-hips.

The effects of rationing hadn't only been restricted to paper.

Colin screamed again, this time not hearing the sound. Fortunately none of the cannibals appeared to have heard either. Indeed the audible detection of any activity was utterly precluded by the low-lying grumble that had struck up overhead. Colin glanced high, just as the things did. Dark shapes, large as houses, slid with solemn grace across a brooding sky. He swallowed what little moisture he had left.

The Luftwaffe had arrived.

There was irony in the fact that now he might be saved. Again his books had come to the rescue. Colin knew that the woods were directly east of his grandparents' home, and that if one extended the line on an atlas it would reach Coventry. That was surely where the planes, with regimented organisation, were headed. All he need do was run in that direction.

This he did, dodging and leaping – until an object, squat and solid, floored him completely. At first he thought he had tripped over a felled tree-trunk. Then as he scrambled to his feet (in his peripheral gaze, the ogres had also stood, though remained stationary, waving bits of their families high above what passed for their heads) Colin noticed the sheen of metal lodged in a narrow aperture. Was this a bomb? It looked too advanced for anything the Germans might have developed, but who knew what went on in laboratories? A yard from end to end and a foot in diameter, it didn't seem sufficient to lead to much damage, yet what might have been onboard: a chemical that effected unspeakable transformations in men? Colin had read enough fiction about war to realise the layperson knew but little.

He must move on. The aircraft had shrunk to ominous crosses sailing away boisterously. Their men had come to kill our women and children, and now ours had lent a hand – a seven-fingered one at that! He bit back hysteria, turning away from the gleeful swine, and then started on his passage east. It was another half-hour before he reached the rim of the woods, the sight of the farmhouse on a blazing horizon.

Once he had made the back door, distastefully encircling the neglected pig pens, he discovered what all the fire was. The world from which he had travelled only this morning was alive with flame. Thunder that wasn't anything of the sort boomed across a landscape, which was blacked out and quivering in heat haze. It was a truly terrible spectacle. A hand fell on his shoulder.

"Ugh!" was how Colin greeted the touch, and then he spun round to see nana filling the frame of the doorway. Had the din of battle disguised her emergence? Immediately he was able to say, "Nana, we've got to—"

But she interrupted. "Oh my goodness, *there* you are! Where on earth have you been? I've been worrying myself sick. Come inside at once!"

"Nana, you don't understand. It's not safe for any of us. We must—"

"So you do have *some* sense. Quick, get in!"

She had dragged him into the kitchen that was dark as a grave. His travel bag had gone, presumably into the second bedroom, though his book lay flat upon the work surface. Nana must have brought this in from the step. She was shutting the door. Nightlight flickered, and then a delayed rumble shook the crockery on the Welsh dresser.

"Nana, all the men in the village have... have changed," Colin sputtered. "They're not what they were any more, and they might be coming for *us* next."

She looked incredulous, halting momentarily in her busyness. "What? Changed? How do you mean?"

He drew breath before continuing. "They're all *monsters*."

Nana rolled her puffy eyes – she was clearly tired and upset – and strutted across the room to snatch up the M. R. James. "What did I say to you about reading *this* kind of thing? I think there's bed for you, young man. Any nightmares, you've brought on yourself!"

"But nana—"

That was all she allowed him. Tossing aside the collection as if it were toxic, she wrestled him into the hall-passage, she was too big and strong to resist. As they reached the entrance to the bedroom the coin was ejected from his pocket, to roll haphazardly over the carpet, fetching up against the door behind which granddad must still be sleeping. The rap must be a prompt to the opening of his own, because then he was thrust through.

Not just dark: black. Colin cried out.

Nana was saying, "What's the matter? What's the matter?"

"They'll come here, I know they will..."

"Oh, I didn't mean what I just said about nightmares." She

must be calmer now that she had him again under her auspices and realised this. "But if it helps, I can light you a tiny weeny candle."

He nodded, happy to see her gone for a while. He didn't care for her patronising manner, though he guessed a little light might help him cope. The curtains were drawn, and there was no guarantee that the travesties in the woods would make their witless way to such a remote building. In any case, he was certain that nana would lock the exterior doors. Here she came, back from elsewhere, holding a stick of wax and a square box of matches. She coaxed a flame, setting the beacon upon the bedside table. The room grew queerly luminous, a limited pool of light. But he could see his bag sat on the floor, open-mouthed beneath the mattress.

"Come along then. Into your jimjams."

Colin raised his eyebrows, a communication that had nana shaking her head as she rotated. "You boys grow up so quickly! You'll be a man before long."

As he struggled into his pyjamas, he thought: *Not around here, thanks!* But he said nothing.

She went on, "The quicker you are, the more likely I'll be to persuade granddad to come wish you goodnight."

There was a treat worth fighting for! Colin climbed into the bed, the better to precipitate fulfilment of the promise. The rustle of sheets had nana trudging his way, kissing him wetly on the forehead.

"You miss your dad, don't you?"

What else could he say but, "Yes."

"Well let me see what I can do by way of male company."

She slipped away. Colin experienced a powerful temptation to call her back – everything seemed so horribly wrong – but he couldn't find the words. He heard her creep along the hall-passage, falter, begin to speak.

"George? Geeoorge?"

A delay – and then an artless scuffle of movement. Finally a voice, deep as the fracas from outside of the window,

225

answered, "*The transformation is well under way.*"

Perhaps nana had taken this as a question, because she replied, "Well, he's in his nightwear, if that's what you mean. And in bed."

"*Good. Ready.*" Was granddad's last word a reference to his self? He was adding sluggishly, "*Stand aside – out of sight. I'll chew you later.*"

The illness must be mixing up his language; he was having difficulty expressing himself. If what he had were contagious, rather he would *see* her later, most sensibly at a distance. But that wasn't any kind of reassurance. Why in that case would he risk coming in to Colin?

The kitchen door clapped, and then another opened: one out and then one into the hall-passage. A maladroit shuffle before the bedroom door swung ponderously inwards; a shadow lumbering into the room.

"H–Hello?"

Granddad didn't respond. The only truth of him was a silhouette, etched by trembling candlelight. It didn't look right. Were there slippers, or had his feet become lumpy and enlarged? The body was barely contained within a strained nightgown. Perhaps his face had been tugged out of shape by the condition. He trotted towards the bed, attended by a gruff laboured breathing, and suddenly Colin knew.

"You're, you're one of them, aren't you?"

He wasn't nervous, even when the ill-lit hand – what had been the natural right – stretched his way. There was ink between the knuckles, one letter to each digit. LOVEAND, Colin read, willing the fourth and fifth fingers apart. The men in the woods had entirely lost their humanity: was granddad gone that far yet? As the seven divisions of the left hand also began reaching for him, he wondered, in terror, if the old man had added a full stop after HATRED

MORTBURY PRESS

The horror anthology publisher

The Black Book of Horror

"Black Book stands squarely in the great literary tradition of horror and supernatural fiction..."
Peter Tennant, Case Notes, Black Static #2

"A superior example of its type."
Guy Haley, Death Ray, issue 10

The Second Black Book of Horror

"...this is an excellent anthology of solid, enjoyable, pleasantly scary fiction."
Mario Guslandi, The Harrow

Tales of terror and the macabré, the supernatural and the occult, the gruesome and the ghastly.

Selected by Charles Black

http://www.freewebs.com/mortburypress/

mortburypress@yahoo.com

Printed in the United Kingdom
by Lightning Source UK Ltd.
130458UK00001B/64-75/P